About the Author

Mike Royko has won the Pulitzer Prize and the Heywood Broun Award. His column is carried in almost two hundred papers across the country.

mike royko

SEZ WHO? SEZ ME

INTRODUCTION BY STUDS TERKEL

WARNER BOOKS

A Warner Communications Company

The columns in this book dated before March 4, 1978, appeared, in slightly different form and often with different title, in the *Chicago Daily News;* columns since that date appeared in the *Chicago Sun-Times.*

WARNER BOOKS EDITION

This Warner Books Edition is published by arrangement with E.P. Dutton, Inc.,
2 Park Avenue,
New York, N.Y. 10016

Warner Books, Inc.,
666 Fifth Avenue,
New York, N.Y. 10103

A Warner Communications Company

Printed in the United States of America

First Warner Books Printing: December, 1983

10 9 8 7 6 5 4 3 2 1

For Terry Shaffer, Jon Foreman, Ellen Warren, Paul O'Connor, Wade Nelson, Hanke Gratteau, John Fennell, Patty Wingert, and Helen McEntee—my Dr. Watsons, Igors, Tontos and most valued friends.

CONTENTS

2 THOSE DAMNED BUREAUCRATS

3 JOCKS AND JERKS

7 OLD BLUE-EYES AND OTHERS

8 OVERSET

Now hear this:

> *The distinctive atmosphere was provided by the lunchtime clientele, which included lawyers, judges, traffic court fixers, bondsmen, bailiffs, bagmen, aldermen, and other Loop wildlife. Nobody ever talked above a whisper, for fear of being overheard and indicted. Many of the customers seemed to be communicating solely by winking, nodding, and passing unmarked envelopes.*

> *One day a waitress reached to pick up what she thought was a remarkably large tip. A judge gave her a karate chop on the wrist.*

It is not the voice of Heywood Broun. Nor Murray Kempton. Nor, for that matter, Lincoln Steffens recounting the shame—and raffishness—of cities. It may be the spirit-sound of all three and yet the voice is uniquely Mike Royko.

Five days a week, Royko puts together a column on page two of the *Chicago Sun-Times*. For years, he had done this job on page three of the now-gone and still-mourned *Chicago Daily News*. He may be, pound for pound, the best all-around columnist on the premises. In the country, that is. Ask just about any Chicagoan you may pass on the street.

It is more than his sense of indignation, invariably directed at solemn fools in power and on the side of those up against it. It is more than his antic sense; he's as funny as they come; he can spot the absurd while the others in his trade still ponder its seriousness. It's something else that makes him singular. It is his insatiable hunger to encompass all aspects of contemporary life, the real and surreal.

Much like a wide ranging shortstop, say Marty Marion, he goes after balls others wave at. Naturally, he bobbles a few. To mix a metaphor, there are times when he wings the sparrow rather than the vulture. But these are rare occasions. In a robotesque time, he is daringly flesh and blood. In the spirit of Nelson Algren, the Chicago bard he most admired, he always walks on the wild side and thus infuriates, amuses, deeply touches and enriches his readers.

What is often overlooked is Royko's skill and doggedness as an investigative reporter. Like a famished alley mutt, he digs away at the bone of truth. Observers can point out scores of stories he has uncovered that might otherwise have been safely interred. Usually they have concerned the "ordinary citizen" or the wholly dispossessed, the one without a clout (a Chicago idiom he has made universal), pushed around by Authority. At such times, he appears possessed by a demon.

I have seen him in his cubbyhole of an office. His glasses have slipped down toward the tip of his sharp nose, his cigarette's smoke choking up the joint. He is a man of excess (Can Blake be right—"The road of excess leads to the palace of wisdom"?)

He is listening. Some nobody is at the other end of the phone. Sometimes it's a cry for help. Sometimes it's an astonishing tip. Sometimes it's just a funny story. Other calls may be from fat stuff with clout, whose venality he has exposed to light. Always his response is a growl, more of a grunt. But don't let it fool you. He's not missing a beat.

The human comedy has Mike Royko on the hip and we're all the better for it.

Studs Terkel

SEZ WHO? SEZ ME

1 | BOILERMAKERS AND BAR STOOLS

Midnight Cocktails—
with a Twist

March 25, 1974

It was 1:30 A.M., a half-hour to closing time in Billy Goat's Tavern, which is in a basement on Hubbard Street near the Chicago River.

A dozen or so people sat at the bar. Most of them had finished work at midnight, so it was their cocktail hour. But people who finish work at midnight aren't full of smart cocktail talk. They don't even drink cocktails, at least not in Billy Goat's, where the "in" drink is still a shot and beer.

A couple of printers argued about who was better, Santo or Melton.

The others stared at the TV-movie or their drinks. Owner Sam Sianis counted the cash register's contents. Big Warren, the bartender, drew a beer.

Then the door opened and closed. A few heads turned to see who would be coming down the steps. There are mostly regulars at that hour.

They couldn't see who it was because a cigarette machine blocks the view of the landing.

Suddenly a bloodcurdling scream filled the place. It was a terrible sound, a man's high-pitched voice screaming as if something frightful had been done to him.

Everybody froze. The scream stopped for a moment. The place was absolutely silent.

Then the scream began again, and it was even louder and more agonized.

Nobody wanted to get up and look to see what was at the top of the stairs.

They knew that whoever it was, he had just come in from the night. And there, in those dark streets under Michigan Avenue, anything could have happened.

The way he was screaming, they knew that he had to have been hit with a brick, a knife, an ax, or worse, and would be covered with gore.

So they sat there, staring in the direction of . . . holy smoke, what?

Down the stairs the figure came, and he was still screaming.

Then he stood there, facing them all, his arms held out as if he were being crucified.

He was a tall, rather thin young man. And there didn't appear to be anything wrong with him.

Except that he was stark naked.

The shock was so great that nobody moved. They just stared.

The naked young man grinned. That was even more shocking. This isn't one of those sophisticated places on Rush Street. It is the closest thing to a neighborhood bar that you can find in that part of town. And the people who go there, especially after midnight, aren't used to being grinned at by naked men.

The horror slipped from Sianis' face, and was replaced by a look of realization.

It was a streaker. A screaming streaker at that. And in his tavern.

Sianis, a bull-like young man who was born in Greece, inherited the tavern from his uncle, the original Billy Goat Sianis. He also inherited Billy Goat's strong sense of decency. Billy Goat used to hit male customers with his cane if he saw them staring at female customers in miniskirts.

Sianis picked up a beer bottle and shouted at the naked young man: "You dirty sommabeesh, I'm gonna kill you."

Waving the bottle over his head, he ran around the end of the bar.

The naked young man, recognizing that he would soon have something genuine to scream about, dashed up the steps.

Sianis was only a few steps behind, screaming, "I'm gonna kill you, you sommabeesh."

A car waited at the curb; the door opened. The young man leaped inside, and the door slammed just as Sianis got there. He peered in and saw three other young men, also naked.

"You're all crazy," he raged as the car roared away.

Back in the tavern, an old man's hand shook so badly he spilled half his shot. He could barely talk. "My God, I never saw anything like that in my life. What was wrong with him?"

"Ees a flasher," said one of Sianis' relatives, who works behind the sandwich grill.

"Naw, he was a streaker," said Big Warren. "A flasher's a guy who doesn't have on anything under his coat and he scares women. A streaker's different."

"Don't you read the papers?" a printer asked the old man. "They're doing it all over."

He shook his head. "No. I never heard of anything like

that. I never saw anything like that. I thought he was some kind of crazy person."

Sianis was still furious. "I never been so scare since time a guy put gun in my face and stick up. What he scream like that for? I think it's a murder."

"That's right," said Big Warren. "I mean, if he wants to streak, he ought to just come in quietly. He don't have to scare people with all that screaming."

Sianis shook his head. "I don't want no streakers in here. Not in my place."

"You're going to have them," somebody said. "You watch."

Sianis thought about it. Then he grinned cruelly. "Good. I hope another one comes in. Then you know what I'm gonna do?"

"What?"

He extended his hand, waist high and with the palm upward. Then he clenched his fingers into a tight fist, as if squeezing. And he rotated his wrist as if twisting.

"That's what I'm gonna do to that sommabeesh. And when I get done with him, he won't streak no more. He won't do nothing no more."

A printer flinched at the thought and said: "You can't do that, Sam."

Sam looked indignant. "Why not? He deserve it, don't he?"

"Yeah," the printer said, "but you serve food here. I wouldn't let you serve me nothing after you do that."

Sam considered that. Then he reached behind him and grabbed a pair of canvas gloves he sells to circulation truck helpers for seventy-five cents a pair.

"I'll put on one of these," he said. "OK?"

"OK," said the fastidious printer.

Sianis put on the glove, snapped his hand shut, and looked happy. "I hope he come back."

Well, at least we'd find out if he had really screamed as loud as he can.

Soaking Up History

March 29, 1979

A young woman shrieked at me the other day. "What makes *you* an authority on this *subject!*"

The subject she referred to was drinking. And what made her angry was my agreement with the raising of the legal drinking age to twenty-one. As you might guess, she was nineteen.

She had come to me for sympathy. Instead, I told her that I was happy I would no longer trip over apple-cheeked little boozers in some of my favorite bars. That brought color to her cheeks. And they turned crimson when I said: "In fact, I wouldn't mind seeing them raise the drinking age to twenty-five."

Which is when she demanded to know what made me an "authority."

That was her mistake. There are thousands of subjects about which I know absolutely nothing. There are thousands of others about which I know next to nothing. There are thousands more about which I know only a teeny bit.

But when it comes to the subject of people bellying up to a bar and making their livers quiver, I am a recognized authority. If they gave university degrees in this subject, I would be a

PhD. Harvard University would probably make me a distinguished professor.

In all modesty, my credentials are brilliant. Here is a very brief career resume:

Age 13 to age 19: Position: Bartender in various Chicago taverns, such as the Blue Sky Lounge (Milwaukee Avenue); Twilight Inn (Armitage Avenue); Hawaiian Paradise (Ashland Avenue); Twilight Inn II (Western Avenue), Cullerton Tap (West Cullerton Street), and several others. I was able to obtain this employment despite my youth because I was hardworking, industrious, and my old man owned the joints. Additional duties: Accepting bets on horses; preventing customers from falling asleep with head in toilet; admitting regular patrons through side door at 8:00 A.M. on Sunday so they could get over shakes and go to church; answering phone and telling wives that husbands had not been there all evening; appraising wristwatches for payment of drinks in lieu of cash; dispensing hard-boiled eggs, pickled pigs feet, beef jerky, and other gourmet delights; breaking up fights by unleashing a Doberman named Death and letting him gnaw on brawlers until peace was restored; and, finally, giving monthly cash-stuffed envelope to police bagman for assorted favors, such as overlooking a thirteen-year-old bartender.

Age 19 to 23: Served in armed forces with distinguished duty in such theaters of operation as Billy Bob's Bar in Biloxi, Mississippi; Jeb's Bar in San Antonio, Texas; Mr. Clagg's private moonshine still in Bobo, Mississippi; Suzi Wang's Bar and Bathhouse in Tokyo; and Kim Dong's Bar and Social Center in Korea. Experiences included being struck on side of head with bottle in Billy Bob's Bar; on other side of head in Jeb's Bar; atop head by Mr. Clagg's retarded brother, Crazy Clagg; and becoming briefly engaged to be married to a young lady I met in Kim Dong's Bar and Social Center, who decided instead to steal my wallet and boots. Outstanding achievement: Being arrested in two states within one hour. This occurred when a group of us on an eastbound train were celebrating our return from Korea where we had fought to a draw. When we refused to leave the club car, the attendant called an MP, who arrested us while the train was in Washington State. Minutes later, we crossed into Idaho, where the MP turned us over to local police, who arrested us for the second time. And to think that this country once gave returning heroes ticker tape parades.

Age 23 to present: Engaged in field research in an estimated 3,267 bars, cafes, bistros, pubs, taverns, saloons, gin mills, and joints in Chicago, Kansas City, Miami, San Francisco, Burlington, Wisconsin, New York, Washington, England, France, Germany, Cicero, and a few hundred other cities and countries. Saw a one-legged man dance on a bar in Munich. Got winked at by a one-eyed woman in Marseille. Went into Schaller's Pump in Mayor Daley's neighborhood on a St. Patrick's Day and escaped alive. Saw a man win a bet in Milwaukee that he could drink a quart of vodka in five minutes, and helped put him in the ambulance. Saw a man in Cicero wrestle a jukebox and lose. Talked to the man in Wyoming who was arrested for hitting a bartender on the head with a dog. Saw a 130-pound lady bartender named Kitty in Logan Square knock a 210-pound hillbilly unconscious with one punch to his brow. She had a quart jar of Polish pickles in her hand when she punched him.

If space permitted, I could go on and on. But if I described my research in detail it would take a month, and just reading it would give you cirrhosis.

My years of study have taught me many sociological truths, a few of which I'll share: Never talk to someone who drinks with his eyes closed. Never laugh at someone who is weeping while singing a sentimental song about his mother. Don't sit next to someone who leans at more than a forty-five-degree angle. Avoid making eye contact with guys who have bottle scars on their noses and tattoos on their arms. Never

ask a lady in a bar to dance if she has bottle scars on her nose
and tattoos on her arm. Never call a bartender who has an
eighteen-inch neck "my good man" or "fellow." South of
Twelfth Street, don't play the jukebox while the Sox game is
on the TV. In a strange bar, never use the phone more than
twice or they will think you are planning a stickup. Never pet
a tavern dog that has a purple tongue and yellow eyes. Never
flirt with a barmaid who has a purple tongue and yellow eyes;
her husband might be offended.

But of all the truths I've acquired in my studies, the most
lasting is this: As a general rule, a sixteen-year-old who
drinks is likely to do crazier things than a seventeen-year-old;
a seventeen-year-old will do crazier things than an eighteen-
year-old; an eighteen-year-old, more than a nineteen-year-
old, etc., etc., etc.

This is not merely my opinion—it is based on scientific
research done by many expert researchers, such as bartenders,
bouncers, traffic cops, ambulance drivers, and morgue attendants.
They say that as drinkers, people in the younger age group
drive wilder, hit each other with pool sticks more frequently
and with less reason, stand in the street at 2:00 A.M. and
shout louder, and throw up on the floor more often than any
other age group.

I don't know at which age the craziness subsides, but it
isn't at an age when someone, while completely sober, puts
rear tires on his car that are twice as big as the front tires.

Maybe the answer to when a person should start drinking
was best summed up by an old geezer who said: "If they
think they're having fun, they're not old enough."

Hearty 'Hallo' from Greece

November 23, 1973

For days, terrible rumors have been sweeping Billy Goat's Tavern.

They all concerned the recent trip to Greece by Sam Sianis, the owner. He went to Greece, where he was born, to marry a girl named Irene.

But he got there just as the student uprising began and troops, tanks, and martial law moved in.

So everybody in the tavern was saying Sianis was in a Greek prison, or Sianis was trapped at the airport, or Sianis was captured by the students, or that he had fled to the mountains.

One customer summed up everybody's grief when he lifted his face from the bar and wailed:

"He said that when he came back he'd have a big party and the drinks would be free. But if he's in prison, no party. Jeez, those damn students. What a tragedy."

The basis for the rumors was one phone call Sianis made to the tavern after he landed in Athens.

Unfortunately, the connection was bad and the call was taken by one of Sianis' relatives, all of whom work in the tavern-grill.

Nobody knows what Sianis said because Sianis' relatives speak limited English. The ones behind the grill can say only:

"Wan doobla-cheese weet onion." Those who tend bar can say: "Wan stein bee!"

The relative who took the call could only report: "I no no wha' hap, bus eeesh nah goo!"

I was distressed by the rumors because I'm partly responsible for Sianis being in Greece in the first place. I have been playing matchmaker.

When the famed Billy Goat Sianis died, the bar was inherited by Sam, his nephew, whom Billy Goat had brought here as a boy from a small village in Greece.

Billy Goat's funeral was hardly over when many young ladies, and some who weren't too young, began coming to the tavern and making goo-goo eyes at nephew Sam.

Some were sincere in their overtures, since Sam, at thirty-seven, is a fine figure of a man. He is only five seven, but he has a nineteen-inch neck and can lift a bar stool by one rung with his teeth.

Others, however, were attracted by the fact that Sianis' place sells more Schlitz than just about any joint in town, which means he is a man of considerable means.

I feared that one of these women would turn his head with her wiles, and an unfortunate marriage would occur.

So I urged him to go back to his native Greece and find a nice girl who knows nothing of checking accounts, charge accounts, Bonwit Teller, property laws, Gloria Steinem, tennis clubs, and property laws.

My motives were partly selfish. Billy Goat's is my favorite tavern, and a tavern is only as happy as its owner, and a tavern owner cannot be happy with a wife who expects him home before 3:00 A.M.

"Remember Zorba!" I kept telling him. "No henpecked man, he."

So after several vacations in Greece, Sianis returned this summer with a picture of the beautiful Irene and an announcement that he would return in November to marry her.

"She's good woman," he said. "She don't say much."

And that was why he happened to be there this week in the midst of unrest, troops, tanks, and martial law.

Finally the tension became so great that the bartenders were drinking more than the customers, which can happen when they become nervous, and when the owner is out of the country.

That is why I put through a transatlantic phone call, hoping to get some information. One of his relatives gave me a relative's number in Athens. The number was "seesha fy seesha, fy seesha fy fo!"

The call went through. Several voices said: "huh?" Then Sianis himself came on.

"Wash new?" he said.

I told him that the customers feared for his safety and about the rumors.

He said things had, indeed, looked bad for a while.

"When I get off airplane, I look for Irene, but she's not there. I figure that maybe I'm making a mistake if she can't even meet me.

"Then I get in cab and I go two blocks and then the soldiers jump out and surround me.

"I say: 'Wash wrong?' They say: 'We gotta war.' I say: 'Whose gonna win?' They say: 'We gonna win.' I say: 'I'm on your side.'

"Then they tell me that nobody is supposed to be out this late. Ees Marshall's law, I ask them Marshall who? In Chicago, my place stay open till 2:00 A.M., so it wasn't too late.

"They tell me that I better get off the street until the war is over. So I been off the street all week."

Did this mean that he is being kept from Irene, and that the wedding is off, and the Chicago free party, too?

"Nah," said Sianis. "Irene is right here with me. We gonna get married next week. Here, I put her on the phone. Irene, say hallo."

She came on the phone and said: "Hallo!"
I said: "Hello. Are you looking forward to the wedding?"
She said: "Hallo!"
I said: "Do you think you will like Chicago?"
She said: "Hallo!"
Sianis came back on and said: "Her English ain't too good yet."
The tavern will remain a happy place.

The Fluid Side of Modern Art

April 15, 1975

The regular customers in Billy Goat's Tavern seldom get excited about art.

In fact, the last time the subject came up was when two customers got into a brawl over which of them had the better arm tattoo. Everyone agreed that the wife's tattoo was best.

So I was surprised by the intense interest aroused by an exhibition held over the weekend at the city's Museum of Contemporary Art.

This was the highly publicized exhibition by Chris Burden of something called "body art."

It consisted of Burden lying motionless on a floor for forty-five hours under a sheet of glass that leaned against a wall at an angle.

Actually, they weren't impressed by the artistic merit of what Burden did.

"I know guys who have been lying on floors for years," said Big Warren, the bartender. "But they are known as lushes."

Pointing toward the end of the bar, someone else said: "Look at him. He has been sitting there for five hours now with his face resting on the bar, and *that*'s tough on the nose."

"If what he did is art," another critic noted, "then that guy who sleeps in a city salt box under Wacker Drive is an artist, too."

Despite these criticisms, there was one aspect of Burden's performances that had everyone expressing admiration—the reports that he did not visit the men's room even once during those forty-five hours. Or the ladies room, either, which I mention only because in the art world, who knows?

In some circles, especially those formed by wet beer glasses, this kind of self-control is much admired.

Indeed, a man's bowling average, softball ability, or sexual boasting are not considered any greater an achievement than his ability to sit at a bar for hours without having to leave his bar stool, or show discomfort.

"I will tell you theesh," said Sam Sianis, proprietor of Billy Goat's, "I weesh I had customers like heem. A guy who can wait that long could drink enough beer to pay for my license."

Big Warren said: "I've never heard of anyone waiting that long. In a place I used to work, we had one guy who sat for ten hours drinking beer without getting up. The coroner listed him as a drowning victim."

Someone else said: "What amazes me about this Burden is that the stories said he didn't move a finger all that time. You'd think he would have at least crossed his legs."

But Burden didn't. Every news account agreed on that point.

"He ought to be in the *Guinness Book of World Records*,"

someone said, referring to the book that chronicles unusual achievements. "Although I don't know what you'd list him under."

Even experts on this subject were amazed and there are experts on this as there are on everything.

"I absolutely do not believe it," said Dr. David Presman, a urologist, when asked about the forty-five-hour achievement.

"Even with a diminished fluid intake, his bladder would get a certain volume that would make him uncomfortable.

"The average person couldn't wait more than ten or twelve hours without getting damned uncomfortable."

"I'm skeptical about the whole thing. If that's what modern art is about, give me Rembrandt."

Because of the doctor's skepticism, I spoke to an official at the museum to confirm this vital point.

Is it true that Burden did not once visit a washroom?

"That's correct," said a museum spokesman.

How can you be sure?

"Someone was nearby at all times," the spokesman said, explaining there was great concern for Burden's health, since he wasn't eating or drinking anything while he was an art object.

Was it possible that when the person who was watching Burden went to the bathroom, Burden took the opportunity to sneak off himself?

"No. He was never alone. Besides, he was being videotaped. He didn't move during the entire time."

That's remarkable.

"Well, there was one thing that happened. . . ."

What was it?

"You won't quote me, will you?"

Of course not.

"Well. . . ."

What, what?

"He peed in his pants."

Boy, oh, boy; and people said Van Gogh was weird
because he cut off his ear.

How to Insult a Norwegian

September 24, 1978

During a group discussion of the Ali-Italian dispute, a guy
sitting a couple of stools down raised an interesting question:

"How come Norwegians get off so easy?"

Get off what so easy?

"Well, I'm an Italian. And at one time or another, I've
been called everything from a dago to a wop to a spaghetti-
bender, right? And you are part Polish, so you have been
called a polack or a dumb polack, right?"

Once or twice, yes.

"Every ethnic group I can think of has got some kind of
nasty label. It is an American tradition. So how come I can't
think of any kind of name for the Norwegians?"

We all thought about that for a while. Then a little beer
drinker said: "You're right. I can't think of any kind of slur
about a Norwegian. I'm Jewish, and there are more derogato-
ry labels hung on us than anyone else."

"No, there aren't," said a tired-looking liberal nursing a
scotch. "The blacks have the most. Then come the Jews.
And after them, it is a toss-up between a half a dozen groups
for third place."

"How do you know that?" asked the Italian.

"I read about a study a university professor made," the liberal said. "He spent a couple of million dollars in federal funds compiling a list of racial and ethnic epithets. When he finished, he found out that whites have something like 192 different ways of insulting blacks. Gentiles have about twenty-five ways of insulting Jews. After that comes the rest of us. We all have got one way or another of insulting each other."

"Yeah, but did he find a slur for Norwegians?" asked Big Warren, the bartender.

"No, come to think of it, I don't think the Norwegians were on the list."

"See?" said Johnny Shack, the Italian. "They somehow got off the hook."

"Wait a minute," said Charlie, who is Irish. "I heard a guy called a dumb Norwegian once."

"That doesn't count," said the liberal. "You can call anybody a dumb this or a dumb that. It's not the same as being called a wop or a heeb or a polack or a spick or a jig or a mick. No, somehow the Norwegians have been ignored in the Americanization process. They have no slur of their own. I wonder why."

"I'll tell you why," said George, who had been listening quietly. "I'm of Norwegian ancestry. We have no label because we are nice. Everybody likes us."

That offended everyone at the bar.

"What do you mean, you are nice?" asked Charlie who is Irish. "We're nice, too. But people call us micks."

"Yeah," said Harry, who is Jewish. "You don't think I'm nice?"

"Sure, you're nice," said George the Norwegian. "But you all get in some kind of controversy. Or you get in wars. Or something. Not the Norwegians. Besides being nice, we're quiet. When was the last time you heard of Norwegians being controversial? You have never even heard of a Norwegian voting bloc, have you? Name me one crooked Norwegian alderman. We keep a low profile.''

"Knute Rockne did it," said the liberal. "Everybody liked Knute Rockne, so you've had a good image."

"That's right," said Johnny Shack. "And Viking movies. Every movie about Italian soldiers shows them as short losers. But Vikings are always big, handsome blond winners. Hell, the Vikings haven't won a war in a thousand years. We lose one war and everybody makes jokes about us. It isn't fair.''

Everyone glared at George the Norwegian until he bought a round. "I did not make society," he said. "I just live here.''

"You know what you are, George?" asked Johnny Shack. "You are a noogin.''

George looked startled. "A what?"

"A noogin."

"What in the hell is a noogin?"

"It is a defamatory word for Norwegians. I just made it up. I don't know what it means, but it sounds awful.''

"I like it," said Charlie who is Irish. "I have some Norwegian in-laws. They call me a mick. Now I can call them noogins. It will drive them up the wall.''

"Well, I don't like it," said George the Norwegian, downing his drink and standing up. "Nobody has ever called me a noogin before. I don't have to take this kind of abuse.''

And he walked out.

"He's too sensitive," said Johnny Shack. "I've been called worse than a noogin.''

"Yeah, but noogin does sound bad," said the liberal.

The door opened and George the Norwegian came back in. "All right," he said. "If you promise never to call me a noogin again, I'll tell you what they call Norwegians.''

"I thought there was no word," said Charlie who is Irish.

"There is. I just didn't want to tell you. But if you want to insult a Norwegian, you call him a 'herring choker.' ''

"You're kidding," said Johnny Shack.

"No, it's true," said George. "It is because Norwegians eat so much herring. I think the Swedes started calling us that. Norwegians and Swedes always insult each other."

"What do Norwegians call Swedes?" asked Charlie who is Irish.

George shook his head. "There is no word. Dumb Swedes is the only insult I've ever heard."

"All right," said Johnny Shack, "then we have to create a new word for the Norwegians to call the Swedes. It is only fair."

"How about a sweegin," said Charlie who is Irish.

"That'll work," said the liberal. "The noogins against the sweegins. Isn't ethnicity wonderful?"

"What are you?" asked Johnny Shack.

"Me?" said the liberal, heading for the door. "I'm a WASP. I'm just a bystander."

Maeshe's Cafe Menu

July 18, 1977

I just read that Arnie Morton has spent about $1 million to give his newest restaurant a spectacular atmosphere.

That's the trend in the restaurant business. The glittery surroundings are considered even more important than the chow. Today's restaurant critics write more about the interior designer than they do about the chef.

In a way, that makes Morris Saletko—better known as "Maeshe Baer"—a pioneer in the restaurant field, although you will not read it in *Panorama* or *Chicago* magazine.

Maeshe, who passed on last week in the trunk of his car, used to run a restaurant called the H & H, on LaSalle Street, a couple of blocks north of City Hall.

Maeshe didn't go in for fancy decorations. His tables were in understated Formica. The only colors in the place were the varicose veins on the legs of his harried waitresses.

The cuisine was acceptable, if you fancy corned beef on rye, pickles, a bowl of borscht, and potato pancakes.

What made it popular was the atmosphere and the magnetic personality of Maeshe.

The distinctive atmosphere was provided by the lunchtime clientele, which included lawyers, judges, traffic court fixers, bondsmen, bailiffs, bagmen, aldermen, and other Loop wildlife. Nobody ever talked above a whisper, for fear of being overheard and indicted. Many of the customers seemed to communicate solely by winking, nodding, and passing unmarked envelopes.

One day a waitress reached to pick up what she thought was a remarkably large tip. A judge gave her a karate chop on the wrist.

Many of Maeshe's business associates frequented the place, although it wasn't clear what business they were in. They spent most of their time sitting around in dark glasses, golf shirts, and fedoras. They were shy. If you stared at one of them too long, he would take off his fedora and hold it over his face.

Maeshe's magnetic personality was subtle. He was not a backslapper. Anybody he slapped on the back would probably scream and flee.

He seldom said much, except when he answered the phone and whispered: "Which race?"

Most of the time he sat behind the cashier's counter, glowering at anybody he suspected of being honest.

Yet, people flocked to him. It was probably because he was known to be an easy touch. If you needed a few dollars, Maeshe always had it.

Of course, if you were thirty seconds late in making your interest payment, your friends would wind up autographing your cast.

That was one of the reasons people flocked to him. For every person who came in the H & H to eat, another dozen would walk in, hand Maeshe something, and scurry away.

One man came to Maeshe empty-handed. Right in front of the lunch crowd, Maeshe used the empty hand for an ashtray. When the man yelled, Maeshe threw him out for being unruly.

Maeshe was at the H & H for years before his customers learned that his real name was Morris Saletko. They learned this when his picture was in the paper saying that Morris Saletko had been indicted with some syndicate activists who had been hijacking trucks carrying millions of dollars in merchandise.

Maeshe didn't steal the trucks. He was supposed to have helped hide them.

He had a plausible explanation in court. He said a customer came to him and asked if he knew of a good garage where he could park a truck with some film in it. Maeshe recommended the garage where he parked his own car.

"Then I went to the club to get some steam and sun," he told the jury.

That was all there was to it, he said, until the FBI woke him up one night and said he was under arrest. "You must be silly," he told the agents. "I never took no hot film."

After that, Maeshe drifted out of the restaurant business, although they let him run a soda fountain in the Sandstone Federal Prison.

When he came back, he said he was going into the vegetable business. Sometimes he would be seen standing around places like Caesars Palace in Las Vegas, waiting for a radish to grow.

A couple of years ago Maeshe and a friend were standing at Halsted and Jackson waiting for the corn harvest when a big car pulled up and two men started shooting.

Maeshe was wounded in a fingertip. A reporter asked: "Maeshe, who tried to bump you off?" Maeshe said: "I think it was gypsies."

Nobody is sure who put Maeshe in the trunk of his car last week, or even why.

One detective said: "I'm really surprised."

Why?

"Maeshe was pretty big. I didn't think an Olds had that much trunk space."

Sam Bounces to a Record

December 19, 1974

For those who are fascinated by record-setting athletic achievements, a Chicagoan may have set a new national record for bouncing. Or at least I'm going to claim it for him until someone can prove they've done better.

The record was set a few evenings ago by Sam Sianis, when he bounced the same drunken brawler out of his tavern six times in the same night.

Actually, the record should be shared by the man who was bounced, but he was too busy to introduce himself.

The event began when two friends sat at a table in the Billy Goat Tavern, quarreling over the divisive issue of whether Bobby Douglass should be a quarterback, a tight end, or the Frankenstein Monster.

Suddenly they were swinging and rolling around on the floor.

It wasn't much of a fight, so Sam was calm as he came around the bar. Sam, thirty-seven, is only five seven. But he works out by lifting bar stools with his teeth.

Sam believes in using as little force as necessary when resolving a dispute. So he said, "Hokay, break eet up," and gave one of them a kick.

"You keek dem," he later explained, "an' you don't sprain your back."

The kick brought one man to his feet with a yelp and he stepped back peacefully.

But the other man came up with his arms flailing. Sam spun him around, pinned his arms to his side, lifted him, and carried him out the door.

It is a little harder to do that in Sam's tavern because it is in a basement. "I don't mind the stairs," Sam says. "Keeps the legs in shape when you got to carry them outside."

The door soon opened and the battler was back, stumbling down the stairs and heading for his former friend, who was sitting at the end of the bar looking morose.

A moment later, he was again being flung through the doorway.

"You nuts," Sam shouted after him. "Go home!"

The other customers gave him scattered applause.

Two minutes later, the door opened and the brawler ran in and leaped from the landing to the middle of the room.

"Put 'em up," he said to an elderly city bridgetender who was drowsing at a table.

"Don't be goofy, kid," the bridgetender said. "I'm a precinct captain. You could get in big trouble."

Sam reached for him, but he crouched and grabbed for an ankle. Sam abandoned his bearhug-lift technique. Instead, he grabbed him by a wrist and dragged him like a sack of potatoes up the stairs and onto the sidewalk.

The applause was more enthusiastic.

Now Sam sat at the bar, near the stairs. "I'll get him before he gets halfway down," he said. "Watch."

But the brawler was clever. The place is divided by a hamburger grill into two rooms. And there is a door in the other room, too.

That's where he came from. And, fists up, he headed for Sam's cousin, who works behind the grill.

The cousin speaks very little English, so he silently raised a meat cleaver over his head.

Sam reached the man before he could be cleaved. This time he used a headlock with a bit of ear-grinding to haul him out.

The customers sensed a record in the making. "How many times is that?" the bridgetender said. "Four," said Big Warren, the bartender. "Yeah, but he's pretty skinny," the bridgetender said.

The brawler's friend and former adversary looked up from his beer and said: "Maybe, but he's wiry."

The door opened. Sam poised. But it was only two regular customers. Sam relaxed.

Suddenly he was there. He had come in behind them, walking in a crouch.

This time Sam chased him into the men's room.

When they emerged, Sianis was dragging him by both ankles.

"Dees works good," Sam later said of the ankle-drag technique. "When the head bumps on the steps, eet makes them more sober."

Now everyone watched the door. It was something like following a no-hitter into the ninth inning.

He came back. But he walked in quietly and slowly, with both hands held open in a gesture of peace toward Sianis.

"I lost my watch in here," he said.

Sam glanced around at the floor. "Where?"

Pow! The guy landed a sneak punch to Sam's forehead. It wasn't much of a punch, and Sam hardly blinked. But, nevertheless, it was a punch.

Sam finally hissed.

It always begins softly, then it gets louder and louder until it sounds like a broken steam pipe. Everyone in the place froze, including the brawler.

"When I hees," Sam has explained to me, "eet scare hell out of people. I donno why, but it scare 'em bad."

Maybe it is simply because nobody expects a squat Greek to suddenly sound like a broken steam pipe.

But I once heard a brawling, 230-pound circulation driver from Tennessee shout in terror and flee when Sam hissed. He later explained that he has a deep fear of snakes.

While hissing, Sam went into a karate crouch and raised his hand for a chopping blow.

The sneak-puncher staggered backward and fell over a chair flat on his back.

Sam put a foot on his Adam's apple, leaned down and hissed some more. The man's eyes bulged.

After about thirty seconds, Big Warren said: "Better quit, Sam, or he'll die of fright."

Sam let him up and gently walked him up the stairs and out the door.

"He won't be back," said Big Warren. "The hissing always does it."

Everybody congratulated Sam for his achievement. "It ranks with the time Gale Sayers scored six touchdowns," said

ae bridgetender. Sam smiled modestly and said: "Eat was a
nuddy field when Sayers did eet."

Through it all, the brawler's friend sat brooding in his beer.
He finally got up and went up the stairs.

As he went out the door, he turned and pointed a finger at
Sam, saying:

"You just lost me as a customer, Sam. I ain't coming in a
oint where my friends are pushed around."

A Stiff Lesson

April 25, 1978

The young couple had a bitter quarrel. From the angry words
that drifted to others in Billy Goat's Tavern, the dispute
seemed to be over whether he or she was the better racquetball
player. She loudly declared that she was through with him
forever and flounced into the night, leaving him to brood over
his beer.

After considerable brooding, he squared his shoulders and
with a sob in his voice said: "I feel like jumping off the
bridge and ending it all."

A broken-nosed man sitting a few stools down said: "Don't
do it, kid."

The young man shook his head and said: "Why not?
Without her, I don't want to go on. I want to end it all."

The broken-nosed man said: "I'm not telling you not to

end it all. That's your business. Maybe it's even a good idea.
What I mean is, do it a different way. Don't jump off the
bridge."

The young man blinked at him for a moment and said:
"What does it matter how I do it?"

"It matters to other people, kid. It matters to me."

"Why should it matter to you? I don't even know your
name."

"My name's Charlie," said broken nose. "I work down
the street on one of the excursion boats on the Chicago River.
That's why I don't want you to go off the bridge. Show some
consideration for others."

"How does it concern you?" said the young man.

"Because since I've been working on the excursion boats,
I've spotted twenty-five or thirty stiffs in the river and
reported them. It's very depressing."

"That many?" the young man asked.

"Yeah. And what's worse is when they float to my dock.
Then the police pull them out and lay them out and that
makes a mess. Who needs that?"

The young man looked revolted. Charlie went on.

"Just the other day, I was coming in to tie the boat up
when I spotted a floater. I had just painted the dock and I
thought, To heck with that.

"So I put my boat in reverse, gunned it hard, and the
backwash carried the stiff all the way down to the next
landing. Then I called the police and they hauled him out
there instead of at my dock."

The young man was horrified. "You saw a body in the
river and you . . . you . . . just washed it away?" He couldn't
go on.

"Sure," Charlie said. "Why should I be responsible for
everybody who goes in the river? Enough is enough."

The young man shook his head. "What you did was,
was . . . inhuman."

Charlie looked amazed. "What do you do, kid?" Charlie asked. "You know, for a living?"

"I'm in computers," the young man said. He named a large corporation down the street from the bar.

"Uh huh," Charlie said. "Nice clean job, huh? No bodies around where you work?"

"Bodies? Of course there are no bodies," the young man snapped.

"But you think it is OK to mess up where I work with your body. How would you like it if I came to the place you work and stuck my finger in one of your computer plugs and fried myself and you had to take care of it?"

"That's ridiculous," the young man said.

"Think about it, kid. If you are going to knock yourself off, at least have the decency to do it where you won't be a nuisance. Go a few blocks over to the lake and jump off the rocks."

That suggestion brought an angry growl from a hulking man on another stool, who said: "Whatya mean, the lake. Don't tell the kid to jump in the lake."

Charlie shrugged. "I was just trying to help."

The big man said: "Yeah? Well, I fish for smelt. And last year me and some buddies were down by the lake one night, and you know what happened? Not more than five minutes after we put our nets in, we caught a stiff."

The young man gasped. "You caught a body when you were fishing?"

"Yeah, some guy."

"That's terrible," the young man said. "Who was he?"

"I don't know. We threw him back."

"You what? You threw him back in? The water?" The young man's eyes were beginning to bulge.

"Yeah," said the big man. "Whatya expect? If we pulled him out, the cops would have been making reports all night and we would have never caught no smelt. We called when we finished fishing and they got him out anyways. I heard it on the radio."

The young man shook his head. "I can't believe this. They threw him back in the water."

"I'll tell you, kid," said Charlie, "maybe a sewer would be the best thing."

The young man stared at him. "A sewer? Are you serious?"

The big man nodded. "Yeah, you won't mess up the fishing that way."

Just then, the door opened and the young woman came in. In a moment, they had apologized and made up. She suggested they have a drink.

"Not here," the young man said, pulling her toward the door. "Not with THEM."

After the door closed, Charlie said: "That's the trouble with kids today. You can't tell them anything."

How to Ease that Hangover

December 27, 1974

This is the time of year when all sorts of advice is written about hangovers.

The articles usually touch on three key points: What a hangover is, how to avoid one, and how to cure it.

Defining a hangover is simple. It is nature's way of telling you that you got drunk.

I've never understood why nature goes to the bother, since millions of wives pass on the information.

Except for abstinence or moderation, there is no way to completely avoid a hangover.

But there are certain rules that, if followed, will ease the discomfort.

First, stick with the same drink you started with. By that I mean that if you started the evening drinking champagne, beer, and frozen daiquiris, stick with champagne, beer, and frozen daiquiris the rest of the evening.

Drink quickly. If you can do most of your drinking within the first hour of the party and quickly pass out, you will have regained consciousness and be well on your way to recovery while others are still gadding about. By the time the Rose Bowl game comes on, your eyeballs will have come out from behind your nose.

Be careful what you eat, particularly later into the night. Especially avoid eating napkins, paper plates, and pizza boards.

If you follow these rules, you'll still have a hangover. So the question is, how to get through it with a minimum of agony.

It should be remembered that part of a hangover's discomfort is psychological.

When you awaken, you will be filled with a deep sense of shame, guilt, disgust, embarrassment, humiliation, and self-loathing.

This is perfectly normal, understandable, and deserved.

To ease these feelings, try to think only of the pleasant or amusing things that you did before blacking out. Let your mind dwell on how you walked into the party and said hello to everyone, and handed your host your coat, and shook hands, and admired the stereo system.

Blot from your mind all memories of what you later did to

your host's rug, what you said to that lady with the prominent cleavage that made her scream, whether you or her husband threw the first punch. Don't dredge up those vague recollections of being asleep in your host's bathtub while everybody pleaded with you to unlock the bathroom door.

These thoughts will just depress you. Besides, your wife will explain it in detail as the day goes on. And the week, too.

If anything, you should laugh it off. It's easy. Using your thumb and forefinger, pry your tongue loose from the roof of your mouth, try to stop panting for a moment, and say: Ha, ha. Again: Ha, ha. Now pull the blanket over your head and go back to sleep.

The other part of a hangover is physical. It is usually marked by throbbing pain in the head, behind the eyes, back of the neck, and in the stomach. You might also have pain in the arms, legs, knees, elbows, chin, and elsewhere, depending upon how much leaping, careening, flailing, and falling you did.

Moaning helps. It doesn't ease the pain, but it lets you know that someone cares, even if it is only you. Moaning also lets you know that you are still alive.

But don't let your wife hear you moan. You should at least have the satisfaction of not letting her have the satisfaction of knowing you are in agony.

If she should overhear you moaning, tell her you are just humming a love song the lady with the prominent cleavage sang in your ear while you danced.

Some people say that moaning gives greater benefits if you moan while sitting on the edge of your bathtub while letting your head hang down between your ankles. Others claim that it is best to go into the living room, slouch in a chair, and moan while holding a hand over your brow and the other over your stomach.

In any case, once you have moaned a while, you can try medication.

Aspirin will help relieve your headache. But it might increase the pain in your stomach.

If so, Maalox will help relieve the pain in your stomach. But it will make your mouth dry.

Water will relieve the dryness in your mouth. But it will make you feel bloated.

So it is best to take the aspirin, the Maalox, and just hold your tongue under the kitchen faucet. Or rest it in the freezer compartment of your refrigerator.

If you don't like to take pills, then the headache can be eased by going outside and plunging your head into a snowbank. BE SURE IT ISN'T A SNOW-COVERED HEDGE.

If you eat, make it something bland, such as a bowl of gruel. I don't know what gruel is, but it sounds very bland. If you don't know what gruel is either, then just make something that you think it might be.

Most experts recommend a minimum of physical activity, such as blinking your eyes during the bowl games, and moving your lips just enough to say to your wife: "Later, we'll discuss it later."

On the other hand, you might consider leaping out of bed the moment you open your eyes, flinging the windows open to let the cold air in, and jogging rapidly in place while violently flapping your arms and breathing deeply and heavily.

This will make you forget your hangover because it will bring on a massive coronary.

Toast to a Freeloader

February 8, 1980

People who haven't been in Big Wally's Tavern for a while
will order their beer, then look around and ask where Freddie
the Freeloader is.

Wally Tibor or his wife, Evelyn, will shake their heads as
they break the sad news.

"Freddie has passed on."

"No kidding. What from?"

"He just got old, I guess."

Then they will talk about what a heroic creature Freddie the
Freeloader was. And about the cold night he saved Old Jake's
life.

And Evelyn or Wally will say: "I never had a better dog.
No tavern ever had a better dog."

That is a strong statement, since tavern dogs are probably
the bravest, most useful of all dogs.

Some of them have become legends, such as Bruno, a
Milwaukee Avenue tavern beast. He was a cross between a
Doberman and a chow, and he had red eyes and a green
tongue. One night a robber came in and with one bite Bruno
performed a rather crude but effective vasectomy on the
felon.

Then there was Duke of Armitage Avenue, a huge, mean
mixed breed that had lost one ear in a fight with a dozen cats.

It was said that if Duke even licked your hand, you could die of blood poisoning.

Duke was unusual in that he didn't like to bark. So a teenage burglar who broke in one night thought he had clear sailing. He was emptying the cash register when Duke put his paws up on the bar, stared into the kid's eyes, and made growling, slobbering sounds.

When the owner showed up in the morning, he found Duke still growling and slobbering, and the teenage burglar still standing with his hand in the register. The owner swears that the kid's hair had turned pure white.

But as noble as these dogs were, Freddie the Freeloader was something special.

Freddie was born to be a tavern dog. He just wandered in off the street one day and made himself at home, mooching potato chips, boiled eggs, and hunks of barroom pepperoni. That's how he got his name.

He could do everything expected of a good tavern dog— never biting a regular customer, sniffing suspiciously at strangers or people who asked for credit, breaking up fights by biting all brawlers equally, and growling at wives who came looking for their husbands.

He could do it all—plus something I've never heard of any other tavern dog doing.

At night he would walk customers home from the tavern at 2259 North Greenview. Nobody trained him to do it. He just seemed to know that a dog is a drunk's best friend.

A regular named Leo was the first to notice it. One night Leo told Evelyn: "You know, when I leave here, that son-of-a-gun always walks me to my door."

It became kind of a joke. Evelyn or Leo would tell people: "Don't worry about getting rolled on the way home. Freddie will get you there."

And he did. The regulars would leave one at a time—Leo, then Shorty and Teddie and Donnie and Marty.

They would stagger down the street with Freddie at their sides. As soon as one of them lurched safely into his house, Freddie would trot back to the bar for another.

Evelyn recalled: "Sometimes one of them would be leaving, and I'd say: 'Wait, Freddie's not back yet from taking Tony home.' So they'd have another drink and wait for Freddie."

After a while, Freddie knew where most of the regulars lived, which is more than some of the regulars knew at 2:00 A.M. So all they had to do was follow him and he'd get them there.

Nobody kept track of how many times Freddie got people safely home. Hundreds, even thousands. And not one of them was mugged or pinched for vagrancy.

Think about that. A Saint Bernard named Barry is in history books because he rescued forty people during a blizzard in Switzerland in 1800. Freddie provided safe escort for that many people on any busy Saturday night.

Then there was the incident with Old Jake. Even now, when somebody mentions it, everybody at the bar drinks a silent toast to Freddie.

It was late one night during last winter's terrible blizzard. Old Jake had been drinking boilermakers to brace himself for the long walk home. By midnight, he had braced himself enough to walk to Alaska.

"When Jake got up to leave, I told Freddie to go with him," Evelyn said. And off they went into the fierce cold and deep snow.

About ten minutes later, Freddie returned. But instead of mooching a piece of pepperoni, he stood near the door and barked.

"Lay down," Evelyn said. But Freddie kept barking and barking.

"I said: 'I wonder what's wrong with that crazy dog,'" recalled Evelyn.

Somebody opened the door and Freddie went outside. But

he just stood there barking. So a couple of the regulars went outside to see why he was acting that way.

Freddie ran down the street and they followed him. He turned at the next corner, then stopped and stood wagging his tail.

There, lying in a snowbank, almost covered with new snow, was Old Jake.

He had passed out. And if Freddie hadn't brought help, Jake might not have been found until the spring thaw.

"Freddie saved his life for sure," said Evelyn. "When he sobered up, Jake even came back and thanked Freddie. Gave him a whole bag of chips.

"I swear, if I could afford it, I'd have a statue made of that dog."

There have been statues made of devoted dogs. So if some sculptor out there wants to make one, Evelyn and Wally would be glad to put it in a place of honor. Maybe next to the cash register.

It wouldn't have to be big or even artistic. Just the prone figure of a man—with a pint bottle in his hand. And standing over him in a noble pose, a mixed-breed mutt.

But don't put a brandy keg under Freddie's chin. That's for Saint Bernards.

For Freddie, maybe just a piece of pepperoni sticking out of his mouth.

2 | THOSE DAMNED BUREAUCRATS

Memo(ries) Are for Real

January 26, 1973

I'm a bureaucracy buff. Whenever I can, I enjoy watching bureaucrats in action because they are so orderly.

They live by the book. They communicate through the memo. And when they go home at night, their desks are clean.

On the other hand, my desk is sloppy and I hate writing memos because it is just as easy to yell something across an office.

But, of course, yelling across the office defeats the whole system because you can't put a yell into a file. And maintaining a complete file is part of an effective bureaucracy.

I recently obtained a fine specimen of the bureaucrat in action.

It consists of a series of four memos sent within the offices of Southwest City College, 7500 South Pulaski Road.

To be fully appreciated, the memos should be read in their proper sequence, as they are presented below.

I think they tell the entire story.

MEMO ONE
Dec. 19, 1972
Memo to: Marilyn Mayer
From: M. Gaines
Subject: Meeting—Spring, 1973 Librarian Schedule
There will be a meeting Friday, Dec. 22, at 9:00 A.M. in Conference Room A, Building 100, to discuss the five-day schedule for Learning Resources Center faculty, Spring, 1973.

MEMO TWO
Memo To: Marilyn Mayer
From: Wesley E. Soderquist, Provost
Subject: Attendance of Meeting of Dec. 22, 1972
Date: Jan. 2, 1973
On Dec. 22, 1972, a meeting was called to discuss the Spring, 1973, schedule for the library faculty.
You did not attend this meeting.
Please indicate to me, in writing, the reason why you did not attend.

MEMO THREE
Memo To: W. Soderquist, Provost
From: M. Mayer, chairman, Learning Resources Center
Subject: Attendance of Meeting of Dec. 22, 1972, in response to Soderquist memo of Jan. 2, 1973.
Date: Jan. 2, 1973
On Dec. 22, 1972, two-thirds of the LRC librarians were not scheduled to be on campus. This fact was apparent in the schedule submitted to you some weeks ago.
Our department asked for the meeting to be rescheduled for a time when the staff would be present, but this request was denied.

It was also not made clear, though requested, why this subject could not have been discussed at our regular weekly meeting of Dec. 18, when you, Mr. Conway, and Miss Gaines were present and yet dismissed the meeting after five minutes.

In lieu of granting of these requests, I did send in writing a note designating Mr. Hensley as my representative. I presume you accepted this as I did not receive any word contrary to this.

You are aware, I am sure, that on other occasions, I have attended meetings called by the administration even when they did not fall within my schedule.

This date, however, as you are also aware, was particularly important to me, apart from Southwest College.

It was my wedding date—and I am incredulous that, knowing this, you still scheduled a meeting of the Learning Resources Staff.

MEMO FOUR

Office of the Provost

Memo To: Miss Marilyn Mayer, chairman, Learning Resources Center

From: Wesley E. Soderquist, Provost

Subject: Attendance of meeting of Dec. 22, 1972, response to Miss Mayer's memo of Jan. 2, 1973

Date: January 4, 1973

You may consider this memo as a reprimand for not attending a meeting called by the administration.

Neither Miss Gaines nor myself were notified of your wedding on that day.

In the future, please inform us of any event that prevents you from fulfilling your obligation to the college.

I further suggest that you adjust your library attendance form to effect a day of Personal Leave for Dec. 22.

End of memos. The file is up-to-date.

Incidentally, Miss Mayer says that three days before her wedding, at a faculty dinner, she told a group of people about her wedding plans. She says Mr. Soderquist was among them.

But things people say are unreal. Only memos are real.

A Faceless Man's Plea

December 10, 1973

Leroy Bailey had just turned twenty-one. He was one of seven kids from a broken family in Connecticut. He had been in the infantry in Vietnam only one month.

Then the rocket tore through the roof of his tent while he was sleeping and exploded in his face.

He was alive when the medics pulled him out. But he was blind. And his face was gone. It's the simplest way to describe it: He no longer had a face.

That was in the spring of 1968. He went to an army hospital, was discharged and shipped to Hines VA Hospital, west of Chicago.

After three years and much surgery, they told him there was little more they could do for him. He still had no face.

Now Bailey spends most his life in the basement of his brother's home in La Grange. The brother moved here from the East to be near him while he was hospitalized.

He knits wool hats, which a friend sells for him. He listens to the radio or to a tape player.

Because of his terrible wound, most of the goals and pleasures of men his age will always be denied him.

But there is one thing he would like to be able to do someday. It isn't much, because most of us take it for granted.

He would like to eat solid foods.

Since 1968, he has eaten nothing but liquids. He uses a large syringe to squirt liquid foods down his throat.

Last year, through some friends of his brother, Bailey met a doctor who specializes in facial surgery.

The doctor, Charles Janda of Oak Brook, said he believed he could reconstruct Bailey's face so that he could eat solid foods.

But it would require a series of at least six separate operations, possibly more.

Bailey eagerly agreed, and the first operation was performed at Mercy Hospital.

Then Dr. Janda and the hospital sent their bills to the Veterans Administration.

They did this because Bailey and his brother were under the impression that the VA would pay for any treatment he needed that wasn't available in the VA.

The VA refuses to pay the bills. The reason was explained in a remarkable letter sent to Bailey by a VA official. (The italics are mine.)

Dear Mr. Bailey:

Reference is made to the enclosed invoice for services given to you for selective plastic surgery done on Sept. 22, 1972.

It is regretted that payment on the above cannot be approved, since the treatment was for a condition other than that of your service-connected disability.

Outpatient treatment and/or medication may only be authorized for the treatment of a disability which has been

adjudicated by the Veterans Administration as incurred in
or aggravated by military service.

Any expense involved for this condition must be a
personal transaction between you and the doctor.

It is astonishing, I know, but the VA actually told him that
he was being treated for something "other than that of your
service-connected disability."

How can this surgery be for anything else but his "service-
connected disability?"

Until he was hit by a rocket, Bailey had teeth. Now he has
none. He had eyes. Now he has none. He had a nose. Now he
has none. People could look at him. Now most of them turn
away.

Bailey believes that the VA thinks he wants the surgery just
to look better, that it is "cosmetic" surgery.

Even if that were so, then why in the hell not? If we can
afford $5 million to make the San Clemente property pret-
tier, we can do whatever is humanly possible for man's
face.

But Bailey insists it isn't his appearance that concerns him.
He knows it will never be normal.

He explains his feelings in an appeal he filed months ago
with the VA:

The only thing I am asking for is the ability to chew and
swallow my food.

This was the purpose for the whole series of painful and
unsuccessful operations I underwent in Hines Hospital between the day of my injury on May, 1968, and my eventual
discharge from the hospital in 1971.

At the time, I was told the very depressing news that
nothing further could be done.

I will never be able to accept this decision . . .

In some bureaucrat's file cabinet is Bailey's appeal. It has been there for many months.

Every day that it sits there, Bailey takes his syringe and squirts liquid nourishment down his throat.

If his appeal is turned down, he will spend the rest of his life doing that. Not even once will he be able to sit down and eat at the dinner table with his brother's family, before going back down to the basement to knit hats.

The VA Does a Fast Reversal

December 11, 1973

A year after giving the brush-off to blind, faceless Leroy Bailey, the Veterans Administration has reversed itself in almost a matter of minutes. Monday, after I wrote about Bailey's case, the VA bureaucrats suddenly found new energy, compassion, and ability to make a decision.

The VA says it now has decided to pay the medical bills Bailey incurred in trying to get his face rebuilt enough to eat solid foods.

It was an interesting study of a governmental bureaucracy in action.

Late in the morning, we were called by Don Monico, a VA public relations man.

He couldn't answer questions, but he said we should talk to Vern Rogers, a bigger VA public relations man.

Mr. Rogers, in turn, said that he was not speaking for himself. He was speaking for Alton Pruitt, director of the West Side VA hospital.

(In a bureaucracy, it is usually done like this, if possible. That way, nobody is actually speaking, since Mr. Rogers is not speaking for himself, and Mr. Pruitt isn't really speaking.)

Anyway Rogers-speaking-for-Pruitt said the whole matter was being referred immediately to some mucky-muck board in Washington.

"It will go to Washington for an administrative review. And whether or not payment will be made will have to be determined by a board of medical examiners."

This, of course, was laughable. Why was a big review needed to make the decision to let Bailey chew food?

Rogers-speaking-for-Pruitt wasn't sure about that.

But a moment later he said that Mr. Pruitt would actually come on the phone and speak for himself. Which he did.

"I was just on the line to Washington," Mr. Pruitt said. "The VA is going to go ahead and pay. We also are going to ask him to come in so we can make a complete assessment of his needs."

Just like that. It shows how efficient a government agency can be—a year late—if its inefficiency is suddenly splashed across a newspaper.

But that still doesn't explain why the VA originally wrote Bailey that his facial surgery "was for a condition other than that of your service-connected disability."

I tried to get an answer.

That letter had come from Jack Pierce, chief of the medical administration service at the West Side VA.

But it wasn't signed by Mr. Pierce. It was signed by a J. Funches "FOR" Mr. Pierce.

Mr. Pierce wasn't available to discuss it. So we contacted Josephine Funches, who signs letters for Mr. Pierce.

She didn't remember too much about the case. "I think I

may have read an article about him in the paper,'' she said.

But you wrote a letter to him.

''I may have signed a letter, but that letter was just sent out over my signature, that's all.''

Do you follow this procedure? Mrs. Funches signed the letter for Mr. Pierce. But she says the letter was somebody else's creation.

So we tried the public relations man again, Rogers-who-speaks-for-Pruitt.

''That [the letter] was an error on the part of the Veterans Administration,'' said Mr. Rogers.

Any idiot can see that. The question is, who made the error?

''A clerk made the mistake,'' said Rogers.

There's your bureaucracy. If what Mr. Rogers says is true, a clerk decided that Bailey's terrible injury wasn't the result of the war. And he typed Mr. Pierce's name. And Mrs. Funches signed the letter for Mr. Pierce.

If that is the way they do things, there must be a lot more Leroy Baileys out there.

Snakes Alive

May 11, 1974

The postmaster in a small town in Montana recently received his regular manila envelope from his superiors at regional headquarters in San Francisco.

It always contains pep talks, brochures, interoffice memos—the usual junk executives use to plague subordinates.

The postmaster opened the big envelope and dumped the contents on his desk.

Two eighteen-inch snakes fell out, one red and the other a bluish color. They landed on the desk top and wriggled.

The elderly postmaster did what most people do when surprised by snakes, especially in an unlikely place.

He cried out, jumped up, and ran halfway across the office. His pulse rated quickened, his breathing became heavy, and his adrenalin flowed.

Then, from the other side of his office, he stared. He cautiously approached his desk. The snakes were still. He got closer and saw that they were made of rubber.

He pawed through the written material that had been in the envelope, looking for an explanation as to why the Western Regional Office of the United States Postal Service would send him two rubber snakes.

He found a collapsible corrugated box, with precut air holes in the side. It appeared to be a cage for the rubber snakes.

And he found a brochure. He read it and it sounded so crazy that he called me.

"Don't use my name," he said, "because I've only got a year to go to my pension.

"But as far as I can tell, they want postmasters to put those snakes around the post office to scare employees, so they'll be on their toes, or something like that.

"Or maybe it's to remind them that they should always be alert so they don't hurt themselves in industrial accidents.

"I'm not sure which, from reading the brochure.

"But I'll tell you, it sure scared hell out of me. I mean, with letter bombs and things like that, the first thing I thought when I saw them was that some maniac was out to get me. That's a crazy thing to do, don't you think?"

I should say so. I've never sent anyone a rubber snake, although I once planted one in the bunk of a friend of mine when we were in the service. He jumped out of the window and sprained an ankle. I also put a rubber worm in another friend's mess hall stew, and a rubber roach in an acquaintance's martini.

But I am known to have a crude sense of humor. Something more should be expected from our U.S. Postal Service.

I called Washington to find out why a postmaster would receive rubber snakes.

"They are only being sent out in the Western region of the country," the public affairs officer said. "They have the explanation."

So I called San Francisco and talked to James Speck, the regional manager of public affairs.

"Yes, we have sent some of them out," he said.

"How many?"

"About five hundred."

"Why are you sending out snakes?"

"Actually, we don't call them snakes. We call them hazard adders. They are symbolic of danger—the danger of on-the-job hazards.

"We have regular safety campaigns and the hazard adders are the symbol of our most recent one."

I told him that one of his postmasters was almost scared to death by the snakes, which would seem to be a safety hazard in itself.

"Well, they aren't supposed to fall out that way," he said. "They are supposed to be in a package."

Are they supposed to be hidden about the post office, to keep postal employees alert?

"No. Somebody might slip on them. And that would just defeat the purpose."

Then how are they to be used?

"The postmaster or his safety officer is supposed to call the employees together and give a talk on hazards. During the talk, the snake is supposed to be used as a symbol.''

Of course. The postmaster calls his employees together. Then he gets up and makes a speech, with a snake in each hand. Or maybe wrapped around his neck.

I'm sure that would make employees aware of dangers on their job, especially the danger posed by a crazy postmaster.

Mr. Speck didn't say what the next safety campaign's gimmick will be.

But they ought to give some thoughts to the old hotfoot.

Bureaucrats Are at It Again

May 26, 1976

I like stories like these two. They confirm my theory that for every honest, inoffensive, harmless citizen, there is a bureaucrat waiting for a chance to goof him up.

Or, as Joe Louis once said about his opponents, "They can run, but they can't hide.''

Janet Noble was in the supermarket. She walked away from her food cart to talk to the butcher. It took only a moment.

When she walked back to her cart, she yelled: "My purse is gone!''

The store's employees ran around looking for the thief, but it was too late. The police came and filled out their reports.

Over dinner that night, Janet and her husband, Dick, a car salesman, were glum. They are young and the loss of $100 hurt. And replacing charge cards, keys, licenses, and worrying about bouncing checks is a bother.

A few days later, the store manager called Mrs. Noble. Somebody had written a bum seventy-five dollar check, forging her name.

And one of her credit cards had been used at another store.

Two policemen came to her apartment to get more information about the contents of the stolen purse.

They sat down in the living room and talked. Then one of the policemen noticed something on the living room bar.

"Say, is that a slot machine?"

"Yes," said Mrs. Noble. "We got it as a wedding gift."

She explained that some friends had given it to them. It was quite old and her husband liked to tinker with it.

"It's a conversation piece," she said.

"Does it work?" the policeman asked.

"I'm not sure," Mrs. Noble said. "Sometimes it does, sometimes it doesn't. I keep quarters in it for the laundry room washers and driers. The back of it is open."

The policeman reached in and got a quarter, put it in the slot, and pulled the lever. Two cherries and a lemon came up, and the machine paid out five quarters.

"This is an illegal gambling device," said the policeman, "and we have to confiscate it."

So they picked it up and hauled it away.

Then they got a warrant and Mrs. Noble was arrested on a charge of possessing an illegal gambling device.

She went to the police station and was fingerprinted, photographed, and her picture was put in the files with forgers, purse thieves, and people of that sort.

When she went to court, the case was dropped. But the police said they wanted to destroy the slot machine. Her lawyer won, and the machine was returned. But now Mrs.

Noble has hidden it away with friends in case the police come after it again.

As for her stolen purse—remember her stolen purse?—the police haven't found it yet. Mrs. Noble has a new purse now. But she is careful not to put it down in stores. She might be pinched for littering.

The Farris brothers are in the heating and air-conditioning business in Springfield. The business has been in their family since 1899.

They advertise on the radio. The manufacturer of some of their products provides them with commercials.

They recently used a commercial that said: "You may have to live with outdoor air pollution for a while yet, but you don't have to live with indoor air pollution." The commercial suggested the purchase of some kind of air-filtered air-conditioning unit.

Not long after that the Farris brothers received a letter from the Illinois Environmental Protection Agency.

It was a very official letter, since this is a very official state agency. It said:

Recently it was brought to the attention of the Illinois Environmental Protection Agency that WFMB-FM radio in Springfield, Illinois, was airing a Farris Bros. commercial, which, in describing an air conditioner, stated that although we can't do anything about the dirty air outside, we can make the inside air clean.

Illinois EPA is concerned with the quality of Illinois 'outside air' and is concerned with all references to such air, even those included in private advertisements.

The letter went on to ask who had developed the ads, and whether there were plans to use such ads in the future.

And it asked for an answer "by the end of the month."

It was signed by Ernest K. Nielsen, attorney for the "Enforcement Section of the Division of Air Pollution Control."

The letter made the Farris brothers nervous. Like any small businessmen, they are sensitive to official letters from governmental agencies.

They wondered what kind of regulation they might have violated by "referring" in a commercial to the air we all breathe.

As it turned out, they hadn't done anything wrong. It appears that the pollution agency was just trying to intimidate them. The bureaucrats don't like people talking about pollution.

The attorney who wrote the letter admits that his supervisor told him to do so. But he won't say who the supervisor is.

For two days, we placed about a dozen calls to officials in the Environmental Protection Agency, trying to learn who ordered the letter written and why the antipollution bureaucrats are harassing businessmen about advertising. All of them, from Director Richard H. Briceland down, refused to accept the calls or answer questions.

I know an old lady who, when surprised, says: "As I live and breathe!"

I'm going to tell her to be careful about that.

He's Lazy, Not Disturbed

May 12, 1978

You wouldn't have to be a shrink to know that something was wrong with Miguel Maldonado, twenty-four.

Just the look in his eyes was a tip-off. Sometimes his eyes were glazed. Sometimes they were wild. But they seldom looked normal.

Then there were the voices that he heard when people weren't around. The voices told him he wasn't of much use to anyone.

Whatever his inner problems were, they had started early. By the time he finished grammar school, he was getting drunk, smoking marijuana, and popping whatever kind of pills the neighborhood pushers carried. And around Humboldt Park, the pushers carry almost a complete pharmacy in their pockets.

As Miguel got older, he moved to Uptown, did odd jobs, and slipped into the drug world. He apparently tried just about everything, including Angel Dust. That is a very pretty name for a tranquilizer usually prescribed for cows and horses.

Apparently all of these harmful additives didn't make him happy. He brooded a lot, was depressed, and occasionally talked about killing himself.

He drifted around the country for a few years. His family doesn't know exactly what he did or where he went, but a trip within his trip took him to an Iowa mental hospital.

And when he came home, his travels hadn't made him any happier.

"He was not an addict," said a brother, Ray. "But he was an abuser.

"Many times, he would not be high. When he lived with me, I was with him most of the time, and I know he was not high.

"But he would have this glaze over his eye. He had this dangerous look."

Lately, his brother says, Miguel's mental problems seemed to be getting worse. He confessed that he sometimes sold himself as a male prostitute to buy dope.

He began hearing those voices when nobody was around. Hearing voices is never good. But in Miguel's case, the voices were giving him bad advice. They were telling him that he ought to kill himself.

So he and his brother agreed that Miguel needed professional help.

First they went to a drug rehabilitation clinic. But the people at the clinic said that he needed more than drug rehabilitation, and suggested he go to a mental hospital.

So Miguel went to the Madden Mental Health Center. He was there for about five days, but then he signed himself out.

He went back on the street and into dope for a couple of weeks. And when he showed up at his brother's house again, the voices were really jabbering to him.

His brother had him examined by a doctor at a city Board of Health clinic.

"The doctor told us that Miguel was actively hallucinating, that he could hurt himself or hurt others. He wrote that in his report."

Miguel didn't argue with that, his brother says. "He told me he needed help, that he wanted help."

The doctor wrote a letter, stating that Miguel should be hospitalized, and Ray took him to the Chicago-Read Mental Health Center, 6500 Irving Park Road.

Chicago-Read, which used to be known as Dunning, is run by the state. Throughout its history, somebody or other is usually issuing a report that conditions aren't good. Only a few days ago, the Mental Health Association of Greater Chicago said that many patients who are poor live in close company with roaches, rats, and each other. Their dormitories are filthy, smell bad, and are filled with trash. And they aren't getting much help for their mental problems.

But Ray did not know about that report. And even if he'd known, he wouldn't have had much choice. People who don't have a lot of money either use places like Chicago-Read or they wander the streets talking to themselves.

When they got to Chicago-Read, Ray talked to a doctor. He told him about Miguel's problems and showed him the referral from the Board of Health doctor. And Miguel said that the voices were telling him to kill himself.

Ray did not expect his brother to be treated like a paying guest at the Drake Hotel. But he didn't expect the kind of reception he said they received.

"After we talked to the doctor, he said Miguel didn't need hospitalization. He said Miguel's problem was that he was lazy and that he belonged in jail instead of in the hospital. He said that our family was just tired of him and we were trying to put him in the hospital to get rid of him.

"When I started to argue with him, he picked up the telephone and said he would call the security guards if we did not leave. So we had no choice but to leave."

That sounds like an insensitive attitude, even for Chicago-Read. We tried to confirm Ray's account of the conversation, but the doctor refused to return numerous phone calls.

Anyway, Ray went home with his troubled brother Miguel, who was still hearing those voices.

And at noon the next day, Miguel took the voices' advice.

He went downtown to the Clark Street Bridge, climbed over the railing, jumped into the Chicago River, and drowned.

Now: Talk Like an Educator!

January 9, 1973

Until now, only professional educators knew how to speak Educatorese, that mysterious language with which they befuddle the rest of us.

But now, for the first time, anyone can learn to speak it.

All you need is the new guide: "How to Speak Like an Educator Without Being Educated."

And as a public service, the guide is being printed in its entirety below.

In a moment, I'll provide instructions on its use. But first, a word of credit to its creators.

The guide is the work of two rhetoric and speech teachers at Danville (Ill.) Junior College, Barbara Stover and Ilva Walker. They compiled it after years of wading through administrative circulars.

They did it for fun, but some of their students have found that the phrases are useful in preparing papers for sociology classes.

The guide is simple to use.

Take one word from each of the five columns. It doesn't matter which word. Take them in any order, or in no order.

For instance, if you take the second word of Column "A"; the fourth word from Column "B"; the sixth word from

Column "C"; and the eighth and tenth words from the last two columns you will have:

Flexible ontological productivity implement control group and experimental group.

That doesn't make sense, does it? But now add a few connecting words, and we have:

"Flexible and ontological productivity will implement the control group and experimental group."

That still doesn't make any sense. But it sounds like it does. Which means it is perfect Educatorese.

You can do it with any combination of the words. As an example, use the first five digits of my office phone: 321-21.

This works out to:

Adaptable reciprocal nuclei terminate total modular exchange.

Add a few little words and you have a splendid sentence, worthy of at least an assistant superintendent:

"Adaptable and reciprocal nuclei will terminate in total modular exchange." And you can quote me on that.

Go to it. With this guide you say things like:

"The interdisciplinary or supportive input will encapsulate vertical team structure."

Or "Optimal ethnic accountability should facilitate post-secondary education enrichment."

Try it yourself. Once you get the hang of it—who knows? —you might wind up with Superintendent Redmond's job.

A	
comprehensive	conceptual
flexible	ideological
adaptable	optimal
culturally	minimal
perceptual	categorically
evaluative	unequivocally
innovative	intrapersonal
interdisciplinary	interpersonal

B

cognitive
reciprocal
stylistic
ontological
prime
supportive
workable
resultant
behavioral
judgmental
ethnic
attitudinal
multicultural
encounter
counterproductive
generative
cognate

C

nuclei
interaction
focus
balance
chain of command
productivity
conformance
panacea
rationale
input
throughput
accountability
feedback
objective
resources

C (Continued)

perspective
curricula
priorities
diversity
environment
overview
strategies
posture
methodologies
introversion
posits
concept
Gestalt

D

indicates
terminate
geared
compile
articulate
verbalize
facilitate
implement
incur
sensitize
synthesize
integrate
fragment
maximize
minimize
energize
individualize
encapsulate
orientate

E
total modular exchange
in-depth discussion
multipurpose framework and goals
serial communication
serial transmission of applicable cable tools and
    instrumentation
post-secondary education enrichment
changing needs of society
motivational serial communications
high potential for assessing failure
control group and experimental group
student-faculty relationships
identifiable decision-making process
sophisticated resource systems analyses
vertical team structure
translation in depth
classroom context
individual horizons

The Virtues of a Butterfly Net

February 14, 1973

Although I am against the ownership of guns, I think every
citizen should be equipped with a large butterfly net.

Then we could throw the nets over all the strange people
we meet and take them where they belong.

With that introduction here are two stories to illustrate what I mean.

THE UNION ORGANIZER

June Rapp plays and sings at the piano bar in the Red Carpet Restaurant, 28 West Elm. She is very good, according to fans of piano-bar music.

Not long ago, a man from the Musicians Union came into the Red Carpet. He asked Mrs. Rapp, who was not performing at the moment, who the piano player was.

She said that she was.

He asked her if she was a member of the Musicians Union.

She said that indeed she was, and has been for a long time.

In that case, he said, why hadn't she signed a union contract with the owners of the Red Carpet Restaurant.

For a very good reason, said Mrs. Rapp. The owners of the Red Carpet Restuarant happened to be she and her husband, Stan. She had joined the union before they bought the Red Carpet and while she was working somewhere else.

But now she was working in her own place.

Therefore, she would be signing a contract with herself.

The idea struck her as funny.

"I play the piano when I feel like playing. When I don't feel like it, I don't play.

"With that kind of attitude, I would have to fire myself if I was living up to a contract.

"And if I think I'm working too hard, who should I go on strike against? Myself?"

Unfortunately, the Musicians Union has no sense of humor. As it has proved so often in the past, it has little sense at all.

And so, as of right now, Mrs. Rapp has been charged by the union with the following:

- Imperiling the interests of the union.
- Violation of union rules.

- Failure to remit payments for the welfare fund.
- Failure to use proper contract form, submitted to local recording secretary before scheduling engagement.

In other words, the Musicians Union wants Mrs. Rapp to sign a contract with Mrs. Rapp.

I called the union to ask how a person can sign a contract with herself. Leo Nye, the recording secretary, said: "All matters concerning publicity must go through the office of the union president, Mr. Daniel Garamoni."

"I will speak to him."

"He is not here." Click.

Mrs. Rapp doesn't know what to do now. She fears that if she signs a contract with herself, she might then go on strike and picket herself. Which means that if she decides to go inside her own joint, she will have to hit herself on the head with her placard.

My advice is that she go on the way she is. But she should keep a butterfly net next to the piano, just in case the union man comes around again.

THE HIGHWAY MENACE

Joseph Mascari, twenty-three, took his car to Bob and Lee's Car Wash at Peterson and Crawford.

It is the kind of car wash in which you remain in your car while the machine moves it through the brushes and suds.

He said he was about halfway through when the steering wheel suddenly spun and the car hopped off the track, banging against the side barriers.

They turned the conveyer off and one of the attendants told him to back the car back onto the track. He did, and the wash was completed.

Then he got out and looked at the side of the car. There appeared to be about $100 damage to the door and fenders.

"You must have turned the steering wheel," the attendant told him. "The sign says you should not turn the wheel."

"I saw the sign and I did not turn the steering wheel," Mascari said. "I have been through the car wash before. I know not to turn the wheel."

"The machine does not make mistakes," the attendant said. "You must have turned the wheel."

Then the attendant picked up a phone and called the police.

A policeman arrived. He wrote a ticket and gave it to Mascari.

The ticket says that at the time of the violation, Mascari had been "east-bound on car wash rack at 4000 W. Peterson."

It also described the general motoring conditions at the time.

"Road conditions: Wet.

"Light conditions: Daylight.

"Weather: Clear.

"Traffic: Light."

The charge: "Negligent driving."

Mascari posted his license as bond and will appear in court in several weeks.

I will go there and let you know how it turns out. The car wash manager will probably be there. So will the policeman.

I had better bring at least two butterfly nets.

Wrong Mom? Tough!

November 18, 1979

Mrs. Fran Lasota is in real trouble. She has been formally accused of abandoning her own baby. And she has received a summons, ordering her to appear in court and to bring the neglected baby with her.

Fran's friends and neighbors in the town of Marengo will probably be shocked and dismayed to read that Fran would abandon her baby in Chicago. Especially since Fran is in her forties and hasn't had a baby for many years.

It came as a shock to Fran, too, when her phone rang a few weeks ago and a bureaucrat from the Illinois Department of Children and Family Services asked her why she had abandoned her baby.

"My what?" asked Fran.

"Your baby," the bureaucrat said.

"What are you talking about?"

The man told her that a week-old boy had been brought to a Chicago hospital to be treated for a rash.

The hospital cured the rash, but the mother never came back for the baby.

"Why do you think it is my baby?" Fran asked.

"Is your name Frances Lasota?"

"Yes."

"Well, that's the name of the mother," the bureaucrat said.

Fran told the man that he had the wrong Fran Lasota. And she asked him how she had been chosen as the errant mother.

From what he said, she gathered that he had just looked in phone books for people named Lasota until he found one named Fran.

"Well, you'll have to keep looking," she said, "because it's not my kid."

She thought that would be the end of it. But recently she received a registered letter.

It was the summons, telling her that she had to appear in court on a neglect charge. And it said she should bring her baby with her.

Naturally she was flustered. She called the Cook County state's attorney's office, which prosecutes neglectful parents, and explained her problem.

"He told me I had better show up in court," she said.

She called a lawyer in Marengo and asked him what to do.

"He told me I should get a Chicago lawyer to defend me."

She called the Marengo Police Department to see if it had any advice.

"They told me that I should probably go to court. If I didn't, I might be held in contempt of court for not showing up with the baby I don't have."

She called the Department of Children and Family Services and tried to explain her problem.

"They didn't seem to understand what I was talking about."

Now she doesn't know what to do. It's a long trip from Marengo to Chicago, and Fran doesn't see why she should have to come all that way for something she hasn't anything to do with. Nor does she want to spend money on a lawyer.

But she is afraid if she doesn't show up, she will be held in contempt and will be in even worse trouble.

So she sought my advice, which was a wise thing for her to do, since I've had a lot of experience in dealing with bureaucrats.

My advice to Fran is that she had better go to court.

And she had better bring a baby with her.

Believe me, if you show up without a baby, they'll just get suspicious. They'll think you dropped the kid on his head and don't want to admit it, and you'll be in deeper trouble.

So borrow one. Somebody must have a baby you can use for a day. Go in there, show them the kid is healthy and happy, and maybe they'll let you off with just a stern warning.

On the other hand, they might decide you are unfit and take the baby away from you. Then you'd have to go back to your friend and say: "Sorry, but your kid's in a foster home. But thanks for trying to help."

That wouldn't be good because your friend would probably be miffed. So I'll have to come up with another plan.

OK, here's what you do. Go rent a monkey. There are places you can get them.

Put the monkey in baby clothes and take it to court and say to the judge:

"OK, Your Honor. I admit it. I abandoned my baby. But look at this kid. He looks like a monkey. It's from his father's side. If you had a kid this ugly, Your Honor, wouldn't you abandon him? I mean, he's got hair on his feet."

Chances are, the judge will be sympathetic and let you go, especially if the monkey bites him.

The worst that can happen is that they will declare you an unfit mother and take the monkey away from you and put it in a foster home.

You'll be out one monkey and the Department of Children and Family Services will be stuck with a foster baby that bites, climbs the drapes, and has hair on its feet.

And who knows—someday you might be proud. The kid could grow up to be an alderman.

That 'Nothing to Hide' Game

March 31, 1975

The man's voice sounded smug over the phone. "I don't see what the big fuss is about. If people don't have anything to hide, why should they care if somebody investigates them?"

In a friendly tone, I asked him what his name was. He hesitated for a moment, then told me.

"And your address?" I said.

"What do you want that for?" he said. "I just called to tell you what I thought. You don't need my address."

"Well, if you're ashamed of where you live. . . ."

"I'm not ashamed of where I live," he said indignantly. And he gave me his home address.

I began sounding officious. "Where are you employed?"

"Hey," he said, "I just called to tell you what I thought."

"That's what YOU say. But how do I know what your real motives were?"

"What do you mean, my real motives? I'm giving you my opinion."

"Sure, but what's behind it?"

"There's nothing behind it."

"Then tell me where you work."

"For what?"

"I'd like to do some checking on you."

"On ME?"

"That's right. Who do you work for? Who do you associate with?" I was starting to sound like a professional interrogator.

"What the hell is that to you?"

"Tell me, do you belong to any organizations? Do you own stocks, bonds, real estate, and what is your relationship with your wife?"

"My wife?"

"How much income tax did you pay last year and on how much income? Let's have the facts. C'MON."

"You're nuts," he said, and he hung up.

I don't blame him. I guess I did sound a little nuttier than usual.

But my approach had worked again. Every time somebody gives me the old "if a person has nothing to hide" routine, I counter by asking them personal questions. There was the lady who sent me the letter in which she said that she didn't see why Bill Singer or anyone should object to being followed if he wasn't doing anything wrong.

I looked her up in the phone book and called.

"What is your age please?" I said.

"Why do you want to know that?" she said.

"If we publish your letter, we would like to include your age."

"I'd rather you didn't," she said.

"But I need your age in order to fill out this form."

"I don't understand. What form?"

"An opinion form. You see, when you express an opinion, as you did in the letter, I'm supposed to fill out a form."

"Oh, I didn't know that."

"Oh, sure. We can't have people expressing personal opinions without checking on them."

"Well, I'd rather not," she said, believing my nonsense.

"Just a few facts. What is your husband's income, his

take-home pay? Have you ever been married before? If so, what was the reason for your divorce?''

She answered with what I assume was a gasp.

"Please give me the names of the people you normally associate with during a year's time. What banks do you use and how much do you have in your account? Do you or your husband ever DRINK? If so, how MUCH?"

She sounded outraged. "I'm not telling YOU anything."

"Could you at least tell me the make and color of your car?"

"Our car?"

"Yes, that would make it easier if we have someone follow you in order to get this information."

She shrieked: "You leave us alone or I'll call the police." Then she hung up.

Now there is a very, very suspicious character. She didn't even say good-by.

The Eighty-three-Year-Old Desperado

June 10, 1979

At eighty-three, Irving Naiditch is a fine old geezer. He says what he thinks, is amused by the foolishness of humans, and takes joy in simple things.

For example, Mr. Naiditch boarded a Clark Street bus a few days ago. He was pleased to see the sign that said senior citizens could ride for twenty-five cents. Like most older people, he likes bargains.

So he dropped his quarter in the box and moved slowly toward a seat, leaning on his cane.

Then the bus driver said: "I need to see some identification."

"Sure," said Mr. Naiditch, and he took out some ID showing his age.

"No," said the driver. "There's a special card from the CTA you need to have."

Mr. Naiditch did not have the CTA identification card because he lives in Minnesota and was here visiting his two sons.

He told the driver: "The sign up there doesn't say anything about a special card. It just says you have to be a senior citizen. I'm a senior citizen."

The driver said: "You need a special ID card."

Mr. Naiditch said: "Where does it say that on the sign? Show me."

The driver said: "It's the rules."

Mr. Naiditch said: "Show me the rule. All I see is the sign and it says I can ride for a quarter."

The bus driver shook his head: "You have to put in another quarter."

Mr. Naiditch said: "Don't I look old enough for you?"

The driver said: "Put in another quarter or get off the bus."

One of the privileges of old age is being stubborn. Mr. Naiditch said: "OK, give me back my quarter, and I'll get off the bus."

The driver said: "I can't give you the quarter. It's in the box."

And Mr. Naiditch said: "Why should I get off the bus if you won't return my quarter? I want my quarter or I want my ride."

The driver said: "Look, if you don't get off the bus, I'm going to call the police."

"So call the police," said Mr. Naiditch, walking to the rear of the bus and sitting down.

A sensible man would have shrugged it off and driven his bus. A sensible man wouldn't have argued with an eighty-three-year-old man about a quarter in the first place.

But bus drivers sometimes think they are captains of ships. So this driver stood up and told everyone to get off and take the next bus. After pointlessly inconveniencing these people, he found the nearest phone and called the police.

Two squad cars pulled up, and several policemen boarded the bus. The first one had his billy club out.

Mr. Naiditch, sitting alone in the back of the bus, smiled at the policeman and said:

"I'm the desperado."

Mr. Naiditch and the driver told their stories to the policemen.

"And that's what you called us for?" one of the cops said to the driver, looking disgusted.

The driver, filled with a sense of power, said: "Either he pays another quarter or he has to get off the bus. It's the rules."

"I'll get off if he gives me my quarter back," said Mr. Naiditch.

"I told you, it's in the box," said the driver.

The policemen put their heads together, then one of them reached into his pocket and said to Mr. Naiditch: "I'll give you a quarter."

Mr. Naiditch, his sense of logic now in high gear, shook his head and said: "That's not fair. Why should you give me your quarter? The bus has to give me my quarter."

The policemen held another huddle. And it would be nice if I could report that they then hit the bus driver on the head and arrested him for public stupidity.

But they did the next best thing. They asked Mr. Naiditch where he was going.

"I'm going downtown to have lunch with some old friends," he said.

"C'mon," the policemen said. "We'll get your ID card."

So Mr. Naiditch got to ride in a squad car all the way to the

Merchandise Mart, where the CTA has its offices. And one of the policemen accompanied him right to the counter where they issue the ID cards to senior citizens.

However, they wouldn't give him an ID card.

"You need a picture of yourself for the card," a bureaucrat said.

"What about his quarter?" the cop said.

The bureaucrat conferred with his superior and the decision was made to refund Mr. Naiditch's quarter.

"Thank you," said Mr. Naiditch.

When Mr. Naiditch got downstairs, the policeman asked where he was going.

"To see my old friends," said Mr. Naiditch.

"How you going to get there?"

"On the bus. And all I'm going to pay is a quarter."

"Good luck," said the policeman, jumping in his squad car and driving quickly away.

Mr. Naiditch got on a bus, dropped a quarter in the box, and said: "I'm a senior citizen."

The driver looked at Mr. Naiditch and nodded. He didn't know how lucky he was to be a sensible man.

Don't Let the Food Bug You

July 7, 1978

The lady had been eating a box of raisins when she found two bugs. So she put them in a jar and brought it downtown for me to see.

"Look," she said. "You can see them in there. Two bugs."

I peered into the jar, and she was right. They were tiny and appeared lifeless, but they were there, all right.

"You're right," I said. "There are two bugs in your jar."

"Well, what do I do about it?" she said.

"There are a lot of old vaudeville jokes about finding bugs in your food. Should I tell you one?"

"I'm serious," she said. "This has happened to me with food before. Hasn't it ever happened to you?"

It may have, but I've never noticed. I try not to look at food that closely, just so I'll avoid knowing too much about it.

Or even thinking about it. I had a friend who used to think about his food too much. He'd sit at lunch, munching a sandwich, and say things like: "You know, I'm calmly chewing on a piece of ham that came from the dead body of a poor creature that, in its own simple way, once enjoyed living. It had feelings. It knew fear, sexual cravings, fatigue, the pleasure of a good simple meal. And here I am, devouring its body. And we consider ourselves civilized?"

Once, when he was eating a lambchop and poignantly describing the sweet, gentle nature of little woolly lambs that happily frolic in the green meadow, I demanded to know why he didn't just shut up and become a vegetarian.

"Because they spray chemicals on vegetables," he said, "and I've already got enough to worry about eating meat."

So it's best not to think about such things. But to get back to the lady with the bugs in her raisin box.

"Who can I complain to?" she asked.

"The people who package the raisins," I suggested.

"What good will that do?" she said. "It's their product, so you can bet that they know they have bugs in it without my telling them."

"But they'll probably give you a free box. Maybe a whole case of boxes. Ralph Nader has made them all nervous."

"I don't want a free box of this buggy stuff," she said. "I want to get them in trouble for this."

Ah, then there is only one place to go for that. To the federal government. If there is anything our government loves, it is causing trouble for private corporations. It is now estimated that the federal government does more in one week to slow down our national productivity than all of the German saboteurs did during World War II.

"Who do I see there?" she asked.

I had no idea, never having complained about bugs myself. But there had to be a federal agency that did nothing but count bugs in our food, and I urged the lady to go find it.

She called a couple of days later. "It didn't work," she said. "It wasn't above the defect level."

The what?

"They have levels of how many bugs are allowed. This wasn't above it."

I had trouble believing that, but it is true. I've since checked and found that there is a bug guideline put out by the federal government.

It is called "The Food Action Levels—current levels for natural or unavoidable defects in food for human use that present no health hazard."

Under each of the foods listed, there is a "defect action level." Anything below this level the Food and Drug Administration considers "no hazards to health."

And under raisins, it says: "Insects: 10 whole or equivalent insects and 35 drosophilas eggs per eight ounces of golden bleached raisins."

Since the finicky lady had found only two insects in her package, she still was eight whole or equivalent insects short of having a grievance. Plus those 35 drosophilas (fly) eggs. She hadn't found any of those. What was she complaining about?

In case you are the kind of person who studies food closely, looking for tiny black specks and other things that will upset you, here are a few other "defect action levels."

Apple butter: "Average of more than four rodent hairs per 100 grams of apple butter or average of more than five whole or equivalent insects."

(Don't ask me why they allow fewer insects in apple butter than in raisins, but more rodent hairs. I guess it's a matter of taste.)

Fig paste: "Over 13 insect heads per 100 grams of fig paste in each of two or more subsamples."

(That's another puzzler: In fig paste, you count only the insect heads. But what does a person do if he finds thirteen pairs of insect feet in his fig paste? Or thirteen pairs of insect ears? Is he supposed to just overlook it? It seems to me that the federal government is splitting insects, if not hairs.)

Peanut butter: "Average of 30 or more insect fragments per 100 grams, or, average of one or more rodent hairs per 100 grams, or, gritty in taste and water-insoluble inorganic residue is more than 25 mg. per 100 grams."

(No wonder most people also use jelly.)

Frozen broccoli: "Average of 60 aphids, thrips, and/or mites per 100 grams."

(I've always wondered why I disliked broccoli; you're better off with fig paste.)

I could go on, but why bother? Just try not to look too closely at what you eat. As the Food and Drug people wrote in their defect action level guide:

"It is not now possible, and never has been possible, to grow in open fields, harvest, and process crops that are totally free of natural defects. The alternative to establishing natural defect levels in some foods would be to insist on increased utilization of chemical substances to control insects, rodents and other natural contaminants."

So it is either bugs or spray. And we know what happens if

they spray too much. We might turn into bugs ourselves.

As Julia Child says: *Bon appétit!*

That Old, Gray Area

December 20, 1976

It can be infuriating the way minor government officials take their power and flaunt it.

For example, my driver's license expired, so the other day I went to the secretary of state's office on Elston Avenue to get it renewed.

A little lady behind the counter was filling out the application form. Height . . . weight . . .

"Color of eyes?" she asked.

"Brown."

"Color of hair?"

"Brown."

She glanced at my head. "Brown?"

"Uh-huh. Brown. I've always had brown hair."

She looked dubious and said: "I'd say it is, uh, gray."

"Well, in this light, I suppose there's a little gray mixed in with the brown."

She squinted her eyes, studied my head more intensely, and said:

"No, it's mostly gray."

"On the sides, yes. I'm probably getting a little gray along the sideburns."

"Sir, you don't have much hair anywhere but on the sides."

"Look," I said, "what's the big deal? This is just a form."

"I know, sir, but we're supposed to try to get it right. For identification purposes. So I'll put down . . ."

"How about grayish brown?"

"I'm sorry, we can use only one color."

"That's a ridiculous rule. There are many colors that can't be described in one word."

"I don't make the rules, sir."

"Well, this is silly."

Which it was, of course. All my life, on every piece of identification I have ever had, the color of my hair has been listed as brown.

And suddenly this woman, who obviously had weak eyes, the way she squinted, was being arbitrary.

I showed her my company identification card. "See, right there it says brown.

"That's not official, sir."

"Look at my company ID photograph. Does the hair look gray? It's brown. Almost jet black, as a matter of fact."

"Is that you?"

"Of course it's me."

"My, you used to be a nice-looking man."

"Oh, for Pete's sake," I said, which is all a person can say when they are dealing with someone that negative.

A supervisor walked over and said: "Some kind of problem here?"

"Yes," I said. "I don't want my driver's license to contain inaccurate information."

The woman looked indignant and said: "Just a moment, sir!"

The supervisor said: "What kind of inaccurate information?"

"Oh, it's not that important," I said. "Let's get on with it."

"The gentleman says his hair is brown," the woman said.

The supervisor gawked at my hair, shook his head, and said: "It is gray. What there is of it."

"Ha!" I said. "My father always told me that you can't fight City Hall."

"This isn't City Hall," the supervisor said. "This is a state office."

"Look, I don't have all day," I said. "Can't we get this over with?"

(I knew there was no point in arguing. These government people always band together against us. My hair could have been purple and he would have agreed with her.)

"All right," the lady said. "I'll put down gray."

"You couldn't make it pale brown?"

"I'm sorry, sir, but it's really. . . ."

"Oh, go ahead."

And she did. She actually wrote it down. Gray. GRAY! On my driver's license.

Not that I care. Who is ever going to see it, really? Nobody. Except maybe a traffic policeman.

What is the policeman going to think, seeing "gray" on a driver's license that belongs to a guy with all that thick, bushy brown hair?

And what if it is a policewoman?

Later that evening I was having dinner with some friends and told them about the incredibly color-blind license clerk.

"Don't feel bad," one of my friends said. "Paul Newman is almost entirely gray."

I felt better.

"And Marlon Brando is getting fat," another friend said.

"And Steve McQueen is getting all wrinkled," someone else said.

I really felt good.

"So," one of my friends concluded, "you've got it all—gray, fat, and wrinkled. You're a superstar."

3 | JOCKS AND JERKS

The National Pastime

June 25, 1981

For days we've been reading thousands of angry words about the greed of ball players and team owners.

Sportswriters have worked themselves into a lather about the evils of greed, greed, greed.

The fans, too, have poured out their rage at greedy ball players who would deprive them of their baseball satisfaction, and greedy owners who charge them too much for tickets.

Greed has never before been under such vicious attack, not even when oil companies announce their profits.

I'm puzzled by this attitude. It's about time somebody spoke up in defense of greed.

Greed is what made this country great. Never mind the spirit of adventure: the earliest explorers came here to find something that belonged to somebody else, and to grab it.

Every time the Indians turned around, they were either being offered a bag of dime-store jewelry in exchange for

Manhattan or were being chased off their land because there might be gold under their teepees.

The tattered immigrants were welcome because business-men wanted cheap labor to drive rail spikes and sling slag for their mills and dig their mines, not because they were eager for the company of hordes of garlic-chompers. The inscription of the Statue of Liberty should read: "Send us your poor—especially those who will work sixteen hours a day for twenty cents an hour."

And for every immigrant who came for political or religious freedom, a thousand others walked off the boat, looked around and said: "Gimme mine."

The great cities were built by swindlers and hustlers. The first arrivals cheated the Indians. The second arrivals were the real estate hustlers who swindled the first arrivals out of their land. The third arrivals were the nickel-biting merchandisers who went into partnership with the second arrivals, then cheated them out of their share.

Today, their descendants live in Lake Forest and are in the *Social Register.*

And nothing has changed. The most sought-after college degree is the master of business administration. A kid doesn't go after an MBA because he's seeking beauty and the meaning of truth.

Yesterday's idealists are driving Mercedes-Benzes. The last time I looked, Bob Dylan had finally discovered what was blowing in the wind, so he found himself a good accountant and some tax shelters.

America leads the world in number of lawyers and in volume of lawsuits. At any given moment, half the country is in court demanding money from the other half.

The Teamsters, who represent working people, recently held a convention and voted to pay the thugs who lead them $200,000-plus salaries. And the members were happy to do it because the thugs promised to blackjack somebody in their financial behalf.

When Chicago went condo-crazy, tenants screamed because they had to buy their apartments. Three years later, they sold that $30,000 flat for $90,000, and wept because they had to pay capital gains before they could put the profit into 16 percent yields in the money market.

So why has greed suddenly become so unpopular?

All the ball players and the team owners want is everything they can get, which is what most people want.

The fact that the average baseball player earns $172,000 a year—and some make millions—is irrelevant. Some people might think that it is outrageous for someone to become a millionaire by buying and selling pork-belly futures on LaSalle Street. Others might think it outrageous that it costs twenty-five dollars an hour to hire someone to install a doorbell.

Americans measure their heroes by their net worth. Just look at *People* magazine, which has become the new Who's Who. A recent issue featured a hillbilly singer who just traded in his $13 million mansion for a $15 million mansion. Only greed could make him that rich. And his fans love it. But if the story said he was living in a furnished room in Uptown, they'd decide he was a loser and toss his records out. If *People* magazine ever started doing stories on people who empty bedpans in hospitals for $172 a week, its circulation would disappear.

Sure, ball players are greedy. That's what has made baseball more popular than ever. As soon as Reggie Jackson became the highest-paid player in the game, the fans said: "Wow, he must be great if he's making all that money." If he was playing for five dollars an hour, they'd throw hot-dog wrappers at him.

One of the great athletes of our time was named Paul Haber. You've never heard of him? Of course you haven't.

Although he was the top handball player in the world, in his best year he earned about $10,000, including side bets, so nobody was impressed except other handball players. But if the sports page headlines suddenly said: "Haber Inks Pact for $5 Million," sports fans would have lined up for miles to see him, even if they didn't know what game he played.

Actually, the most greedy people involved in the baseball strike are the fans who are screaming about the greed of the players.

Most people see their baseball on TV, where it is free. And now they're upset because they are being deprived of free entertainment.

And when someone screams that he's being cheated because he's no longer getting something for nothing, that, my friend, is greed.

Finley in the Billy Goat

December 15, 1976

Every time I turn to a sports page, somebody is saying something bad about Charles Finley.

If it's not his former players, then it's the other owners or the writers or fans complaining about how mean and nasty and sly and avaricious and ruthless he is.

It may be true. Nobody's perfect.

But there is another side to Finley. This story has never

been told, but Finley was responsible for one of the most remarkable religious events I have ever witnessed.

He brought the message of goodness and decency to a place that is notorious for the sinfulness of its customers—Billy Goat's Tavern.

This is how it happened. Late one evening, a couple of years ago, the door opened and about two dozen men and women filed into the place.

The regular customers—at least those among them who could raise their heads—were surprised to see so large a crowd arrive on a weeknight.

The appearance of the group was different. The men had short haircuts and shiny shoes. The women wore expressions of prim disapproval.

Leading them into the saloon, which is not far from where I work, was Finley. The visitors were from a small town in Indiana and all were members of a Baptist church. They had been Finley's guests at a night game between the A's and the White Sox at Comiskey Park.

Now he was showing them the seamier side of life in the big city.

The church group sat at a long table and looked at the regular customers—printers, office sweepers, off-duty doormen, the crew of a Lake Michigan excursion boat, and a few guys who do not discuss the nature of their work unless they are under oath.

A few of the regulars stared back. They had never before seen twenty-five people drinking Cokes.

Finley stood up and told his guests they were going to have a special treat. His manager, Alvin Dark, was going to make a speech and answer questions.

Dark rose and talked for a couple of minutes about the strategy of that evening's ball game. But then he got to the main subject of his speech.

Dark said that at one point in his life he had become a

sinner. He said he had engaged in most of the vices that are frowned upon by good Baptists.

When he admitted this, the church people shook their heads and a few of them even said: "Tsk, tsk."

On the other hand, some of the regular customers began listening closer. A couple of them leered in anticipation of maybe hearing details of some of Dark's more interesting sins.

But then Dark's voice got louder and he told how his sinning days had ended. He revealed that he had been born again.

He told of how his eyes had been opened and how he no longer chased after women, or got liquored up, or had mean thoughts about his fellow men.

He told of the importance of clean living, clean thinking, and being righteous and pure.

"Amen, brother," one of the church members said.

"This is very depressing," said one of the regular customers.

Another looked down at his shot glass and mumbled something about having failed his mother.

Big Warren the bartender looked worried and said: "Preaching is very bad for business."

But Finley looked around and said: "You can all learn something from this man."

Dark was really going. He quoted from the Bible. He told of how he felt when he had finally seen the light.

And he finished by calling upon everybody to live clean, think clean, and be clean.

The church group applauded. The regulars looked morose. A half-hour earlier, they had been swearing, telling lewd stories, making bets, arguing, having a fine time.

"I came in here feeling good," one of them said. "Now I might jump off a bridge."

The church members were asking Dark questions about

living the clean life in sports. Dark said clean living makes for better athletes.

From a corner table, a gravelly voice was heard. It came from a small, red-eyed man sitting over a beer glass and racing sheet. He focused his crimson eyes on Dark and said:

"You mind if I ask you a question?"

"Go ahead sir," said Dark, looking benign.

"I saw you play. You were a helluva ball player."

Dark looked modest. "Thank you, sir."

And Finley cut in: "He was an outstanding player."

"Yeah," the red-eyed man said. "What I wanna ask you is this. Ain't it true that Babe Ruth used to run around with all kinds of low women, and that he drank lots of booze, and he ate like a pig, and was a real disgusting sinner?"

Dark looked sad at the thought of Ruth's many sins and nodded: "Yes, I'm afraid that is true."

"Uh-huh," said the man with red eyes. "Well, then tell me this. If a team was made up of nine Alvin Darks, and it played against a team made up of nine Babe Ruths, who would win?"

Dark looked startled and said: "Well, I suppose the Ruths would. He was the greatest player there ever was."

"Yeah, that's what I think, too," shouted red-eye. "So let's all drink a shot to the memory of Babe Ruth and dirty living."

With that, he stood up, downed his beer, and winked at one of the church ladies, causing Finley to observe: "He's just a bum."

But the regular customers gave him a standing ovation. Those who could stand.

And that's how the spread of clean living was checked in Billy Goat's Tavern that day. Hallelujah.

Billy's Right to Punch

November 1, 1979

The case of Billy Martin, who was fired again as the New York Yankees' manager, should not be dismissed as just another mere, noisy sports flap.

No, there are profound issues involved here, involving basic human rights, grand American tradition, and the maintenance of civilization.

The most significant of these issues can be put this way:

- Does not a person have the right to go into a bar and have a drink and mind his own business without having to put up with guff from some pest?
- And if a pest persists in bothering him, does he not have the right to punch the pest in the mouth?

That's what the Billy Martin case seems to be all about, at least if we can believe Martin. The man who was punched—a traveling marshmallow salesman from a Chicago suburb—refuses to discuss it.

Martin's lawyer told me the fight happened this way:

"Billy had just come back from a hunting trip with a friend of his in Minneapolis. They go hunting every year after the baseball season.

"They went to the hotel Billy was going to stay at and

went in the bar. Naturally, people recognized Billy and some of them crowded around and asked for autographs, and everything was just fine because they were acting nice.

"Then this big guy pushes his way in. He's the traveling marshmallow salesman.

"He'd been a pain in the ass, bothering people in the bar all evening. And now all of a sudden he had found himself a real, live celebrity to give a bad time to.

"So he got antagonistic to Billy, real aggravating. He went so far as to bet $400 he could whip Billy's tail.

"Well, somebody like Billy is always the target of guys like that.

"So Billy walked out, but the guy followed him, and he's a big guy, about six two and 210 pounds. Hell, Billy doesn't weigh 150 pounds with his clothes wet.

"And when they got outside the bar, the big guy already had his coat off, and he gave Billy a shove, and Billy found himself in a fight, and that's when it happened."

What happened was about ten stitches in the guy's mouth.

Now this unknown marshmallow salesman has become an object of sympathy throughout the sporting world. I heard people at lunch today chortling with satisfaction that Billy Martin got what he deserved for mistreating an ordinary American citizen.

Well, the marshmallow man gets no sympathy from me. If Martin's version is at all accurate, then the man deserved each and every stitch in his lip.

(I tried to reach the marshmallow man to hear his side of the story. But he's ducking interviews and his wife said she doesn't want to talk, either. She sounded pretty miffed, which may be why the marshmallow man is so silent.)

I don't know if the Supreme Court has ever pondered this issue, but it is an American tradition that a stool in a bar is a place of sanctuary.

Once you sit down and order a drink, you have the

inalienable right to remain silent. You have the right to stare into your glass and brood and ignore the world, including those around you.

This right has been firmly established, if not by a court of law, then by higher authorities, such as the American cowboy movie.

Time after time, we have seen scenes in which a cowboy is minding his own business at the bar when someone intrudes to insist he have a drink, or to demand to know who he is, or call him a low-down sheepherder.

In virtually every case, it is the belligerent drink-buyer who winds up on the floor, as he deserves for intruding.

Of course, this is the twentieth century, and we don't have shootouts in bars, except on Friday and Saturday nights in 80 percent of Chicago's neighborhoods.

Nevertheless, the tradition goes on. Anyone familiar with correct barroom etiquette knows that you intrude on someone, especially a stranger, and give him guff at your own peril.

The fact that Billy Martin is a celebrity is irrelevant. If anything, it makes a punch in the mouth even more justifiable.

Anytime someone like Billy Martin walks into a bar or restaurant, he stands a fifty-fifty chance of attracting the human equivalent of the gnat.

This is a jerk who cannot be in the same public place with a well-known person and not do something about it.

It might only be to interrupt his meal or drink by demanding an autograph, although sometimes they invite themselves to sit down.

If the person is as controversial as Martin, the jerk might decide to let him know what he thinks of him.

The objective is to attract attention, have a moment of reflected fame, and go to the office the next day and brag: "Hey, you know who I ran into last night? Billy Martin, and I told him right to his face that. . . ."

Many jerks believe that this is their right, that someone like

Billy Martin is under an obligation to sit still while they abuse him.

But why should he? The jerks would not expect an off-duty pipe fitter or heavy-equipment operator to meekly take their abuse.

Billy Martin should have the same right as any pipe fitter or heavy-equipment operator to split a lip when it deserves to be split.

Without this discipline, every bar in America would become chaos. The heavily outnumbered bartenders can't be expected to maintain order. The police can't spend their time doing it. Civilized behavior in bars is imposed by the tradition that swift and just punishment will be meted out on the spot to the wrongdoer by the aggrieved party.

So what Martin really did was to strike a blow for civilization and against anarchy.

And for that, he lost his job. It just shows that in the age of jerkism, which we're in, the jerks are winning.

POST SCRIPT: Shortly before this column's deadline, the marshmallow man finally talked. He said that Martin provoked the fight, not him. He said all he did was tell Martin, whose team had a dismal season, what a great job managers Earl Weaver and Dick Williams did. But, gee, the marshmallow man says, he didn't mean to get Martin mad. Ha!

Silence Is the Best Sport

April 14, 1978

I don't have many sports heroes. People who make $250,000 a year ought to feel good enough without me slapping my palms together and shouting hey-hey, wheee.

But I have to admit that I found a modern hero in George Hendrick, a baseball player for the San Diego Padres.

He has a rare quality that every other professional athlete in America should try to emulate.

Hendrick is not the best ball player. Other players can hit harder and farther, throw better, run faster, scratch themselves harder, fidget at the plate longer, spit more accurately, and saunter to the water cooler slower.

But no one is more silent.

Hendrick is in the process of putting together an amazing record of not saying anything in public. He has not spoken to a reporter, a TV babbler, a fan, or anyone else for five seasons. He won't even say hello or good-by, or grunt.

When he is given awards at sport banquets, he doesn't say thank you. That's because he doesn't show up at the banquets.

The people who own Hendrick's team are upset by his silence. So are the reporters in San Diego. But I think it is wonderful. Next to politicians and sports broadcasters, the people in our society who babble the most public nonsense are professional athletes.

In the past, before TV turned sports into a national religion, athletes weren't that way. Athletes used to say harmless, dumb things.

The old-time prizefighter would wipe the blood from his nose and tell a radio audience: "I wanna say hello to my mudder and fadder and to my wife whoozits, and I wanna thank my manager and my mudder and fadder an'...."

The ball player would say: "Well, Jack, my greatest thrill in baseball is just being up there in the big time. This team has what it takes to go all the way. We got a great manager and a great bunch of guys here in Detroit, uh, I mean St. Louis."

But that's over. Now public utterances by athletes fall into two or three categories, all of which cause migraines.

Money: We get interviews that go like this:

"Joe, on that free throw, what caused you to miss the basket and backboard by twelve feet?"

"I'll tell you why. I can't concentrate anymore. I can't concentrate because this organization doesn't appreciate me. They pay me like a dog. I can't play good if I'm not appreciated."

"But you just signed a new multiyear contract yesterday for $300,000 a year. You were happy yesterday. What happened?"

"Sure I was happy yesterday. But that was a long time ago. I'm better today than I was yesterday. I think I'm even taller."

The media: Their complaints often sound like this:

"I'm not going to talk to you press guys no more because you get the facts all wrong. Look at this story. It says I was arrested when I was stopped for going 102 miles an hour and they found twelve pounds of cocaine hidden in my left shoe. See? I was only going ninety-nine miles an hour, and the cocaine was in my right shoe. And you guys wrote that this girl who charged me with being the father of her baby was only sixteen. That's a lie. She was fifteen, and she charged me with rape. What I want to know is, why didn't you mention that I caught two passes in last week's game, but the coach doesn't respect me?''

Religion: A growing number of athletes believe that God is a sports fanatic. After every big playoff game, or World Series, or Super Bowl, the players explain the outcome this way:

"This Big Dodger in the Sky must have been in the batting box with me when I pulled that ball . . . Yes sir, it was the Big Scorekeeper who made the ol' scoreboard explode.''

Or: "When I went back for that fly ball, I knew I was going to catch it because me and my wife read the Bible for three hours last night, and I knew the Lord wanted me to catch that ball. And when I leaped over the outfield wall, I could hear the Big Fan clapping. . . .''

Even some of the losers figure there is a Big Game Planner in the Sky.

"You want to know why I only completed one pass in thirty-eight attempts? It was the Big Coach in the Sky testing me. When their tackle twisted my neck and their linebacker bit off my thumb, I told myself the Big Coach had called that play from the Big Sideline, so I shouldn't feel bad. He was testing my faith. Maybe next year, He'll call my big play. I still have one thumb.''

Listening to them, you get a picture of God as not just a compulsive sports fan, twiddling the knob on his TV set to keep track of every play in every game, but something much worse: He's not content to watch the games unfold—He decides which side will win. In other words, these athletes apparently believe God is a fixer. Maybe they see Him as wearing dark glasses and a pinkie ring. If the nation's bookies

ever start believing it, too, church attendance will boom in
Las Vegas.

The Lusty Art of Eyeballing

November 2, 1973

Many gentle people were shocked when they saw the news
photo of Dick Butkus calmly putting his finger in another
player's eye.

They said it proves that football is nothing but a dirty game
of violence and brutality.

"The man is a beast," said one reader.

"He looks like a gourmet plucking an escargot from its
shell," said another.

At first glance, it looks that way. But is it so?

Remember, there is another school of thought among those
who see pro football as a living art form, despite its roughness.

In a *Time* magazine essay, a writer told of the precision,
skill, and rhythm of the game. He said such things as:

"There is the balletic grace of a halfback on the open field,
pirouetting from tackles with the practiced ease of Nureyev
spinning through a double *tour en l'air.*"

Many deep thinkers have put forth this argument in various
intellectual journals. Of course, none of them has ever had
his optic nerves strummed by Dick Butkus.

When I saw the Butkus picture this week, I figured it was
just further evidence of football's violence.

My question was what he intended to do with the eye had he plucked it from the man's head.

Would he triumphantly slam it to the ground in the end zone, as some players do when they have scored?

Or would he hold it above his head and do a joyous Indian dance, as others do after a touchdown?

I gave it no more thought until an art-loving friend directed my attention to a painting by Malvin Albright, a renowned artist and a brother of the famous Ivan Albright.

The painting, which is of great value, hangs in the private collection of Riccardo's Restaurant and Gallery.

It shows the artist's conception of God giving life to Man, His creation.

And I had to concede that there was a remarkable similarity between Albright's painting and the photograph of Butkus.

"This," my art-loving friend said, "is just another example of life imitating art."

Or, as Elizabeth Browning put it: "What is art, but life upon the larger scale." And nobody would argue that Butkus does things on a large scale, especially the man who owns the eye.

Schiller said: "Art is the right hand of nature." Which is the hand Butkus was using.

Yet, can art be what Butkus had in mind?

I put the question to Robert Billings, author of *Stop Action* the book about Butkus' life and career.

Billings studied both pictures and said:

"In a way, it could be true.

"As you see, Albright's deity is creating life.

"And Butkus' finger surely brought life to this fellow. When Dick let him up, he hopped up and down as lively as anyone I've ever seen.

"Remember, art is beauty. And beauty is in the eye of the beholder. And that's where Butkus put it."

I finally sought an opinion from Willie Hyena, Chicago's poet laureate and an artist in his own right. And he said:

> You ask
> What is art,
> And I say
> I dunno.
> But if this
> Is what it is,
> We do it best
> In Chicago.

He Was Called 'Quick Death'

October 3, 1975

Many sports experts are now declaring Muhammad Ali is the greatest heavyweight fighter "of all time." Ali, of course, says so himself.

That's ridiculous. Ali may or may not be the best heavyweight fighter of our time, but he is not the best to ever live.

That distinction belongs to the late Brza (Quick Death) Smrt, the magnificent Bulgarian boxer who has never received the recognition he deserves.

To those who are familiar with Brza Smrt (pronounced Berzha Shmert), the idea of Ali beating him is laughable. Ali wouldn't have lasted more than a few seconds.

Smrt's record, which I'll go into in a moment, has never been appreciated because he fought before TV and other mass communications made athletes world figures.

(Incidentally, Brza Smrt was called "Quick Death" because that is what the words "brza smrt" mean. It was his real name. Ask any Bulgarian.)

His career spanned the years between 1234 and 1250. Because of poor record-keeping in Bulgaria, his accomplishments later drifted into obscurity.

But thanks to an international group of sports-minded scientists and scholars, his brilliant career has recently been reconstructed.

In fact, his skeleton has been reconstructed. That's why we know today what a superhuman physical specimen he was.

It was through a remarkable bit of luck that his remains—the location of which had not been known—were discovered a few years ago. A Bulgarian farmer was harvesting cauliflower when he found something that looked like a cauliflower, but didn't feel like it. It turned out to be the skeleton of Smrt's ear. This led to excavation and discovery of his tombstone and the rest of him.

Smrt had a remarkable physique. He was almost seven feet tall and his arms hung down to his knees. His reach was extraordinary. And because he was born without fingers, his huge hands were natural clubs.

Scientists say his knees were quadruple-jointed. He could bend them as easily backwards and sideways as the normal way. With this flexibility, he could run as quickly sideways or backwards as he did forward. This made him easily the most mobile boxer in history.

They estimate that he weighed 350 pounds or more—all rocklike muscle—and had tendons in his arms and wrists as thick as those found in the legs of a large elk.

So much for the dry scientific data. It was the way he used his physical gifts that made him so fine an athlete.

Smrt had a simple, but effective, style. He would glide forward, then sideways in a circle at tremendous speed, literally surrounding his opponent. He would throw one punch. And the results were always the same. His opponent went down. Not only out, but dead.

That's one of the reasons Smrt's career got off to a fast start, then lagged. Nobody wanted to fight him. In fact, his first three fights ended before they began because he killed his opponents during the weigh-in ceremonies.

Authorities banned Smrt from fighting because they feared he might decimate Bulgaria's male population and make it vulnerable to attack by the Turks, despite his assurance that he would kill all the Turks himself.

His fans were furious because he was a popular figure. In one way, he was like Ali, who recites poetry.

Smrt didn't recite poems, but he sang. Not just before a fight; he would sing loudly all during the fight. And despite his size, he had an amazingly high voice. He sounded exactly like an operatic soprano. This was disconcerting to his opponents, but it pleased the fans. Even those who didn't enjoy boxing came out just to hear him warble an aria while he punched someone.

The ban was finally lifted when the rules were changed to permit his opponents to wear thick metal helmets that covered the entire face and head.

This made the matches even more popular because the helmets made a loud "gong" sound, and when Smrt really got going, it sounded like a carillon concert. With his soprano voice ringing out at the same time, it was spectacular.

However, these fights also were banned when it was discovered the helmets, while saving the lives of the opponents, made them deaf for life because of the noise. Authorities worried that nobody would hear the Turks sneaking up on Bulgaria.

That's when Smrt's career entered its most interesting

phase. And when we find another parallel between Smrt and Ali.

As we know, Ali taunted Joe Frazier by saying: "He is a gorilla."

That's exactly what Smrt said about his next opponent. Except it really was a gorilla. And Smrt knocked it out with one blow to the chest.

He later fought several bisons, a few hippos, and finally an enormous rhino, winning all by knockouts.

The rhino fight was his last. He quit because the rhino, when it finally came to, was permanently cross-eyed. Smrt, who was basically a softhearted man, said the sight of the rhino's eyes, looking at each other, haunted his conscience and he vowed never to fight again.

I'm sure that Ali's admirers will stubbornly insist we can't be sure Brza Smrt would have beaten Ali, since they have never fought. But it can be proved through scientific means.

Tests have shown that a punch with sufficient force to knock a rhino cross-eyed would not only KO Ali, but would actually separate his head from his body and propel it almost thirty-eight feet into the third or fourth row of seats, and this would not only kill Ali, but might even silence him. Even Howard Cosell might not have the words to adequately describe such a dramatic moment in sports.

So when we talk about the greatest fighter of "all time," I will take Brza (Quick Death) Smrt.

On the other hand, Sven the Beast, a Norwegian who could crack icebergs with one punch, was great back in the early four hundreds. And before him, there was Oooga the Rock Eater, the baddest man in the caves.

After all, "all time" is a long time.

A Great Fish, the Bullhead

January 11, 1977

Those who say the Eastern press is made up of elitists and snobs may have something. I never believed that until I looked at a recent issue of *Harper's* magazine.

I rarely read *Harper's* because it is always full of articles that are significant, serious, even profound. That kind of article always has an unhappy ending.

Also, it has no centerfold picture. And if it had one, it would probably be of Ralph Nader or Margaret Mead.

But I happened to look at an issue because it had a big special section devoted to fishing.

Fishing is something I think a lot about lately. It helps in times of great stress.

For instance, I might be thinking about President Nixon and what will happen if he is removed from office. What will happen is that Gerald Ford will become president.

That thought causes stress. So I think about what will happen is that Mr. Nixon will stay on as president. More stress.

Nixon or Ford. Ford or Nixon.

At this point, foam appears on my lips. So I think about fishing.

Which led me to *Harper's* and that special section. It

contained dozens of articles about fishing, and I read them all.

Since it is a serious magazine, some of the articles were deep and philosophical. I didn't mind that, because I get pretty philosophical about fishing. It has always been my philosophy to cut a worm in half. You save money that way.

But when I finished the last article, I realized that there was something infuriating about *Harper's* special fishing section.

The only kind of fishing that they had written about was trout stream fishing.

And that is the most snobbish, effete, overrated fishing there is. It's the kind of fishing for which you get dressed up in tweed clothes and try to look like David Niven or Ray Milland. You even wear a tweed fedora covered with artificial gnats and fleas, which you use as bait.

If you want to experience the ultimate snobbery of being a trout fisherman, just go to Abercrombie & Fitch and tell them to outfit you for trout. A tailor will come out and measure your inseam, while the salesman asks you if you want your little trout basket monogrammed.

But tell them you want some gear for catching a big carp in the Lincoln Park lagoon. The salesman will quiver his nostrils and refer you to Sears.

Why do snobs like trout fishing? Probably because it is safe, since most of it is done in shallow, narrow streams. The trout fisherman has no stomach for venturing out into the vastness of the Chain of Lakes and facing the treacherous water-skier and the dreaded drunken speedboater.

I think some foppish types become trout fisherman because those cute artificial gnats and fleas are used as bait. How would it look to have a lot of fat worms attached to a tweed fedora?

But mostly, it gives a New Yorker a chance to go to

Abercrombie & Fitch and spend his money before a drug addict takes it from him.

These have to be the reasons. What sensible person would actually prefer wading in cold water, endlessly casting a gnat, when he could be fishing like a true sportsman, sitting in a rowboat, drinking beer, and waiting for the bobber to be pulled down by the finest fish of them all?

I am speaking of the noble bullhead.

Yes, I am a bullhead fisherman. I have pursued him from Lake Calumet on the south to Big Mud Lake in the north, from the Lincoln Park lagoon all the way to Crystal Lake.

Why do I prefer the bullhead above all others?

Because he is one of the few fish that actually exist.

The legendary muskie does not exist. All those muskies hanging above the bars in Wisconsin resorts are made of plastic in Japan. And even if they did exist, who would want to pull one into a boat? They go for the throat. Fishing is supposed to be relaxing.

The bass is another myth. Those stories of huge bass, leaping high and biting at the sky, are fabrications of companies that manufacture expensive bass lures that look like baby owls, baby monkeys, and baby babies.

I know the bullhead exists because I have caught him. I have fished for muskie, bass, walleyes, bream, crappies, gar, tarpon, snook, coho, steelheads. You name it. I've never seen it.

But whatever I have fished for, I have caught bullheads. And I've learned to respect him, the way he flops on the bottom and hides in the mud when he is hooked. And the burping, grunting sound he makes when you drag him in. He kind of reminds me of Slats Grobnik.

I concede that some other fish exist. The carp is real, and very big. But he also is very dirty because he likes to eat muddy stuff. To cook a carp you must first let him swim in

your bathtub for many days to get clean. Some fishermen do
this, but I find that a carp makes it difficult for me to unwind
in a hot tub.

The northern pike is also prized by some sportsmen. But
when you remove the hook from his lip, he will try to bite off
your thumb. Why fool with an ingrate?

So I prefer the bullhead above all others, and especially
above the overrated trout. Try catching a trout on a piece of
salami. They bite only at gnats, fleas, and flies. Yet I once
caught a bullhead on a piece of salami.

Common sense should have told *Harper's* that anything
that prefers eating gnats to salami is really dumb.

A Chilling Hazard
for Winter Joggers

February 18, 1977

Joggers might be interested in a new hazard that has been
discovered by a physician.

It's not as common as the heart attacks, torn ligaments,
broken ankles, dog bites, muggings, and other jogging risks
we hear about.

But it is something that joggers might give some thought to
avoiding, since it can be painful and debilitating.

The physician, Dr. Melvin Hershkowitz of Jersey City,
writes about the hazard in the *New England Journal of
Medicine*. Dr. Hershkowitz, a jogger, was himself the victim.

He said it occurred last December 3rd, when he went for his usual 7:00 P.M. jog in a park near his home.

His clothing—and it is relevant in describing this case—consisted of flare-bottom, double-knit polyester trousers, Dacron-cotton boxer-style undershorts, a cotton T-shirt, a cotton dress shirt, a light wool sweater, an outer nylon shell jacket over the sweater, gloves, and sneakers.

It was an extremely cold evening—eight below zero, which contributed to an even more severe windchill factor.

The first twenty-five minutes of jogging were uneventful, Dr. Hershkowitz reports. He normally jogs at least thirty minutes and has been doing so for many years. He is fifty-four.

However, after twenty-five minutes, he began experiencing an "unpleasant, painful burning sensation."

The pain occurred in a part of his body that might be described as an appendage common to males.

He wrote: "From 7:25 to 7:30 P.M. this discomfort became more intense. The pain increased with each stride as the exercise neared its end. At 7:30 P.M., the jog ended."

Dr. Hershkowitz said he went home and examined the afflicted area.

He said his diagnosis was that he had suffered a case of "early frostbite."

As a physician, Dr. Hershkowitz knew that the way to treat frostbite was to bring the temperature of the frostbitten area back to normal body temperature.

So, he wrote, he took the following steps:

Immediate therapy was begun. The polyester double-knit trousers were removed. In a straddled standing position, the patient created a cradle for rapid rewarming by covering the "afflicted area" with one cupped palm.

Response was rapid and complete. Symptoms subsided

fifteen minutes after onset of treatment, and physical find-
ings returned to normal.

However, Dr. Hershkowitz wrote, there were side effects.
He said they occurred when his wife happened to come
home from a shopping trip and walked in while he was
treating his frostbite.

As he described it, she saw him "standing, legs apart, in
the bedroom, nude below the waist, holding the afflicted area
in his right hand" while, at the same time, flipping the pages
of a medical book with his left hand.

He described his wife's reaction this way: "Spouse's observation of therapy produced rapid onset of numerous, varied,
and severe side effects (personal communications)."

Dr. Hershkowitz analyzed the frostbite this way: "The
syndrome was assessed as tissue response to high air velocity
penetrating the interstices of polyester double-knit trouser
fabric and continuing through anterior opening of Dacron-
cotton undershorts, impacting upon receptor site of target
organ to produce the changes described."

He said he continues to jog, however, but "wearing an
athletic supporter and old tight cotton warmup pants used in
college cross-country races in 1939. No reoccurrences are
expected."

SOME WARM ADVICE

After I read about his experience, I phoned Dr. Hershkowitz
in New Jersey to ask if he had any other advice to offer
joggers.

"Nothing more than that they should dress warmly when it
is cold," he said.

Dr. Hershkowitz said that after his article appeared he
heard from a few other people who had had similar experiences with frostbite.

"Not from joggers. But I heard from a man who rides his

bicycle even in extremely cold weather. He agreed that it was a painful experience.

"And a man in Vermont, who takes long walks in the winter, wrote that this once happened to him. He said he avoids it by walking with his hands over, uh, that area. I would think this might make people wonder about him.

"But the nicest letter I received was from an eighty-one-year-old lady in a nursing home. She said that she and the other elderly ladies read my article and that they were all cackling over it. She thanked me for giving them all a good laugh."

He said his wife has recovered from the shock brought on by his frostbite treatment.

"At first, she did not know what was going on. But after I explained the stituation to her, she understood. I think."

Yankees, Stay Home!

October 6, 1978

A former New Yorker was babbling to me about how great his Yankees are, how they will win, blah, blah, blah, so I told him to shut his big, fat New York mouth.

That made me feel good. If there is anything that can make me feel really good, it is hating the New York Yankees.

That's why I'm glad to see the Yankees become powerful again after many years of being just an ordinary team. There was no satisfaction in hating ordinary Yankee teams.

Some very young baseball fans, who grew up when the

Yankees were temporarily mediocre, might not understand about Yankee-hating. They don't know that it is one of the great traditions of baseball.

Yankee-hating is based on two things.

First, there is the team itself. As far back as I can remember, Yankee teams had the greatest stars, from Ruth through DiMaggio through Mantle, and routinely humiliated everyone else.

It seemed unfair and sadistic, especially to those of us who were fans of feeble teams like the Cubs. There were times when the Yankee groundskeepers were much finer athletes than the Cub players.

So for most people, World Series time was Yankee-hating time. In fact, the Yankees provided the best reason for taking an interest at all. Who, except for their own fans, could get emotionally involved when St. Louis would play Boston in a World Series? But when the Yankees were in the Series, as they almost always were, the rest of the country would sit and radiate good, healthful hatred. And when they'd win, as they almost always did, we could hate them even more, which made us feel even better.

But the Yankee team itself wasn't the only reason to be a Yankee-hater. There is also the City of New York.

Most Americans dislike New York. They consider it arrogant, selfish, wasteful, overwhelming, and overrun by the kind of sinful young women in boots and short skirts that they never meet in their home towns, but wish they could.

The tradition of hating New York began long before it began asking the rest of us to pay its bills while condescendingly viewing us as amusing rustics.

I think one reason for New York-hatred was the movies. There was a time when every movie that wasn't a cowboy movie or war movie was set in New York. Sophisticated movies about cafe society. Dead-end kid movies. Gangster movies. Broadway movies. And the worst of all, the hick-boy-or-girl-goes-to-New York-to-be-a-success movie.

Even the great monster movie, *King Kong*, wound up on the damned Empire State Building.

After a while, the rest of us began to feel inferior. We had our cafe society, our juvenile delinquents, our gangsters, our own hicks who came here to make it big. We had buildings a giant ape could climb on. So why was it always Broadway and Times Square, and those wise-cracking New York cabbies?

To me, the crowning insult was the movie *Somebody Up There Likes Me*. For those of you who don't know prizefight history, it was about a New York fighter named Rocky Graziano, who battled his way from the slums to become champion.

Fine. But the fact is, Graziano got his head almost torn off two out of three fights by Anthony (Tony Zale) Zaleski, a Chicagoan who battled his way out of the steel mills to become champion.

So who got to see himself played by Paul Newman? The tough kid from Chicago? No—the New Yorker whom the Chicagoan almost killed. Is that justice?

I must pause for a moment to take a Maalox. I still get mad every time I think of it.

Actually, I like New York. I enjoy visiting it because it is the most entertaining, exciting city in America. There are far better reasons to hate cities like Cleveland or Indianapolis or Detroit or Dallas.

But I do dislike New Yorkers, most of whom either are intellectual con men, professional wise guys, or self-pitying whiners. Furthermore, most of their legendary cab drivers sound dumb.

Anyway, those are a few of the reasons for the tradition of Yankee-hating, which I hope will again flourish. If a person can't hate Reggie Jackson, who can he hate?

However, there is one problem in modern Yankee-hating that didn't exist in earlier times.

That problem is Los Angeles.

If there is any city that is easier to hate than New York, it is Los Angeles. It is said that most of our modern cultural trends begin in L.A., which explains why this country has such a big national twitch. L.A. is the place that spawned fast-food chains, expressways, youth cultism, the foul-speech movement, most guru tribes. It gave us Richard Nixon, Ronald Reagan, Jerry Brown, and other political warts. Most recently it has given us the "laid-back" lifestyle, which consists of being relaxed, slack-faced, unconcerned, and cool while slowly going insane.

There will be no problem in hating the Yankees if they have to play Philadelphia in the World Series. There may be good reasons to avoid Philadelphia, but none to hate it.

But if it is the Yankees against Los Angeles, a conflict arises. On one hand, there is the grand tradition of Yankee-hating. On the other hand, there is the City of Los Angeles. How can anyone want all those laid-back L.A. loonies to celebrate a championship? Yet, how could anyone want all those hyperactive loonies in New York to celebrate one?

I suppose a person could stay neutral by hating both teams, but that is a lot of hatred to expend, even for a Chicagoan.

It will be a tough decision. So I'll wait and hate that bridge when I come to it.

4 | SMOKE-FILLED ROOMS

A Tribute

December 21, 1976

If a man ever reflected a city, it was Richard J. Daley and Chicago.

In some ways, he was this town at its best—strong, hard-driving, working feverishly, pushing, building, driven by ambitions so big they seemed Texas-boastful.

In other ways, he was this city at its worst—arrogant, crude, conniving, ruthless, suspicious, intolerant.

He wasn't graceful, suave, witty, or smooth. But, then, this is not Paris or San Francisco.

He was raucous, sentimental, hot-tempered, practical, simple, devious, big, and powerful. This is, after all, Chicago.

Sometimes the very same Daley performance would be seen as both outrageous and heroic. It depended on whom you asked for an opinion.

For example, when he stood on the Democratic National Convention floor in 1968 and mouthed furious crudities at smooth Abe Ribicoff, tens of millions of TV viewers were shocked.

But it didn't offend most Chicagoans. That's part of the Chicago style—belly to belly, scowl to scowl, and may the toughest or loudest man win.

Daley was not an articulate man, most English teachers would agree. People from other parts of the country sometimes marveled that a politician who fractured the language so thoroughly could be taken so seriously.

Well, Chicago is not an articulate town, Saul Bellow notwithstanding. Maybe it's because so many of us aren't that far removed from parents and grandparents who knew only bits and pieces of the language.

So when Daley slid sideways into a sentence, or didn't exit from the same paragraph he entered, it amused us. But it didn't sound that different than the way most of us talk.

Besides, he got his point across, one way or another, and usually in Chicago style. When he thought critics should mind their own business about the way he handed out insurance business to his sons, he tried to think of a way to say they should kiss his bottom. He found a way. He said it. We understood it. What more can one ask of the language?

Daley was a product of the neighborhoods and he reflected it in many good ways—loyalty to the family, neighbors, old buddies, the corner grocer. You do something for someone, they do something for you. If somebody is sick, you offer the family help. If someone dies, you go to the wake and try to lend comfort. The young don't lip off to the old; everybody cuts his grass, takes care of his property. And don't play your TV too loud.

That's the way he liked to live, and that's what he thought most people wanted, and he was right.

But there are other sides to Chicago neighborhoods—suspicion of outsiders, intolerance toward the unconventional, bigotry, and bullying.

That was Daley, too. As he proved over and over again, he didn't trust outsiders, whether they were long-hairs against war, black preachers against segregation, reformers against his machine, or community groups against his policies. This was his neighborhood-ward-city-county, and nobody could come in and make noise. He'd call the cops. Which he did.

There are those who believed Daley could have risen beyond politics to statesmanship had he embraced the idealistic causes of the 1960s rather than obstructing them. Had he used his unique power to lead us toward brotherhood and understanding, they say, he would have achieved greatness.

Sure he would have. But to have expected that response from Daley was as realistic as asking Cragin, Bridgeport, Marquette Park, or any other Chicago neighborhood to celebrate Brotherhood Week by having Jeff Fort to dinner. If Daley was reactionary and stubborn, he was in perfect harmony with his town.

Daley was a pious man—faithful to his church, a believer in the Fourth of July, apple pie, motherhood, baseball, the Boy Scouts, the flag, sitting down to dinner with the family, and deeply offended by public displays of immorality.

And, for all the swinging new life-styles, that is still basically Chicago. Maybe New York will let porn and massage houses spread like fast-food franchises, and maybe San Francisco will welcome gay cops. But Chicago is still a square town. So City Hall made sure our carnal vices were kept to a public minimum. If old laws didn't work, they got new laws that did.

On the other hand, there were financial vices. And if somebody in City Hall saw a chance to make a fast bundle or two, Daley wasn't given to preaching. His advice amounted to: Don't get caught.

But that's Chicago, too. The question has never been how you made it, but if you made it. This town was built by great men who demanded that drunkards and harlots be arrested, while charging them rent until the cops arrived.

If Daley sometimes abused his power, it didn't offend most Chicagoans. The people who came here in Daley's lifetime were accustomed to someone wielding power like a club, be it a czar, emperor, king, or rural sheriff. The niceties of the democratic process weren't part of the immigrant experience. So if the machine muscle offended some, it seemed like old times to many more.

Eventually Daley made the remarkable transition from political boss to father figure.

Maybe he couldn't have been a father figure in Berkeley, California; Princeton, New Jersey; or even Skokie, Illinois. But in Chicago there was nothing unusual about a father who worked long hours, meant shut up when he said shut up, and backed it up with a jolt to the head. Daley was as believable a father figure as anybody's old man.

Now he's gone and people are writing that the era of Richard J. Daley is over. Just like that.

But it's not. Daley has left a legacy that is pure Chicago.

I'm not talking about his obvious legacy of expressways, highrises, and other public works projects that size-conscious Chicagoans enjoy.

Daley, like this town, relished a political brawl. When arms were waving and tempers boiling and voices cracking, he'd sit in the middle of it all and look as happy as a kid at a birthday party.

Well, he's left behind the ingredients for the best political donnybrook we've had in fifty years.

They'll be kicking and gouging, grabbing and tripping, elbowing and kneeing to grab all, or a thin sliver of the power he left behind.

It will be a classic Chicago debate.

He knew it would turn out that way, and the thought probably delighted him.

I hope that wherever he is, he'll have a good seat for the entire show. And when they are tangled in political half nelsons, toeholds, and headlocks, I wouldn't be surprised if we hear a faint but familiar giggle drifting down from somewhere.

The Hollow Ring of Peace

January 24, 1973

Mike, the newsstand man, was alone at State and Madison, shivering in the cold night.

"Nah, nobody's been around celebrating," he said. "What's to celebrate?"

The end of the war. Mr. Nixon said it on TV, half an hour ago.

He shrugged. "That so? Now maybe we can take care of things in this country, huh?"

A young couple came around the corner, heads down in the wind. They disappeared down the subway ramp and the corner was again empty.

It wasn't like 1945, when the end of the war brought a million people downtown to cheer.

Now the president comes on TV, reads his speech, and without a sound the country sets the clock and goes to bed.

And that's as it should be. There is nothing to cheer about this time, except that it is over. Even the announcement could have been put more simply. Mr. Nixon's efforts to inject glory into our involvement were hollow. All he had to say was that it is finally over.

"Peace with honor." He had to use the wilted phrase that has been with us most of the war. He said we obtained it.

It is hard to see the honor.

We have just finished ten years of pounding a little country that most of us hadn't heard of until we were there.

We threw everything, short of The Bomb, at them. At one point we put more than half a million troops into it. We killed them up close on the ground and from high in the air. We used old-fashioned infantry tactics and modern electronic warfare. We scorched their forests and bombed their cities. Nobody will ever know how many of them we killed.

With all that, we got a draw.

Before it ended, the word "frag" was introduced into our vocabulary. That's when enlisted men murder their own officers. Drug addiction replaced VD as the GI's ailment. Before it ended, we had put our own men on trial for murdering civilians; pilots were refusing to drop any more bombs.

After all that why even talk about honor?

"Let us be proud," he said, "of those who sacrificed, who gave their lives that the people of Vietnam might live in freedom."

More hollow words. Almost twenty years ago another war ended in a draw and we were told that our boys had died for somebody's freedom. Now the South Koreans live under a dictatorship.

And so will the South Vietnamese. If it isn't communism, it will be some other form of iron rule. They will be told what they can say, write, read, or think. They are almost there already. When they step out of line, they will be tossed in jail.

Why kid ourselves? They didn't die for anyone's freedom. They died because we made a mistake. And we can't justify it with slogans and phrases from other times.

It was a war that made the sixties the most terrible decade in our history. It tore us internally. It left many with a lust for revolution, and others with a lust for repression. It saw young people crossing borders or going to prison rather than fighting.

If we insist on looking for something of value in this war, then maybe it is this:

Maybe we finally have the painful knowledge that we can never again believe everything our leaders tell us. For years they told us one thing while they did another. They said we were winning while we were losing. They said we were getting out while we were going in. They said the end was near when it was far.

Maybe the next time somebody says that our young men must fight and die somewhere, we will not take their word that it is for a worthy cause. Maybe we will ask them to spell it out for us, nice and slow, and nice and clear.

And maybe the people in power will have learned that the people of this country are no longer willing to go marching off without having their questions answered first.

I hope we have learned these things, because there is nothing else to show for our longest war. If we haven't, then we are as empty and as cold as the intersection of Madison and State.

What 'Clout' Is and Isn't

June 7, 1973

In order to understand Washington pundits, the rest of us have had to constantly absorb those words and phrases that become "in."

There was charisma, viable, input, low profile, opting, nitty gritty, game plan, and keeping the options open.

So you would think they, in turn, would learn to use a Chicago word properly.

That word is "clout," and it has been part of the City Hall vocabulary for years.

A while back, a mascara-smeared editor at *Vogue* magazine wrote an item about it—getting the Chicago meaning thoroughly goofed up-and "clout" was snatched up in New York and Washington and other provinces.

Soon it came tripping off the lips of TV commentators, and was being tossed knowledgeably about the Washington Press Club. And most of the time the meaning was confused.

Now, even someone of the stature of David S. Broder, the syndicated columnist, has seized upon the word. And like the others, he uses it without knowing what it means.

But worst of all, Broder's brazen misuse of "clout" appeared in a Chicago paper.

In Wednesday's *Sun-Times*, Broder was writing about the political potential of U.S. Attorney James R. Thompson.

In trying to explain Thompson's sudden prominence, Broder wrote:

". . . His sudden fame and reputation as the most feared wielder of that special Chicago commodity called 'clout' rests on his work in the field of public corruption."

And a little further down, he says:

"What makes even skeptical politicians here take Thompson seriously as a threat to Daley's control of Chicago is the reputation for 'clout' he has developed."

No, no, no——NO!

If what Thompson has is "clout," then charisma is some kind of Spanish soup.

Thompson, if anything, has been a complete enemy of clout.

What Thompson has is law enforcement power. And what

"clout" is in Chicago is political influence, as exercised through patronage, fixing, money, favors, and other traditional City Hall methods.

The easiest way to explain clout is through examples of the way it might be used in conversation.

"Nah, I don't need a building permit—I got clout in City Hall."

"Hey, Charlie, I see you made foreman. Who's clouting for you?"

"Lady, just tell your kid not to spit on the floor during the trial and he'll get probation. I talked to my clout and he talked to the judge."

"My tax bill this year is $1.50. Not bad for a three-flat, huh? I got clout in the assessor's office."

"Ever since my clout died, they've been making me work a full eight hours. I've never worked an eight-hour week before."

"My clout sent a letter to the mayor recommending me for a judgeship. Maybe I'll enroll in law school."

Get the idea? Clout is used to circumvent the law, not to enforce it. It is used to bend rules, not follow them.

That is why Thompson can be considered as anti-clout.

In the racetrack scandal, Otto Kerner and Ted Isaacs were caught clouting for the racetrack industry. Eddie Barrett was caught clouting for the vote-machine company that gave him money. In most of the trials of public officials Thompson has conducted, their clout is what got the politicians in trouble.

I hope this makes everything clear for Broder and the local copy editors who permitted this shocking mistake to slip into their paper. We must try to preserve the purity of Chicagoese and defend against efforts to cheapen one of the world's most beautiful languages.

If we don't, soon people won't understand what a simple Chicago sentence, such as this, means:

"So this beef comes in from a goo-goo that I asked him to

make the drop, but just when it looked like I was gonna be vised, my Chinaman clouted for me downtown and it was all squared."

Which, in a foreign language, would mean: A complaint was made by a do-gooder that I solicited a bribe from him, but just when it appeared that I would be fired, my sponsor intervened in my behalf, and the complaint was suppressed in City Hall.

Or as a pious payroller might say: The mayor is my clout; I shall not want.

Anything Can Happen!

December 4, 1973

One of the worst things about an economic crisis is that we are forced to turn to the professional economists for enlightenment.

But it is easier to read a physician's prescription than to understand an economist. And to make things worse, no two economists ever agree. If they sense an agreement, one of them quickly shifts position. They realize that if they agreed, it could drive down the market value of both of them.

But at last I have found one of them who makes complete sense.

He is John Kenneth Galbraith, the eminent thinker from Harvard.

A few days ago, while discussing the economy, he came right out and said:

"I think we can pretty well count on almost anything happening."

That's exactly what I've been saying all along. And it is reassuring to know that a Harvard professor feels the same way.

In fact, I have gone so far as to say it is almost certain that almost anything will happen.

Some time ago, I said that to a friend of mine.

He scoffed, saying: "How can you be almost certain?"

"Just watch," I told him.

And sure enough, within the next couple of days, almost anything almost happened.

My friend told me: "You were right, but how could you have been almost certain?"

"I just had a feeling," I explained.

Later, this same friend asked me if I thought something specific would happen.

"We'll see," I told him.

Sure enough, before long we did see.

"You were right again," he said.

I just chuckled.

The next time I saw him, he was worried.

"The thought that anything might happen really scares me," he said.

Many people feel this way and you can't blame them. It is awesome.

But I told him not to worry. "Most things probably won't happen," I said.

"Are you sure?" he said.

"I think we can pretty well count on it."

The events of the next few days proved me correct again. Most things did not happen.

"How do you do it?" my friend asked.

He was visibly relieved, but I warned him not to become complacent.

"Remember, there is no way we can be sure what might happen."

He phoned me later and said: "It is just as you said. I haven't found any way to be sure. You are uncanny."

"Not really," I said. "It is fundamental economics—knowing what to look for."

"And what is that?" he asked.

"Almost anything," I said.

Of course, it is one thing to count on almost anything happening, as Professor Galbraith and I do.

It is another matter to prepare for it.

As I explained to my friend, "It is the same with economics as with natural disasters. If you were preparing for a hurricane, what would you do?"

"I would hide in the cellar," he correctly answered.

"And if you feared a flood?"

"I would get up on the roof."

"Right. But what would happen if you prepared for a hurricane and instead got a flood?"

"I would drown."

"Of course," I said. "Now you understand."

"Understand what?"

"That making preparations can be wise, but it can also be stupid."

"But how can I be sure?" he asked.

"By the way it turns out."

"And that is economics?"

"I'm almost certain."

A Star-Spangled Word or Two

July 3, 1974

Tomorrow is the birthday of this nation, so it might be appropriate to consider the words of some of our Founding Fathers. They could really turn a phrase.

And while we're at it, we might also think about some of the profound thoughts of our present statesmen.

JOHN HANCOCK: "I thank God America abounds in men who are superior to all temptation, whom nothing can divert from a steady pursuit of the interest of their country, who are at once an ornament and its safeguard."

RICHARD M. NIXON: *People have a right to know whether or not their president is a crook. Well, I'm not a crook.*

HANCOCK: "I have the most animating confidence that the present noble struggle for liberty will terminate gloriously for America."

H. R. HALDEMAN: *You know where the Watergate story is in the Washington Post today? Page 19.*

PRESIDENT NIXON: *I know, I know. And it'll be page 19 five months from now if we handle it right.*

THOMAS JEFFERSON: "In a government like ours, it is the duty of the Chief Magistrate to endeavor by all honorable means to unite in himself the confidence of the whole people.''

NIXON: *That leaves you to your third thing.*

JOHN DEAN: *Hunker down and fight it.*

NIXON: *Hunker down and fight it and what happens? Your view is that it is not really a viable option.*

DEAN: *It is a high risk. It is a very high risk.*

NIXON: *Your view is that what will happen on it, that it is going to come out. That something is going to break and—*

DEAN: *Something is going to break and—*

NIXON: *It will look like the president . . .*

DEAN: *Is covering up . . .*

NIXON : *Has covered up a huge (unintelligible). . . .*

DEAN: *That's corrct.*

HALDEMAN: *But you can't (inaudible).*

NIXON: *You have now moved away from the hunker down—*

JEFFERSON: ''The whole of government consists of being honest.''

NIXON: *Is it too late to go the hang out road?*

DEAN: *Yes, I think it is. The hang out road. . . .*

NIXON : *The hang out road (inaudible).*

DEAN: *It was kicked around. Bob and I and. . . .*

NIXON: *Ehrlichman always felt it should be hang out.*

DEAN: *Well, I think I convinced him why he would not want to hang out.*

JEFFERSON: ''I have never been able to conceive how any rational being could propose happiness in himself from the exercise of power over others.''

NIXON: *I want the most comprehensive notes on those who tried to do us in. They didn't have to do it. If we had a very close election and they were playing the other side, I would understand this. No, they were doing this quite deliberately. And they are going to get it. . . . We have not*

*yet used the (presidential) power in these four years. . . .
We have never used the bureau [FBI] and we have not used
the Justice Department. But things are going to change
now. And they are going to do it or go.*

DEAN: *What an exciting prospect!*

JEFFERSON: "It is error alone which needs support of
government. Truth can stand by itself."

NIXON: *What's your scenario?*

JEFFERSON: "No duty the Executive has to perform is so
trying as to put the right man in the right place."

NIXON: *Damn dumb Gray! Director of the FBI in the
position of having two White House people say he got an
envelope and he doesn't remember.*

JEFFERSON: "When a man assumes a public trust, he
should consider himself public property."

NIXON: *Yes (expletive deleted). Goldwater put it in context when he said (expletive deleted) everybody bugs everybody else. You know that.*

DEAN: *It was priceless.*

BEN FRANKLIN: "Half the truth is often a great lie."

NIXON: *(to press secretary Ron Ziegler): Just get out
there and act like your usual cocky, confident self.*

JEFFERSON: "Whenever a man has cast a longing eye on
office, a rottenness begins in his conduct."

NIXON: *That's why, for your immediate things things you
have no choice but to come up with $120,000 or whatever
it is, right?*

DEAN: *That's right.*

NIXON: *Would you agree that that's the prime thing you
damn well better get done?*

ALEXANDER HAMILTON: "The more I see, the more I find reason for those who love this country to weep over its blindness."

NIXON: *Will they write it and use it?*

EHRLICHMAN: *I don't know. I mean we're having briefings and all that baloney.*

PATRICK HENRY: "Is life so dear or peace so sweet as to be purchased at the price of chains and slavery? Forbid it, God Almighty! I know not what course others may take; but as for me, give me liberty, or give me death."

DEAN: *You have to wash the money. You can get $100,000 out of a bank, and it all comes in serialized numbers.*

NIXON: *I understand.*

DEAN: *And that means you have to go to Vegas with it, or a bookmaker in New York City.*

HANCOCK: "Some boast of being friends to government! I am a friend to righteous government, to a government founded on the principles of reason and justice."

RICHARD M. NIXON: *(Expletive deleted)*

A Perfectly Clear View of Baseball

July 5, 1979

Former President Richard Nixon recently said that he would like to be a sportswriter. In fact, he said that if he had a second life, that's what he would do with it, which is probably cheering news to voters who believe in reincarnation.

If sports writing is what Mr. Nixon wants to do, I would hope that some sports editor would give him a shot at it.

A baseball story written by Mr. Nixon would probably have a distinctive touch. It might go this way:

"My fellow sports fans:

"I, your sports reporter, have come to you today to give you a full and frank report on the state of the game that was played last night.

"I will not pull any punches. I will not conceal any of the facts. I will give you the bad as well as the good because I know that you are strong enough to take it. I will level with you, as I always have.

"Remember, your sports reporter is not a liar.

"First, I would like to make something perfectly clear: We did not lose that game.

"Yes, there are those who would tell you we lost it because the other team scored more runs than we did.

"But that game was not lost. It was stolen from us.

"I know that is a serious charge, and I do not make it lightly. As I write it, in fact, I am making chopping motions with my right hand to emphasize how serious it is——and that makes it difficult for me to type.

"This theft occurred——and the record will bear me out——in the ninth inning, when the score was tied.

"A runner from the opposing team was on first base. Now, let me say in all fairness that he deserved to be there. I did not want him there. You did not want him there. Most decent, honest fans did not want him there. But he had singled cleanly to the outfield and, under the rules, he had the right to be there, whether we liked it or not.

"But then he stole second base. While our pitcher was not looking, he ran to second and slid in. And because of that theft, he eventually scored the winning run.

"Now, I ask you: Is it the American way to win by stealing? To sneak into a base while the pitcher is not looking? To slide in the dirt to avoid being tagged?

"I am aware that the rules allow stealing. But that doesn't make it right. That isn't the way the decent, honest sports fans of this city want it. And the majority of you sports fans are decent and honest.

"This rule makes it possible for a small minority of players who like stealing to impose their will on the majority of players who are satisfied to stay on their own base where they belong.

"I am not going to quarrel with those who made the rule, or the umpires who permit it, or the managers and coaches who encourage players to steal. If they believe that stealing is right, they must answer to their own dirty consciences.

"But I know this: As a poor boy in California, I once tried to steal a base. And my mother and father said to me: 'Richard, if you cannot reach a base with your head held high, do not crawl on the ground to steal it. You'll get your pants dirty.'

"And I never forgot those words. Often, I have stood on life's first base and thought: 'How easy it would be to steal life's second base.' There were those who said to me: 'Steal the base. If you don't, someone else will.'

"But the words of my mother and father always came back to me: Keep your head high and don't dirty your pants. And I did not even take a long leadoff.

"And let me make this point perfectly clear: The stolen base was not the only miscarriage of justice in that game.

"If we look back to the second inning, we find a turning point. I have always believed that turning points can occur at any point where events can turn. I have said that to Pat often, and she has always agreed, as she does in this case. As I write this, she is nodding.

"At that point in time, our pitcher threw a ball that hit an opposing batter in the head because he did not try hard enough to get out of the way.

"Make no mistake about it: I do not condone hitting opposing players with a pitch. But we all know that both sides do it. Lyndon Johnson's favorite team did it. John F. Kennedy's favorite team did it. Oh, they denied it. But I've read the box scores. I've seen the instant replays. There is nothing new about it. They all did it. But it's only when my team does it that somebody tries to make something sinister out of it. When their team did it, it was strategy. When my team does it, it is dirty tricks.

"Now, when it happened last night, the batter was knocked unconscious and was unable to get up and go to first base. In fact, I believe he is still unconscious.

"I have studied the history of America. Hardly an evening passes when I do not turn up my air-conditioning and sit in front of a roaring fire and read the history of this great land of ours.

"And I have learned one lesson above all others—that when Americans are knocked down, they pick themselves up out of the dust and fight twice as hard. When the going gets tough, the tough get going.

"But that batter didn't pick himself up. He didn't even try. He just stayed on the ground with his eyes closed, waiting for someone to come along and stick a hand out to pick him up.

"That's not the spirit that made this country great. America was not built by people who lie around waiting for a handout.

"Let me make this perfectly clear: Despite the fact that he did not have the gumption to get up and go to first base, the umpire awarded him the base anyway, and somebody else went in to run for him. And that led to one of the key runs of the game.

"So in closing, I can say only that it is a sad thing for this country and our team when a baseball game can be won by a (expletive deleted) thief, and an (expletive deleted) who waits for a handout.

"As for the final score, it was. . . . I'm not sure what it was. It somehow got erased from my notes. Strange."

An Attorney for the Fix

October 23, 1975

At a party attended by a lot of politicians, lawyers, judges, and other Chicago folk creatures, I got into a conversation with an attorney. He had had a few too many.

I asked him what kind of law he practiced.

"I fix," he said.

At first I wasn't sure if I had heard him correctly.

"You what?"

"Fix."

He said it so casually—the way a lawyer might have said he specialized in probate, personal injury, or patent law—that I still wasn't sure what he meant.

"You fix cases?" I asked. "Judges?"

He nodded. When he saw the look of surprise on my face, he looked amused. And he said that if I quoted him by name, he would naturally deny it and sue the pants off me. Naturally.

Now, I wasn't surprised that a lawyer would be a fixer. I've known several, and suspected a lot of others. Everybody knows that the city has fixers. Those people Jim Thompson was shipping off to jail weren't corner grocers.

But this man was the first one who ever came right out and admitted it.

Actually, "admitted" isn't the right word. He just stated it, as if he were describing an acceptable practice. And when he explained how he became a fixer, I could understand why he felt that way.

He got into it in the most natural way. His father was a fixer of judges before him. So he grew up knowing which judges were fixable, how much various levels of the fix cost, how one went about putting in the fix with proper style.

Style, he explained, is important because even when a judge is being fixed for a sum of money, he wants to maintain his judicial dignity. You can't walk in and slap a wad of bills on his desk. Envelopes must be used, the contents never opened in the presence of both persons, and the transfer of the envelope must be done so casually that it could be a cigarette or a stick of chewing gum.

He learned these things from his father at so early an age that by the time he finished law school he was able to set himself up as a full-time fixer. And he said, with some pride, that he probably wouldn't know how to write a routine will or file a lawsuit or appear in a courtroom to argue a case, because he has never had to do so. He has done nothing but fix.

He's been at it for years, and has been highly successful. One of the reasons for his success is that the level of fix-ability has remained constant among judges. As old judges retire or die, new ones step forward to snatch the falling wallet.

The system of selecting judges assures him of success, the fixer said. Most are selected by the machine on the basis of their political loyalty and obedience. Once they have made a few judicial decisions on the basis of friendship and political loyalty, it isn't a long step to making a decision for a buck.

And because so many have been aldermen, county commissioners, or held other political jobs and offices, the fix isn't foreign to them.

So going on the bench means things change only in that somebody no longer says: "Here's your envelope, Alderman." Instead they say: "Here's your envelope, Your Honor."

Once a judge becomes fixable, the fixer said, he usually

remains that way. His standard of living grows to meet or exceed his income. He learns to count on a certain number of fixes to cover his expenses.

Surprisingly, the fixer said, not all judges suspected of being fixed really are. Often people become suspicious of a judge because he makes a lot of weird rulings. But he might be completely honest and make strange rulings only because he is dumb.

On the other hand, he said, one of the most brilliant legal minds in Chicago's judicial history was also one of the most fixable. But he handled matters so adroitly that he was seldom suspected.

During our conversation, the fixer wouldn't discuss specific judges or cases he had fixed. He didn't think that would be ethical.

Besides, he said, he hopes to write a book about his legal career after he retires, and he wants to save his material for that purpose.

I hope he does. As a title, I'd suggest something like: *Chicago—A Complete History.*

Gerald Ford Is Truly Unique

November 5, 1975

The man's voice was filled with indignant anger. He had just read my views on President Ford's refusal to help New York and he didn't like them.

But more than that, he disapproved of what he considered to be my lack of proper reverence for Ford.

"Can't you show some respect for OUR PRESIDENT?" he said.

Well, the fact of the matter is, it's pretty hard.

When I look at Ford, I have trouble thinking of him as "Our President." My reaction is: "Whose President?"

It's nothing personal. He seems like a nice enough man. But I can't forget how he got his present job. Woody Allen could have written the script.

First, Spiro turned out to be a pious plucker of plunder, and had to quit as vice president.

So President Sneaky had to find a replacement and he chose Ford.

Millions of Americans greeted his choice with a thunderous: "Who's he?"

Ford, of course, was leader of his party in Congress. But that's not as imposing as it sounds. To become a leader in Congress, you have to do the following:

- Find a safe district and keep getting re-elected.
- Don't die, so you can pile up a lot of seniority.
- Stay in the mainstream of your party, even when it does something dumb.
- Don't make enemies.
- Don't throw strippers or any other females into the Tidal Basin.

You don't have to be brilliant, or even smart. You can even be dumb, just as long as you don't get defeated. Some congressmen have become leaders just about the time they became senile.

So Ford, who was widely recognized in Washington for being very average, was suddenly the vice president.

Then when President Sneaky took it on the lam, Ford

moved up one more step and presto, he was being serenaded with "Hail to the Chief."

And suddenly we were being led by a man with the most peculiar political credentials in our history. He had never run for vice president or president. The biggest political victory of his life came when the voters of Ionia and Kent counties in Michigan gave him 106,000 votes in 1960. There have been years when Mayor Daley's gang found that many votes in graveyards.

Most of our presidents got the job because they wanted it and went after it, beating down competitors, wheeling, dealing, surviving. President Sneaky, a political Sammy Glick, was the best example.

A few others, such as President Eisenhower, had the office more or less thrust upon them because they had built great reputations in some other line of work.

But Ford is unique. He never had shown an interest in running for president. And that didn't bother anybody because nobody else showed any interest in seeing him run for president. You can't have a more unanimous opinion about a man's prospects than that.

Yet, there he is, popping up on prime-time TV to tell us why he is playing musical chairs with his cabinet or lecturing the people of New York on their wicked ways. (I like hearing a Yale Law grad telling people with dirt under their nails they have been too loose with their cash.)

Due to the itchy palm of Spiro and the strange workings of President Sneaky's brain, we are going to observe our 200th anniversary as a nation under a president who has never run for national office.

So, yes, I do have trouble working up a case of goose bumps when I see Gerald Ford, the pride of two counties in Michigan, standing beneath the presidential seal.

And now that he's been there, the Peter Principle, which

runs rampant in politics, has infected him. He had decided that he is the big man for the big job after all.

And there is an excellent chance he will be elected to a full term, since Americans hate to throw out an incumbent president, even if he didn't run for the office in the first place and probably would have been defeated if he had.

Well, I think Gerald Ford's original instincts were correct— when he aspired to do nothing more than to keep piling up congressional seniority. And the original instincts of his party were correct—when they thought his original instincts were correct.

Please, don't bother to tell me about how a man can grow into a big job. The presidency ain't a pair of baggy pants.

A Senator's Scary Letter

February 5, 1976

A friend of mine recently received a frightening letter from a United States senator. He rushed over to show it to me.

"Look at this part," he said.

The paragraph he pointed to said:

"Your taxes are being used to pay for grade school courses that teach our children that cannibalism, wife swapping and the murder of infants and the elderly are acceptable behavior."

"Do you think it is true?" my friend asked.

"I don't know. Have your children been eyeing you strangely?"

"No, but if this is true, we ought to do something about it. I don't want my children behaving this way."

Me neither. A little swearing and a sniff of weed, maybe. But cannibalism is far too hip for my tastes.

The letter looked authentic. It had a U.S. Senate letterhead and was signed by Senator Jesse Helms, the conservative Republican from North Carolina.

And when I read the letter, I was sure it was authentic. Senator Helms was asking for money.

He was asking for contributions so conservatives could defeat liberal politicans who want our children taught that cannibalism is acceptable conduct.

But just to be sure that some nut wasn't using a senator's name (sometimes it is hard to tell), I called his office in Washington.

The lady who answered the phone said: "The senator is on the floor. Can I help you?"

"Sounds to me like you ought to help the senator."

"I meant the floor of the Senate."

"Oh. I'm calling about a letter the senator has sent out."

"What is it about?"

"Cannibalism."

"Cannibalism?" (She sounded surprised.)

"Yes. You know, when people eat each other."

"The senator sent a letter about THAT?"

"Yes. He says he's against it."

"I'm sure of that. But can you give me any more details?"

"He says our children are being taught that being a cannibal is OK. And to swap wives. And kill old people and little babies. I want to find out more about it, so if my kid becomes a straight-A student I can hide from him."

"Oh, I think I know the letter you mean. But our office didn't handle that. It was prepared by another organization— the National Conservative Political Action Committee."

I called that outfit. A young man came on the phone and said:

"Yes, we sent out the letter."

"Is it true about the cannibalism?"

"Yes. We got that information from a publication called *Human Events*."

At the library I looked up back copies of *Human Events*.

It turned out to be a very conservative publication, with Ronald Reagan's TV-anchorman face on most of the covers.

And in one of last year's issues I found the article that had provoked Senator Helms' fund-raising indigation.

It seems that federal funds have been used to develop a course of studies that includes, among other subjects, the ways of the Netsilik Eskimos.

And it appears that the students learned that when things were really tough way up North, the Eskimos sometimes engaged in infanticide, senilicide, and even cannibalism. And they were casual about sex.

But I found nothing in the article to indicate that our children are being taught that they can bump off granny or little brother, or make a snack of the kid next door.

In studying primitive tribes from any part of the world, we could probably find conduct that would shock Senator Helms. And if primitive tribes in other parts of the world looked at some of our habits, they would probably wonder if we are nuts.

If Senator Helms is worried about the things children learn today, he might try twirling his TV knob night after night. On show after show, there is more violence and kinky sex than you'll ever find in any igloo.

And if Senator Helms is alert, he will probably note that these shows are being sponsored by big corporations, the kind that are usually dominated by men of conservative political beliefs.

So I wonder why Senator Helms hasn't sent out letters

denouncing these corporations and the men who run them for providing nightly bedtime stories about murder, arson, and rape.

I'm sure that Senator Helms would get a big response. Even the Netsilik Eskimos might send him a few bucks. After all, whatever they did, they never called it entertainment.

Rally Round, Gun Lovers

March 24, 1976

I'm not surprised that the National Rifle Association is thinking of moving its headquarters out of Washington, D.C., to a safer environment because two of its employees have been shot.

It serves the NRA right. And this wouldn't be happening if they had joined in my crusade when I first asked them.

A long time ago, I asked all the pro-gun lobbies to help me campaign for a change in the gun laws.

My proposals were simple: We must legalize the possession of sawed-off shotguns, portable and fixed machine guns, bazookas, flamethrowers, hand grenades, mortars, and light artillery.

My reasons for this are obvious.

Handguns are here to stay. Because of the efforts of such fine, patriotic organizations as the National Rifle Association, we will always be able to get our hands on pistols.

I'm all for it, of course. I've always loved pistols. They are fun to shoot, fondle, and play with. Why, I've always considered the phallus to be a pistol symbol. I have always felt sorry for women because they don't have a pistol symbol. Maybe that's why they don't like guns as much as men do.

But because handguns are here to stay, somebody who has one is always going to be walking up to somebody who doesn't and saying, "Stick 'em up," and maybe shooting him.

So the question is, if we are always going to have handguns, how does a decent, honest citizen go about protecting himself?

With another pistol?

No. The pistol is the most inadequate of defensive weapons.

For one thing, carrying it concealed in the pocket or purse is illegal. And by the time you get it out, chances are that you have already been shot. So the best you can hope for is that you can live a few seconds and shoot the person who shot you, so the two of you can bleed to death together. This, at best, is only a moral victory.

Carrying it openly in a holster? That's a slight improvement and it is legal. But it is also inadequate. Most pistols of any stopping force are not accurate. Beyond a few feet, most people can't hit a thing.

That's why they are of little use for military purposes, except in movies. Officers carry them only to intimidate enlisted men.

Ah, but a sawed-off shotgun. There's a defensive weapon. Any nearsighted, trembly-handed novice can effectively use one. The pellets separate when they leave the barrel, forming a large, lethal cloud. If you aim at somebody's chest and miss, chances are you will still blow off a goodly portion of his head, hip, arm, or foot. That's why it is highly favored by knowledgeable crime syndicate assassins.

It is also convenient to carry. You can tuck it into a shopping bag, a large open-topped purse, or have a tailor sew an extra-long pocket into your topcoat. It isn't even necessary to remove it when it is used. Just raise the barrel, pocket and all, pull the trigger, and you are sure to hit somebody—if not the fiend who is threatening you, then someone else who probably deserves it anyway.

The machine gun can also be used this way, and it is particularly effective as a defense against large numbers of assailants. Even if you don't hit them all, just spraying the immediate vicinity with bullets would be enough to set them to flight.

The other weapons I mentioned earlier are recommended primarily for use in defending one's happy home. Once again, the pistol is inadequate for this purpose. And the rifle, while an improvement over the pistol, requires some accuracy and doesn't fire rapidly enough.

But a tripod machine gun, a bazooka, a flamethrower, or hand grenade—with these in the parlor, anybody is more than a match for ruffians who might batter down one's door.

More important, they are what we need if we are to protect our country against invaders, which is one of the basic reasons handguns are legal.

What kind of invaders? That depends. For some people, the threat is from the Communists—Chinese and Russian and Albanian hordes who might land any time they think Americans aren't well armed.

As gun lovers have often pointed out, it is not the threat of nuclear retaliation, our army or navy that keep them from our throats. It is the thought of all those pistols in America's dressers and rifles in our closets.

Others have feared, especially in the late 1960s, that heavily armed Black Panthers might suddenly launch an invasion of their suburbs. For a while there was some concern that Abbie and Jerry might lead America's Yips and Dips on a full-scale revolution.

Well, wherever the invasion comes from, the pistol is not the answer. Will you stop a Russian tank with a .32? Will you force a regiment of well-armed Black Panthers to retreat from your suburban shopping center with a .38?

Of course not. But if the invaders knew that every household in America was armed with a bazooka, a machine gun, a box of grenades, or a mortar, they would think twice before smarting off.

So, once again I call upon the NRA to join with me in urging the broadening of our restrictive gun laws.

Then you can stay in Washington and fight, instead of running away. After all, it is your battle. In fact, I can't think of anybody who can take more credit for it.

Honest Abe and Sexy Sam

May 28, 1976

Samantha Fudley Crick, who at 133 is believed to be the oldest woman in the United States, has disclosed to me in an exclusive interview that she once had "an intimate relationship" with President Abraham Lincoln.

"I suppose you could say he was my lover," said Mrs. Crick, who now lives in a nursing home. "It lasted three years. I don't regret it. He was a wonderful human being and a beautiful person."

Her reminiscences will be published in a forthcoming book called: *Me and Mount Rushmore.*

Mrs. Crick said she met Mr. Lincoln in 1862 when she visited the White House with her father, who was in charge of mule procurement in the Lincoln administration.

"Naturally, I was awed by him, with his reputation as the Great Emancipator and all that.

"He was so tall and somber. I remember saying: 'The burdens of your office must be very tiring, Mr. President.' He sighed and said: 'Yes, they are, young lady, but it beats splitting rails for a living.'

"He later invited me to visit him at the White House alone, and my father encouraged it. My father was an ambitious man and hoped that when the Civil War ended, Mr. Lincoln would appoint him as urban renewal director of Richmond.

"At first our relationship was just friendly. I used to play the harmonica for him. His wife hated harmonica music, but he enjoyed it. He said it relaxed him and helped him ponder great decisions. The day he wrote the Gettysburg address, I played 'Turkey in the Straw' and 'Eatin' Goober Peas'—two of his favorites—over and over again.

"But Mr. Lincoln, despite his image, was like any normal man. I was young and pretty, not wrinkled and toothless as I am now, and his friendship began to turn into something more personal. I believe he began seeing me as a sex object. I suppose that I began, to use a modern expression, turning him on.

"One day he said to me: 'Samantha, do you think of me as old?' I was surprised by the question, and I said: 'No, Mr. President, you are ageless. Why, if you shaved your beard you'd look years younger.'

"But I don't think he believed I was sincere. He went to a closet and took out an ax and several rails, which he kept around for luck, and split them in a jiffy, right there in the Oval Office.

"When he finished, he said: 'There, I'll bet those young dandies and whippersnappers you meet at parties can't do that.'

"The exertion gave him a stiff neck and he was in considerable pain. Like many young ladies of that time, I was skilled in folk remedies, so I gave him a sharp tap on the back of the neck with my harmonica.

"It was that intimate physical moment that drew us together. Our romance began.

"Naturally, after we became close, he asked me to stop calling him 'Mr. President.' I called him Abe, but he really didn't like that name. He thought it sounded Jewish and he worried that people already thought he was too liberal.

"Throughout our relationship, I found him to be a warm, sincere, genuine person, and I enjoyed his company. Naturally, we couldn't be seen together outside of the White House because he was so recognizable due to his height. He was six feet four, you know. That used to bother him. He thought it might cost him the short vote.

"Because I was young and impetuous, I used to try to persuade him to change his image a little, to smile and wear more casual clothes.

"But he really liked those dark suits and that stovepipe hat. Do you know, during those three years, he never once took off that stovepipe hat, even when we were together?

"Our relationship ended when the war was ending. He became so busy binding the nation's wounds that he didn't have time for little old me.

"I built a new life, marrying Mr. Crick, a fertilizer dealer. I told Mr. Crick the entire story, and he was a kind man and said he understood. But he never voted Republican.

"I shall never forget the last time I saw Mr. Lincoln, and we both knew it was our last time together.

"It was a sad and tender moment. He asked me to play 'Turkey in the Straw' for him on my harmonica, just one more time. I began to weep and did not want to play it. But he insisted. He said:

"'Play it again, Samantha.'"

Oh, Jimmy, Be for Real!

July 16, 1976

NEW YORK—I hate to get corny at this late date in a cynical life, but the arrival of Jimmy Carter at the affectionate, emotional bedlam of Madison Square Garden, staged as it all may have been, was one very memorable experience.

This was a guy who, less than two years ago, was almost considered some kind of kook. An unknown Southern local politician, a peanut picker, a man with virtually no power base, setting out almost like a traveling salesman with a dream to be president of the United States.

Now he was walking into his party's national convention to get the nomination, and the delegates, including the most established powers, were on their feet cheering their heads off. Some were even crying.

Less than two years ago, Carter came to visit a Chicago newspaper office to talk to the editorial board about his high hopes. The editor was embarrassed because the meeting was so poorly attended, and he had to run around at the last minute getting people into the room. During those days, when Carter would drop in to see political writers wherever he went, they weren't always in. So he'd leave his material with someone else, sometimes a copy boy.

Now the cameras in the hall were all focused on him, and the signal was being sent everywhere in this country, and far beyond its borders. The most influential publishers, editors, and journalists in the country were stacked in seats to his left and behind, wondering if they'd be lucky enough to arrange for a brief interview sometime between now and November, or ever.

Carter is a calm, controlled man. But if the contrast between what he was only a short time ago and what he was on Thursday night in New York City didn't do something to his emotions, then I'm sorry for him. It did something to mine.

The American dream of anybody making it to the highest positions in our country is a beautiful concept that most of us don't believe in anymore. We feel anybody who makes it big in politics has strings attached to him, and we figure he's in it for what he can grab for himself and his backer.

So, in our Bicentennial year, of all times, along comes this grass roots character from a small town in Georgia, and nobody can figure out where the strings are attached, much less who's on the other end pulling them. He has got a background of bootstrap pulling that might have been written for an inspirational tract. He's from a family that has been tilling the same American soil for six generations, and not a one of them ever went to college until he came along.

We've grown used to politicians appealing to our baser instincts—telling us whom we should hate, suspect, run away from, turn against, turn away from, and turn in.

But here comes this guy who dusts off an old word like love, and isn't embarrassed to say that this is part of what he's all about. And he has managed to persuade the most cantankerous group of individuals in the country—the Democratic Party—to practically fall into one another's arms.

So when Carter walked into the hall, the entire convention—delegates, press, and everybody else—knew it was witnessing something unusual, maybe even special, in modern politics. Stripped of the modern marketing techniques that are now part of the game, it was still the story of a small, unknown guy achieving an enormous triumph over impossible-appearing adversity and against all the odds.

It was the cornball American dream come true, and it was something to see and remember.

And it would be so nice if it turned out that Jimmy Carter was everything he said he was in order to achieve his triumph—a man of decency, honor, compassion, love, and truth.

Because if he isn't all the things he says he is, then he is just the opposite—he is the single most cynical, deceitful, dishonest man in America.

There can't be any in-between—not with the kinds of virtues that he is claiming as his own.

I hope he can be believed. We don't need any more highly skillful liars. We've already been pushed to the brink of a national nervous breakdown by that kind. We deserve a break.

Memories of Wallace

July 14, 1976

NEW YORK—when the moment came for Governor George Wallace to get up in Madison Square Garden and make his convention speech, a Chicagoan named Don Rose was standing in a distant corner of the hall, leaning against a wall and listening with a humorless smile on his face.

Wallace's voice brought back memories for Rose—of a dozen years ago during an early hot spring in Alabama.

"You know what I remember?" Rose said, as Wallace's petulant voice echoed through the hall and poured out of tens of millions of TV sets.

"I remember a bunch of sons of bitches on horses with clubs in their hands riding down decent people on a bridge. I remember a bunch of hot, sweaty churches and sleeping under pews. I remember thinking that cocky little bastard is trying to become America's Hitler. And I remember singing 'We Shall Overcome,' and believing we would. Now, when I see that same cocky little S.O.B. up there talking as if none of it happened. I realized that we didn't overcome—he did."

Rose, a writer and independent political strategist, was less charitable to Wallace than were most of the people in the convention hall and on the other end of the TV signal. Most of the delegates applauded Wallace's speech, which was about breaking down the federal bureaucracy. Some blacks even shook his hand. Those who weren't enthusiastic were courteous, at least.

Then again, Rose isn't here as a unity-hungry Democrat, but as a curious onlooker. So he isn't obsessed, as most of them are, with projecting a toothy, public relations image of being one big snuggly family. He remembers what Wallace represented and he isn't going to let the party's script writers convince him that Wallace is now some kind of elder statesman drifting off into the political sunset.

Well, that seems only fair. Wallace has never admitted that he was wrong in any way. So why should those who believe he was a truly evil influence in American life now buy the pitch that he is anything more.

In the years that have passed since that warm spring, it's become easy to drift into thinking that Wallace's position has been composed of words, elections, ideas, and votes, debates, press conferences, talk shows, and slogans. We forget that his position was formed by such basic realities as a smashed head.

The civil rights movement that took shape in the South was made up of people trying to use reasonable persuasion, not force, and conscience, not intimidation. They weren't bomb-throwers and they didn't make outlandish demands. They sang, congregated peacefully, and walked. The average Southern football crowd is rowdier. Today, it is hard to imagine that their presence could have gotten anyone upset.

And they were asking for such unremarkable privileges as the right to vote without being blocked by unreasonable laws or harassed by malicious stalling tactics. Think of that. It was the 1960s, a century after the Civil War had been fought, and the big deal was that some natural-born citizens were asking for the right to vote.

Because it was so obviously just and because it was asked for in such reasonable tones, you would have thought it wouldn't have caused a ripple. Instead, the worst elements of Southern beer-belly manhood were allowed to provide the response. They did it with whips and clubs, galloping horses and fast cars in the night, snipers' bullets and bombs.

Before it was over, someone like the Reverend James Reeb was a victim. His name is forgotten, I'm sure, by most of those unity-minded people who grabbed Wallace's hand. But I remember Reeb. A decent, idealistic clergyman who said good-by to his wife and kids in Boston and went to Selma to join hands and sing. Some bums jumped him outside a cafe and smashed his brain.

In last night's speech, Wallace whined his usual line about making the streets safe for the citizenry. I don't recall that he was concerned about the lack of safety on his streets for people like Reeb.

His idea of leadership at the time was to help churn up the yahoos to further violence. No man in America did more to provide a forum of respectability to the haters. He became their official rallying point.

Had it not been for Wallace, the pushing might not have led to the shoving. The entire pattern of race relations in this country could have been different, better. All the progress that we've made since, because of people like Reeb, could have come faster and with less national pain.

Wallace made it bitter, tougher and bloodier. That's his legacy, although for the sake of unity nobody here would dream of saying it. And if this is his fade out from public life, it's just too bad that it couldn't have happened a dozen years earlier.

Mr. Grobnik and the Three-Martini Lunch

October 21, 1977

The U.S. Chamber of Commerce has predicted that if the write-off for the three-martini business lunch is threatened by President Carter's tax reform, anger will sweep across the nation. People will be so mad that Carter's entire tax-reform package might be toppled.

I doubt that. Over the years, I've done some research on this general subject. Not taxes, but the drinking of martinis and other refreshments. And it is my impression that the average American is self-reliant and independent, and manages to get sloshed without any help from the federal government in the form of a write-off.

So why would they care if corporate boozers no longer get what amounts to a federal subsidy every time they have a squirt?

And they probably don't buy the argument that the three-martini lunch or post-work cocktails are essential to doing business.

People do business all the time without buying each other martinis. I have holes in my roof, so a roofer recently came around to look at it and quote a price. He didn't take out a pint and offer me a swig. If he had I don't think he would have been able to deduct that swig from his taxes.

So why do we have this tradition of corporations feeling that the federal government should assume part of the cost of their executives getting loaded at noon or while they are weaving down Rush Street during a convention? If an ordinary sot wanders into a topless joint and buys some young thing a quart of champagne, he winds up with a hangover and a screaming wife. The conventioner winds up with a tax break.

Besides, most of them aren't drinking those three martinis to close a big deal or make a sale. They have them in order to calm their nerves so they can go back and face a harrowing afternoon of protecting their backs from other executives. Or to steady their hand for a try at someone else's back.

So how does that make their three martinis any more a necessity than the eye-opener taken each morning by Mr. Grobnik, Slats Grobnik's father?

Mr. Grobnik could have argued that the eye-opener was a business necessity because he had a nerve-wracking job he couldn't face without a liquid propellant.

He worked for many years as the quality control inspector in a garbage can factory. Every thirty seconds a new can would tumble off the assembly line. Two men would pick it up, turn it upside down, and lower it over Mr. Grobnik's head. He would twirl around five times, looking for holes in it.

That's all he did from morning until quitting time. He spun around and around, peering at the inside of garbage cans.

In order to endure this terrible professional stress, he would begin each day by slipping in the side door of Fat Frank's tavern and having a hard-boiled egg and what could be called a two-shot breakfast.

During his noon break he would have a two-swigs-from-the-Jim Beam-pint lunch.

And after work, to wind down and stop twirling, he would have an apéritif, usually a boilermaker.

These should have been considered legitimate business expenses, since he couldn't pursue the essential business of earning his paycheck without them. But he wasn't permitted to write them off, while the president of the garbage can company could deduct his martinis. And nobody ever lowered a can over the president's head.

This inequity continues today. Millions of workers have jobs that give them frazzled nerves. But they can't claim their lunchtime snapper or after-work six-pack on their tax records. And for many people of modest means, the tax savings probably would mean a lot more than it does to General Motors or Standard Oil. For example, I have an uncle who budgets about 60 percent of his income for something to drink. This causes my aunt to have to hold three jobs to make ends meet. That in turn causes my uncle to drink more because he feels bad that she has to work so hard.

But if he were a corporate executive, he could write off half of those drinks, which would deprive the government of tax revenue. And that would mean that his wife would have to hold only two jobs, which would be a loss of even more revenue. At that rate the country would go broke.

Ending or reducing the three-martini write-off doesn't mean

that executives and businessmen would have to abstain. They could get the same results by buying liquor in bulk quantities, issuing every executive a hip flask, and telling them to sneak a nip when the waiter isn't looking.

I'm really surprised at the Chamber of Commerce people. They are the kind who yell the loudest when they think welfare checks are getting too high. Now they defend a form of welfare for thirsty corporate vice presidents. They must be turning into socialists.

Or maybe they're drinking too many martinis.

The Agony of 'Victory'

August 11, 1978

This month marks the tenth anniversary of one of the most controversial political events in this country's history—the 1968 Democratic Convention.

Before the month is over, millions of words are going to be written or broadcast about what happened, why it happened, what it all meant.

But the question that will be argued longest and loudest is, who was right?

Those who believe they represented established order are saying that they saved Chicago from being overrun by savage hordes of hippies, so some heads had to be cracked in the process.

The anti-war protesters who were beaten, chased, or thrown

in jail say they were the victims of mindless bullying by Chicago's politicians and police.

When the anniversary has passed, and the arguing is over, none will have changed views. Both sides will still believe they were right.

But there can be no doubt as to who won. The forces of established order can claim that honor if they want it. By routing the protesters, they not only retained control of two city parks and a few streets, but they obliterated the issues. The nation wound up arguing about who was right. Mayor Daley and the Chicago cops or the protesters, rather than about whether we should keep sending men to die in Vietnam.

If they claim their victory, however, they really should accept everything that goes with it. Everything that followed, such as . . .

It was May 1969. Ralph Durain wasn't sure why he was there, or why he was fighting. But he was a young foot soldier in Vietnam.

His infantry unit was in the Central Highlands, held in reserve in case it was needed.

The word came. A battalion was pinned down in a valley. It needed help. Durain's outfit was sent in.

The action became fierce, and Durain's unit began to fight its way out of the valley. Durain was told to be the point for his squad.

Crouching low, he ran ahead. He doesn't remember anything after that, except feeling a blow to his back, as if he had been kicked very hard.

A bullet had struck his spine. His momentum carried him forward a step or two. Those were the last steps his legs would ever take.

July 1978, after midnight. The main street of De Soto, Missouri, a small town an hour's drive from St. Louis, was deserted except for one person, a man in a wheelchair.

It was Ralph Durain, steadily wheeling his chair down the street.

His eyes were slightly glazed. He had been drinking at a friend's house. Durain drinks his share these days. It helps the time pass. There isn't much for him to do. He has no work. His disability check more than covers his needs. But even if he wanted to work, he has no job skills. He was crippled before he was old enough to learn a trade.

He had a wife for a while. But the marriage didn't work out and she went away. So he spends most of his time just killing time. He sees a few friends, does some drinking, and checks into a VA hospital when he isn't feeling well.

That night, after his friend went to bed, he felt like going somewhere. He wasn't sleepy. With his life-style, he can sleep days or nights.

So he went out and was taking a slow ride down the street.

A wheelchair must use the street in De Soto. The sidewalks slant and the curbs are high. But there was almost no traffic, so he wasn't concerned.

He had gone a couple of blocks when a police car came around a corner and caught him in its lights.

The policemen asked him why he was in the street. Ralph told them that he was just taking a ride, just as most people take a stroll.

The policemen said he couldn't do that. He'd have to use the sidewalk.

Ralph got angry. He has a short temper. He berated the policemen for the kinds of high curbs the town has. A wheelchair can't get up those curbs, he said.

The policemen told him he couldn't stay in the street. It wasn't safe, and it wasn't legal. They asked Ralph where he wanted to go. Ralph told them he didn't want to go anywhere with them. He just wanted to be left alone.

So they arrested Ralph, lifting him into the squad car, and folding his chair and putting it into the back.

When they got to the station, Ralph said he wanted to make a phone call. He said they told him he couldn't. They put him in a cell and left him there.

During the night, he fell asleep and toppled out of his wheelchair. He couldn't climb back in, so he spent the night on the jail floor.

He has a bladder problem from his war wound. He uses a plastic bag. But the bag filled, and he was unable to go to a washroom all that night, so he developed a bladder infection.

In the morning, they let him out. They told him he would have to appear in court in a few weeks.

He asked them what he was charged with, what law he had broken.

It was a traffic law and this is what it says:

"Use of coasters, roller skates and similar devices restricted: No person upon roller skates, or riding in or by means of any coaster, toy vehicle or similar device, shall go upon any roadway except while crossing a street on a crosswalk. . . ."

For Ralph Durain, that's what it all came down to in the Central Highlands: roller skates, coasters, toy vehicles—or a wheelchair. Now they're all the same in the eyes of law and order. . . .

And to the victors of the 1968 convention go the spoils: people like Ralph Durain. What else do they have to show for it?

The Me-Me Non-Voter

November 8, 1978

I've never been bothered that droves of people don't vote. Not once have I ever written a column before an election urging people to exercise that right.

But what does bother me is when I'm forced to listen to some bore explain to me *why* he doesn't vote. Many non-voters find something profound and important in what they don't do.

It happened again a couple of days ago. This time it was a man about thirty years old. Unmarried. Big-paying job. High-rise apartment. Cushy life-style. Self-ordained ladies' man.

"I'm not going to vote," he said, without being asked. "And I'll tell you why. It doesn't matter to me who wins because it doesn't affect my life. It has nothing to do with the way I live. It won't change my life in one way or another.

"It may be important to people in the news business because they make their living writing about elections. And it is important to people in politics because it has to do with their egos. But to most of us, it is irrelevant. Regardless of who is in office, nothing changes. At least nothing that affects me personally."

Well, I made a mistake. I tried to answer him.

I began to talk about the Vietnam War, and how we might

have avoided or shortened that bloodbath had we given more thought to the kind of people we sent to Washington. Had there been more brain and less bluster in Congress, we might have been out of there sooner. Who knows how many lives would have been saved?

But then I remembered that, despite his age, he had managed to avoid being touched by the war. He came from that fortunate upper-middle-class background whose members were so adept at finding loopholes in the draft laws, the generation that left its social conscience behind with the abolition of the draft. Thus he, like so many of his peers, had spent those bloody war years increasing his knowledge of rock music and savoring the pleasures provided by the birth control pill.

So from his safe perspective, it wouldn't make much difference who held office then, since the war didn't touch him, as he said, "personally."

Then I began a small lecture about the fifties and the sixties, and how it mattered a great deal to the black people of this country which candidates happened to be elected to public office during those times. Not only to Congress and the White House, but to the state legislatures, and even various sheriff's offices.

All of that monumental civil-rights legislation, a century overdue, wouldn't have come about if there hadn't been enough people in public office who believed in it. And there were times when it was a close call. One or two more boobs could have swung important votes back a few decades. Luckily, the right kind of votes were there. And this resulted in dramatic changes in the lives of millions of people.

But then I remembered that he wasn't black. He grew up in a wealthy family in a wealthy suburb, and his closest contact to blacks was when the hired help came to clean the house. And the closest he ever got to a place like Selma or to people like Bull Connor was when they might have caught his eye on the color TV set that undoubtedly stood next to his teen-listing telephone in his air-conditioned bedroom.

So he was right. Those who held office in those years weren't significant to his life-style.

I didn't even bother to talk to him about things such as worker-safety laws that have been passed over the years, laws that make it less likely that a workman might have his hand chopped off by a factory machine, although we still have a long way to go in that direction. That, too, doesn't affect him personally.

In fact, I couldn't think of one argument I could give him for voting, because his reasons for not voting were unassailable. As he said, none of it touched him personally. He is part of the me-first, me-second, me-forever, me-me-me-me-me generation. The fact that the outcome of an election might affect others doesn't matter to him, because those people don't matter to him.

What I dislike most about these kinds of insulated me-me narcissists is that when things get rough, they are the first to whine that somebody ought to do *something* to straighten things out. They're the first to look around frantically for somebody, anybody to take care of *them*.

But in the meantime, he's getting his, and what happens to others is of no concern. So he sneers that politics is outside the mainstream.

What he doesn't recognize is that he is the one on the outside. Hopefully, he'll stay there.

'Deep Sadness'
in the Capital

July 26, 1979

A Washington pundit began his weekly essay in a news magazine by saying: "There is a deep sadness in Washington this week."

He went on to explain that the deep sadness is being caused by President Carter's "graceless" cabinet changes and by the doubts these changes have created about Carter.

But deep sadness isn't the only mood of Washington. Other pundits have written that the cabinet shake-up has afflicted the capital with (take your pick) grave concern, serious worry, new levels of uncertainty, apprehension, alarm, dismay, pessimism and consternation, and that everyone in the "shaken capital" is "groping for a satisfactory explanation."

It must be depressing to live in a place like that, with somber people meeting one another on the streets and saying:

"How are you?"

"I feel deep sadness. And you?"

"Grave concern."

"I just ran into Bill Memopads from HEW. He expressed a new level of uncertainty."

"Well, I just talked to Jack Resonant from NBC, and he expressed alarm and dismay."

"Hmm. How's your wife?"

"Deeply pessimistic. And yours?"

"Groping for a satisfactory explanation. How are your kids?"

"They're beset by serious doubts. How are yours?"

"They are filled with apprehension."

"Have you been to that new French restaurant in Georgetown? I hear it's good."

"It is. But the recent events have caused the maître d' to suffer a crisis of confidence. By the way, have you had lunch yet?"

"Just finished. My waitress was profoundly shaken."

"Well, have a nice day."

"I'm taking a wait-and-see attitude about that."

I don't know how to help Washington pull itself together, except to reassure the people of that city that the rest of the country is taking the cabinet shake-up quite well.

I realize that the shake-up has deep and significant repercussions in Washington. The replacement of five cabinet members signifies a profound change in the seating arrangements at dinner parties. It has far-reaching implications for the social coverage of Washington papers. It signifies a devaluation of an invitation to a cocktail party attended by Joseph Califano.

So it's understandable that changes of this kind could cause widespread melancholia, insecurity, and nervous twitches among pundits, high-level officials, unimpeachable sources, top aides, and the other strange creatures who live in the capital.

But to the rest of the country, it ain't that big a deal.

The Washington crowd will probably be dismayed to hear this, but to most people, a cabinet member is just somebody who occasionally appears on "Meet the Press" to respond to pompous, convoluted questions with vague, arid answers.

Only occasionally does a cabinet member take on a real-life quality. The last one was Earl (the Rube) Butz, who became nationally prominent only because he told a racial dirty joke to John Dean, the famed Watergate blabbermouth, who immediately squealed on Butz.

But most Americans aren't silly enough to believe that it makes a great deal of difference which politically connected individuals sit atop the unwieldy federal bureaucracies. The bureaucracies will go on grinding out tons of reports and studies that no one will read, devising new guidelines to make our lives more confusing, and devouring greater quantities of our money.

If anything, most of us outside Washington are slightly confused by the way Washingtonians have reacted to the cabinet shake-up.

For the past year or more, we've been hearing that the trouble with Jimmy Carter is that he is too nice, too easygoing and is not tough and hard-eyed enough to be an effective president. His niceness filled Washington with grave concern and deep apprehension, as well as pessimism, alarm, dismay, and all the other blah-blah.

But now that Carter has taken their advice and become tough and hard-eyed, they are filled with grave concern and deep apprehension because he isn't nice and easygoing anymore.

All of which fills me with grave concern and deep apprehension, as well as pessimism, alarm, and dismay about the mental condition of people in Washington who hyperventilate regardless of what happens.

It may be that the answer to Washington's emotional turmoil is a baseball team.

Most major cities, and even some oversized hick towns, have baseball teams. The teams provide people with sensible concerns. Will Dave Kingman's knee hold up? Will Greg Luzinski regain his fearsome stroke? Will Reggie Jackson murder Billy Martin?

But Washington doesn't have a baseball team. So people there must resort to fretting over whether Califano was treated rudely, whether Schlesinger was a fall guy.

It's the only city in America where people sit down at a drugstore coffee counter and begin a morning conversation with:

"Do you think that Patricia Harris can make the shift from HUD to HEW?"

"I'm pessimistic. What do you think of Duncan moving from DOD to DOE?"

"I'm guardedly optimistic. But I'm gravely concerned about what will happen at DOT."

Frankly, I think that every one of them is a NUT.

Out of the Closet

July 16, 1980

DETROIT—So far, the high point of the convention for delegate Tim Drake has been that nobody has punched him out. Yet.

That's probably a noteworthy accomplishment, considering that of the 1,994 mostly conservative, white, male, upper-middle-class Republican delegates here, Chicagoan Drake is one of only two avowed gays. Drake, twenty-seven, a data technician, was elected from Chicago's Near North Side.

As such, he is something of a curiosity. Not merely because he is gay. Gays in all fields have been tumbling out of the closet in recent years.

But what makes people wonder about Drake is that he is a Republican.

That's what he's constantly being asked: Why would a gay want to be involved with this bunch of cowboy-hat reactionaries? If this bunch can't find it in their hearts to support a woman's issue like ERA, what makes him think they have any sympathy for gay issues?

Drake has become so accustomed to these questions that he didn't even wait for them when he held a news conference. He opened the conference by saying: "I suppose you all wonder why any gay in America would want to be identified with the Republican party."

All fifty reporters nodded. Actually, I wonder why anybody—gay or straight—would want to be identified with this yahoo convention, but that is a broader question.

"Well," Drake said with a smile, "I was born and reared in Indiana, and so I grew up thinking that it was natural to be a Republican."

Everyone laughed. Here was a gay who was not being asked to justify his sexual preferences. But he felt the need to explain that his early upbringing had led him to believe that being a Republican was "natural." And when he said it, he looked doubtful, if not rueful.

What about Reagan? someone asked. Did he have any confidence that the California Cowboy would think of someone like him as anything more than a fruit or faggot?

His answer showed that even gays, when they get into politics, are capable of doing a fast two-step around a tough question.

He laboriously explained that Reagan, while not specifically sympathetic to gay issues, has come out in favor of equal rights for everyone. And that was reason to believe that Reagan would at least be "fair."

Ho ho. If the majority of hard noses at this convention actually believed that Reagan wanted equal rights for everyone in America, they would probably throw him out the back door and nominate a rock head like Senator Jesse Helms.

Equal rights is something these conservatives grudgingly endorse during political conventions, when gullible voters are watching on TV. But what they want is four years of being able to put their feet on somebody else's chest.

Drake seemed to understand that because he said that if he were called upon to vote for a president right now, his choice would probably be John Anderson. Which is the kind of talk that could get him punched out before this convention ends, regardless of his sexual inclinations.

"If the treatment that we moderate candidates received in our caucuses is any indication," Drake said, "then I will vote for Anderson. This platform and convention don't represent the Republican party. The moderates have been trampled. The radical fringe has taken over the convention."

Think about that statement. Here is an admitted gay delegate, which makes him a rather rare political creature. But he considers the majority of Republicans at this convention to be "the radical fringe" of the party. That tells you something about the Reaganites—gays think *they* are weird.

When Drake was asked why there are only two gays out of the 1,994 delegates—and whether this means that the Gay Rights Task Force hasn't been successful in its drive to gain political strength—he said something that could have the Reaganites looking over their shoulders.

"There are only two admitted gays here," he said. "But there are many more than the two of us."

You mean they are gay, but they haven't come out of the closet? Or, more appropriately at this convention, out of the ol' bunkhouse?

"Yes. There are definitely a number of non-admitted gay delegates here."

Somebody asked how he knew that.

"Because some of them have called me and said they wished they could be as open as I am. I won't identify them by name. I wouldn't want to start a witch hunt."

Then he added: "But I can tell you that there is even a Reagan delegate who is gay."

That brought an indignant response from a man who was wearing a Reagan button and a red-white-and-blue hat, and did not appear to be a reporter. From the back of the room he shouted: "What proof do you have that there is a gay Reagan delegate? How do you know that?"

As he moved off the podium, ending the press conference, Drake grinned at the angry man and said: "I know that because he is a friend of mine."

The indignant man looked as shocked as if he ... well, as if he had been pinched.

Epitaph for Jimmy

January 20, 1981

It's just not Jimmy Carter's day. Or week. Or year. Or decade.

Even though it appears that just before leaving office he will finally manage to get the American hostages released in Iran, he's not going to receive much credit for it. The coach whose team wins the Super Bowl will be a bigger national hero.

Already people ranging from national commentators to the man in the street are saying that Carter should have pulled it off a long time ago, or that he should not have paid such a stiff ransom, or that he should have been much tougher all along, and that the taking of hostages shouldn't have happened in the first place.

Some people are even trying to give President-elect Ronald Reagan credit for the hostage release. Among others, William Safire, the *New York Times* pro-Reagan columnist, says that because Reagan called the Iranians a few nasty names a couple of weeks ago, they were frightened into dealing with the milder Carter while they still had the chance, rather than facing the terrors of the Reagan administration.

Maybe they're right. I don't know, because I've never seen anything that lends itself to second-guessing the way the hostage situation has.

But I do know that once the hostages were taken, the most important things that had to be done were to keep them alive while working to bring about their release.

Right from the start, though, there were those who said that preserving our national honor was of equal importance to freeing the hostages.

To preserve our national honor, we would have had to impose a strict deadline and if the hostages weren't out in time, we would have had to go in shooting.

That's what it would have eventually required because it was obvious that the religious fanatics who were running Iran weren't going to be swayed by economic sanctions, tough talk, or even the threat of death. It's hard to frighten someone who is convinced that dying for a cause will provide a one-way ticket to heaven.

But the national honor fever grew, fueled by nightly doses of irresponsible network TV coverage of frenzied but harmless (and staged) demonstrations outside our embassy in Iran. It reached the point where people who had spent the Vietnam War hiding behind deferments were now talking about bombing Iran back to the Stone Age.

And the national honor fever finally got to Carter, goading him into committing the one genuinely stupid act of the entire affair, which was when he sent in the helicopters for a dramatic rescue attempt that failed and caused needless deaths.

From the beginning, the question of our national honor shouldn't have any place in our thinking, any more than police honor and community honor and any other kind of honor has any place in dealing with domestic kidnappers and hostage-takers. Have you ever heard the parents of a kidnapped child talk about preserving his honor?

And how could we talk about honor when our involvement in Iran goes back to the dishonorable act of propping up the rule of a vicious thief like the late shah? (Americans fume when one of our politicians retires from public life with a million or two more than when he began his career, but we weren't able to understand the feelings of the Iranians about a ruling family that stashed billions of dollars in foreign banks.)

How comforting would a sense of unsullied national honor have been if the price had been dead hostages, dead Iranians, dead American troops, and even worse chaos in the world?

But right up to the past weekend there were still those who were talking about declaring war on Iran, going in shooting and other nonsense.

Well, revenge always feels good. But that's not the way things work in the real world.

For example: I no longer hold any grudges against the Chinese because they wanted to kill me during a nervous year in Korea. When Richard Nixon ate egg rolls with them, and said it was time we acted polite toward each other, I went along with it.

Our streets now teem with Japanese and German cars, and Japanese and German tourists. And not too long ago, they gave us a much harder time than the Iranians have.

In less than a full lifetime, our enemies become our buddies, our buddies become our enemies, and our buddies-turned-enemies turn buddies again.

So there's not much point in fantasizing about revenge on

the Iranians. Because of the hostages, they've already made a shambles of their own economy and it might take years for them to straighten themselves out.

Who knows, it might not be long before Americans are taking mid-winter vacations in sunny Iran.

Meanwhile, as Jimmy Carter heads quietly back to Georgia, it's only fair to note that his approach, slow as it was, got the job done.

It's not much of an epitaph, but as a friend of mine put it: "Well, he finally did *something* right."

The *Washington Post* Cover-up

April 26, 1981

I'm sure that by now most normal people are bored by the story of the *Washington Post* reporter who faked a story that won a Pulitzer prize.

By normal people, I mean the 200 million people who don't live in Washington, D.C., or work on magazines in New York.

They're far more concerned with such issues as earning a living, paying the bills, falling in or out of love, keeping their kids off dope, trying to avoid being cheated, robbed, or murdered, planting their crops, hating their boss, and getting through a day without going nuts.

So they have only a limited amount of time to spend

pondering the grave, grave questions that the fake Pulitzer story has raised.

You probably know what all these grave, grave questions are because every columnist in Washington has been gravely wringing his hands about them.

Some of them have written that every journalist in American is somehow tainted by this shabby affair.

Nuts. Only the *Washington Post* is tainted by this shabby affair. After all, when Bradlee, Woodward, Bernstein, and the *Post* became national idols because of Watergate, they didn't say that the rest of us were also national idols. Now that they're bums, they can keep that distinction for themselves too.

And there's been much written about the credibility of the press being endangered because of the faked story, and how the press must be even more alert to this danger.

More nonsense. The credibility of the press is most often questioned by people who find that their particular prejudice is being punctured. When the press was covering the civil rights movement in the 1960s, it was accurate and responsible. But its "credibility" dropped because many whites just didn't want to read about it, so they said it was a pack of lies.

When the *Post* dug up Watergate, millions of Republicans said the "credibility" was no good because they just didn't want the truth coming out.

People have written to me and said things like: "I've been reading you for years, and I always thought you were a fair, responsible reporter. But ever since you began writing about guns, I realize I am wrong. You are a liar, irresponsible," etc., etc.

In other words, because my views conflict with theirs on one issue, I suddenly have no credibility in anything.

So credibility isn't the issue.

And there is no way the press can say this must not be

permitted to happen again. Somewhere there might be a reporter crazy enough to try to fake an entire story. And he or she will be found out and fired. Lawyers are disbarred, doctors lose their licenses, a president is kicked out of office. So who can guarantee that out of thousands of reporters in this country, another one won't get carried away by blind ambition?

But there is one aspect of this fiasco that bothers me. And when a reporter from *Newsweek* magazine called for a comment on the story, it led me to say that any editor involved in approving that faked story should be fired. And not because it turned out to be faked, either. Here's why.

The story was about an eight-year-old boy who was being turned into a heroin addict by the mother's boyfriend.

The reporter told her editor that she actually saw the needle shoved into the boy's arm. But, she said, she couldn't use names because she had promised the mother that everyone would be kept anonymous. Also, the boyfriend had threatened her life if she revealed who he and the others were.

The reporter said she didn't even want to tell any of the editors who the people were.

That editor and others went along with it. The sensational story was written, approved, and went on page 1, and eventually was submitted for, and won, a Pulitzer.

And even when the police commissioner and the mayor demanded the name of the kid, the *Post* refused to tell the reporter to divulge it.

They talked about protecting sources, the role of the press, and all the things editors love to get somber about.

Now, I'll tell you what I would have done if I had been an editor and a young reporter came to me with that same story. I would have said something like this:

"I want the name of the kid now. I want the name of the mother. I want the name of the guy giving the kid heroin.

"We're going to call the cops right now and we're going to

have that sonofabitch put in jail, and we're going to save that kid's life.

"After we do that, then we'll have a story."

And if she refused, I would have told her that she would either give me the information or she'd be fired. And I'd have done it.

They were talking about the life of a child. Or at least they thought they were, the editors not knowing that the story was a fake.

How could they sit there and say, yes, we will keep our word to a mother who is letting her child be slowly destroyed? How could they say that we will protect the identity of a man who is slowly murdering a child?

The reporter was threatened by the dope dispenser? Every day, ordinary citizens witness crimes and say, yes, I'll go into court and testify. Many do it despite serious threats. Some have to be given new identities and relocated in other parts of the country.

A few years ago, I saw a gas station attendant testify against Harry Aleman, Chicago's most feared syndicate hit man. He was terrified. But he said, yes, while walking his dog, he saw Aleman kill a man on a dark street.

But a *Washington Post* reporter can't testify against some degenerate dope pusher?

That's what's really wrong with the *Post* story. It was rotten from the inception because the *Washington Post* acted as if it were protecting a government source who had leaked a secret report that the public should know about, when it was protecting a child murderer.

What would the *Post* have done if it had discovered that a congressman knew an eight-year-old child was being murdered, but had given the killer his word he wouldn't reveal his identity?

I know what the *Post* would have done. It would have demanded that congressman's scalp.

The *Post* and other newspapers just love to deplore the covering up of wrongdoing. At just a hint of a cover-up, they begin baying like beagles.

So what does Mrs. Kay Graham have to say about her editors covering up the slow murder of an eight-year-old child?

C'mon, Kay. Speak up. We might need snappy dialogue for another movie.

A Way Out for the Poor

September 23, 1981

Many people are upset and confused because President Reagan is hacking away at federal programs that benefit the poor while spending more and more on the military.

The pundits are scratching their heads. The economists are scratching each other's heads. Even some of the people in Reagan's administration aren't sure what's going on but are afraid to wake up the president to ask him.

But they wouldn't be upset or confused if they took the trouble to understand and appreciate the crystal-clear logic behind Reagan's approach to federal spending. So I'll try to explain it.

Contrary to popular belief, it's much wiser to take money from the poor than from the rich.

If the government took the foolish approach of extracting more and more money from the rich, eventually the rich wouldn't be rich anymore.

That would be disastrous for this country's international reputation as being a land of plenty. It would shatter the great American dream, which is that anyone, no matter how humble his origins, can become rich if he is frugal, works hard, and has the ethics of a grave robber.

Doing away with the rich would also mean the end of the two-party system in America. Once they were no longer rich, the rich wouldn't have a reason to remain Republicans. They'd probably become Democrats. And that might also destroy the Democratic Party. Who'd want to go to a Democratic rally if people like W. Clement Stone or Richard Nixon started showing up?

On the other hand, if you take money from the poor by reducing their benefits, you don't change their basic financial status. They're still poor. They just become a little more poor.

The change is very slight, really. It's simply a matter of someone who is now saying, "I'm cold, poor, and miserable," saying instead: "I'm colder, poorer, and more miserable."

It's a matter of degree.

Thus, Reagan's approach will achieve one of the basic goals of the conservative: Things remain basically the same. The rich stay rich and the poor stay poor, or even a little poorer.

And by making the poor a little poorer, you provide an added incentive for them to work harder, so they can become less poor, which is better than being real poor, because the next step up from being less poor is being not as poor.

After all, providing people with goals is part of the Reagan program.

As to the next question—reducing the benefits of the poor and giving more money to the military—the logic is so obvious that I don't understand why it is even debated.

First of all, if you make the poor even poorer, they aren't just going to sit around and count their protruding ribs. This isn't India, you know.

America's poor have demonstrated in the recent past that when they get fed up with being poor, or being made poorer, they will show their dissatisfaction by rioting.

So it's reasonable to assume that when Reagan finishes hacking away at federal programs for the poor and for the big cities, which is where most of the poor live, life for the poor will be less fulfilling and there is going to be trouble in the streets of America's cities.

Well, if we're going to have widespread rioting in this country again, then we've got to have a strong military to deal with this kind of insurrection.

So it makes perfect sense to build up the military in the event that the poor riot because their benefits are being reduced in order to build up the military.

On the other hand, if you tax the rich to build up the military, then the poor will be content and won't riot, and then we'll have just wasted the money we will have taken from the rich.

That will leave us with a larger military than we need, which will damage the economy of the better stores and country clubs.

That's not the way to make this country great.

Some of Reagan's critics say that Reagan's military budget is filled with expensive gadgets we really don't need

Take the neutron warhead, as an example. This is the wondrous device that explodes and kills people but doesn't do much property damage. It's the real estate man's dream.

These bombs are supposed to be put in Europe so that we can kill Russian invaders there while not wrecking good tourist attractions.

However, most European countries say they don't want the things around, the ingrates. But that doesn't mean that creating them isn't a good idea, so Reagan wants to go ahead with the project and keep them in this country.

I can only guess why, and it makes sense when one considers the reduced benefits to the poor.

The neutron bomb is probably the ultimate anti-riot device, since it effectively quells rioting while protecting most property.

Remember, many of the poorest neighborhoods, which is where riots occur, were once among the finest in this and other cities. And they are well worth saving.

So after using a neutron bomb to quell a riot, it would simply be a matter of removing the now quiet rioters and setting about restoring the old mansions and stately apartment buildings, and selling or renting them to people in higher income brackets.

This form of ''gentrification''—which means moving out the poor to make way for people with money—would be superior to urban renewal because it's cheaper and you don't have to worry about where the poor people will move once they've been kicked out.

And it would reduce the number of poor in this country, which is something every president wants to do.

So despite the protests of the liberals and others, I truly believe that Reagan's programs will reduce the number of poor.

If nothing else works, his welfare reforms might. Although it's slower, starvation does the job.

Too Far for Whom?

December 23, 1981

The question comes up in almost every analysis of Poland. As *Newsweek* magazine put it in a headline: "Did Solidarity Go Too Far?"

Then the magazine pretty well answered its own question by regretfully concluding that, yes, Solidarity had "sought too much too soon."

. It would have been better off accepting the gains it had made during its seventeen months of existence and not tempting the wrath of the Soviet Union or the Soviet puppets in Warsaw.

"... The union often seemed unable to draw reasonable limits in a real world," *Newsweek* said. "In the end, Solidarity may have been burned by the very fires that gave it life."

The magazine talked of the movement's "dangerous lack of pragmatism" and "a confidence sometimes bordering on arrogance."

And it said that "there remains a nagging feeling that the union overplayed its hand."

That's a very practical view of what has happened in Poland. A very pragmatic, level-headed view.

But coming from any American source—a magazine, a politician, or an ordinary citizen—it's a very arrogant and patronizing view.

Just how far is too far? And just what are reasonable limits? What kind of outrageous, earth-shaking demands was Solidarity making?

It wanted democratic elections.

You've heard of such things. We hold them in this country every four years when we elect presidents. We've been doing it for a couple of centuries.

And we have them in other years, too, electing mayors, governors, judges, congressmen, recorders of deeds, aldermen, sheriffs, and highway supervisors. I'm sure we elect more people to more offices than any country in the history of the world. We make it so easy to vote that you don't have to speak English and can have the IQ of a turnip.

For most Americans, a voting place is within walking distance of their homes. And most don't even have to mark a ballot. We have machines that automatically record and calculate the votes.

In some cities, such as Chicago, a smart fellow can not only vote but he can be paid a couple of bucks for doing it.

And we permit almost anyone to form a party and run for office. We've even had Communist candidates.

We take the right to vote so much for granted that millions of Americans don't even bother to participate. If only half the eligible voters take part, it's considered an overwhelming turnout.

And this was the "unreasonable" demand that caused Solidarity to "go too far." It wanted free elections.

Well, it doesn't seem unreasonable to me, especially since Poland and its democratic traditions go back a lot farther than ours do.

(Even when Poland had kings, the nobility decided that nobody should inherit a crown—the king should be voted onto the throne. It seemed like a pretty good idea, except that it led to royal families in other countries sending bribe money into Poland to buy the election and the throne.)

Of all the countries of Eastern Europe, none has as old a tradition of democratic ideals as does Poland. And that's not an easy course to follow when you have neighbors like Russia and Germany.

So it doesn't seem unreasonable for a social movement that has a membership of one-fourth of a country's total population to be asking for democratic elections. Solidarity has more members than the Communist Party. Far more than the army and the secret police. Many in the army, in fact, belong to Solidarity.

The only other organization in Poland with more members than Solidarity is the Catholic Church, and it wouldn't mind free elections either.

So what's unreasonable about the majority of a country's population demanding democratic elections?

There's nothing unreasonable about it if you look at it from the perspective of the Solidarity members, which is the only reasonable way to look at it.

It's their country. They're the people who have seen their country mismanaged into economic chaos by the bumbling, bureaucratic minds of the Communists. They're the ones who have had to put up with a form of government they despise for thirty-seven years.

Naturally, their demand sounds terribly unreasonable to the Russians and their Warsaw puppets, since there could be only one result of democratic elections—the Communist government would be thrown out.

Sure. And a Mafia extortionist would consider you unreasonable if you didn't pay up. And bank robbers consider the tellers unreasonable if they set off an alarm. Thieves and bullies and despots all have their own one-sided standards of reasonability. But it's ungracious, at the least, for anyone in this country to say that Solidarity wasn't being reasonable and was going "too far."

Going too far has a familiar ring to it. As I recall, Martin

Luther King was always being warned that he was trying to "go too far" and "too fast" and was "pushing too hard." They told him that the day the first black rode in the front of a Southern bus. Fortunately, King didn't pay attention to the warnings.

You could have found many prudent, reasonable, pragmatic people in this country who felt that Washington, Jefferson, Adams, and all the other revolutionary hotheads were going "too far, too fast." If they had listened to that advice, we'd all be rising to sing "God Save the Queen" before football games.

And it is particularly ungracious for any American to tell the Poles that they have gone too far, too fast, since it is to this country's shame that it took part with England in selling out the Poles and other Eastern European countries to the Russians when World War II ended.

We allowed the Russians to make Poland a Communist satellite.

The least we can do is allow the Poles to decide for themselves how far and fast they want to go in undoing the damage we inflicted on them.

A Mangled World

October 8, 1981

Anyone who owns a TV set saw it: The man in Egypt whose arm appeared to be almost gone, although it could have been so mangled, so little of it remaining, that it just looked like it was gone.

He was sitting in the bullet-riddled clutter of the reviewing stand, glancing about him with what appeared to be incredible calm. But, he was probably in shock.

And there was the lingering shot of a bloody hand and arm gripping a chair. The rest of that person was buried beneath overturned chairs and couldn't be seen. The bloody hand and arm was enough.

And a military man, some kind of aide to Anwar Sadat, being helped to his feet, blood pouring from wounds in his face, his eyes wide as if he was amazed by the sight of the dead and the maimed.

But the most chilling sight, to me at least, was during those few seconds when we could see the attackers rushing toward the reviewing stand, then backing away, then rushing in again.

It reminded me of something I once saw in a film about jungle animals. I think they were hyenas. They'd dash forward, baring their teeth and making ferocious sounds, then retreat, then dash back toward their prey.

As terrible as the carnage in Egypt was, I'm glad the cameras captured it, and that it was shown on TV for much of the world to see.

For one thing, it shows that violent death and injury are not quite the way most people see them: in TV dramas and movies, where the blood usually doesn't even show, or in a Sam Peckinpah movie, with wonderful slow motion and special effects so that being shot takes on a graceful dance-like quality.

Egypt is the way it is. Ugly and shocking, with tendons and bones exposed, blood dripping, bodies ripped and shredded, people wandering around with glazed eyes, wondering what happened, not knowing what to do.

You might even say that the film footage could be educational for the majority of those who saw it, young or old, and especially those who have never been in a way and don't know how it is to see human beings torn in half, ripped with holes.

I hope all the world's TV stations show that segment of the film as often as possible this week.

If they do, that great majority of people, in most countries, who do prefer to live in peace and don't like violent death, will see the reality of what they're up against: a minority made up of the fanatics.

It doesn't really matter what deity or political principle is driving the fanatics. The results are the same.

This particular group was probably shooting up the place to please Allah and to strike a blow against the Hebrew deity.

In Northern Ireland, it's the same Christian God, but they blow each other up, and kill and cripple and torture each other in dispute over who really has His ear and favor.

In Iraq and Iran, they too agree on their version of God. But they can't get together on how best to honor Him. So they do their best by killing one another and torturing and murdering their own citizens who don't bend their knees and mutter their prayers in the prescribed way.

Nor does it matter if the killing is preceded by what appears to be thoughtful, rational discussion of the planned killing.

While they use highly technical language that most of us can't understand, and speak without visible emotion, those generals and other war experts who sit in the dignified surroundings of an American congressional hearing room or in the Kremlin's war rooms are talking about the same thing.

Just because they calmly toss off phrases like "first-strike capability" and "interim programs" and "strategic modernization programs" and "multiple shelter programs" and technical or heroic names like "MX" or "Titans" or "B-1s" doesn't mean they aren't fanatics in their own way, or that they aren't talking about the same results.

They're talking about the same kind of things that were shown on the reviewing stand in Egypt: arms torn off, hands dripping blood, bodies slumped with eyes staring at nothing.

The only difference is that they're talking about all those arms being torn off, hands dripping blood and dead eyes on a much grander scale. Millions of arms and hands and dead eyes.

They make their grand plans in Moscow, in Washington, in Peking, and their more modest plans in the less powerful, but equally ferocious, capitals of the other countries.

Meanwhile, most of us—meaning maybe 90 percent, 95 percent, 98 percent of us?—sit as a captive audience, innocent bystanders wanting nothing more than to be left alone.

But we're not left alone because the fanatics seem to have taken control of the world, whether they are spraying a reviewing stand with bullets, lobbing shells across a desert border at one another, or dragging some of the bystanders into the basements of secret police headquarters for some eye-plucking.

Or whether they're sitting in great stone buildings, with guards at the entrances and flags flying proudly. Or what color uniform they wear, or if they are in suits and shirts and ties or how reasonable they make war and death sound.

In one way or another, they're all part of the great international brotherhood of fanatics.

And we saw on TV what they have in mind for the rest of us.

Poor Sadat. All he did was try to drop out of their club.

5 | "LIFE-STYLE"

Flapper Days Are Back

June 8, 1979

While walking across a windy downtown plaza, I saw a pretty young woman and immediately felt sorry for her.

She appeared to be suffering from a physical disability. She walked hunched forward and tilted to one side. Both of her arms were thrust straight down and held rigidly against her right thigh.

As she crossed the plaza, I thought how sad it was that she had to go through life dragging herself around that way.

She entered the glass-walled lobby of the building, and suddenly she began walking normally.

For a moment, I couldn't understand why she had been walking so grotesquely. Then, another woman on the plaza gave me the answer.

This one wasn't hunched over as severely as the other had been. But she leaned to her right side and her hand tightly clutched her skirt.

Of course. She was wearing a slit dress. Both had been

189

wearing slit dresses. But because the plaza was windy, they were preventing their dresses from flapping open in the breeze.

Since then, I've made a point of closely observing women who wear slit skirts. And when the wind blows, almost all of them are overwhelmed by modesty and take measures to prevent their thighs from being exposed.

Most of them do as the two women I mentioned above. Others use the big-purse-or-attaché-case trick, holding it in front of them like a leather fig leaf.

On one particularly breezy afternoon, I stood on the IBM plaza, one of the windiest places in town, and made my observation. It was a terrible thing to see. Half of the women who crossed the plaza walked like Quasimodo, the unfortunate hunchback of Notre Dame.

This forces me to conclude something that might offend a few women, but I have to say it. Despite their liberation, their independence, their many new freedoms of action and thought, a large number of modern female persons still are ninnies.

What else can I think about people who would spend money to buy garments that are clearly designed to display their thighs, then scuttle around like Igor to prevent their thighs from being displayed?

I asked a woman why she would buy a slit skirt in the first place, if not to display her limbs.

She said: "It's the fashion."

Exactly. Millions of women who probably don't even want to flash their flesh in public are buying these slit dresses because some French pervert of a clothing designer has decreed that they are "the fashion."

A scientific experiment I conducted confirms this. The experiment works this way: Whenever I see a woman wearing a slit dress, I make a point of staring at the slit. I mean, I really gawk. I stretch my neck and bulge my eyes and give it an intense leer.

And do you know what the women do? They glare at me. They look angry or indignant or disgusted, as if I am some sort of degenerate.

What does that prove? It shows how ridiculous they are, that's what.

Remember, the idea of a slit skirt is to make a woman look sexy. It is all part of the new fashion trend toward "The Lusty Woman," as *Esquire* magazine ballyhooed it. For months I have been reading about slit skirts in *Time, Newsweek*, the *New York Times, Woman's Wear Daily*, and in this newspaper. I have studied all the picture layouts of models with their slit skirts blowing in the breeze. And not one of the pictures has shown a woman crouched over, frantically grabbing her skirt as if protecting her lower body from a deviate dwarf.

So, if the idea is to make women look sexy, whom are they looking sexy for? A fireplug? Their own mirror? Small dogs?

Of course not. They are supposed to be displaying their thighs and looking sexy for men. That is a law of nature.

Yet, when I respond in an appropriate and perfectly natural way—by leering and gawking at their flashing thighs—rather than being pleased that their slit dresses have had their intended effect, they are indignant.

That is illogical. If they wear dresses that have an exhibitionist intent, then they should be delighted by the attention. They shouldn't scowl at those of us who respond by admiring their limbs.

And when the wind blows, they shouldn't go through all those physical contortions to conceal that which their dresses want to reveal.

This is just another example of how women, while really fine creatures in many ways, are less sensible than men.

Year after year, a handful of suspicious-looking characters who call themselves clothing designers issue their commands: Wear your dresses short and wear boots and look like a hooker. Now throw them away and wear them long and look like a frump. Now dress like a gypsy fortune-teller. Now look like a farm wife. Now wear spike heels. Now show your thighs.

And every time the pimps of fashion give the word, all these enlightened female persons obediently trudge to the clothing stores. With that attitude, they might as well be fetching a pipe and slippers.

In contrast, most men laugh at or ignore changes in male fashions. Except for certain High-Rise Men, who would wear purple leotards if Gucci or Pucci told them to, most of us stay with the classic look that might be called "1955 Robert Hall."

It's true that there are occasional obscene outbursts of male fashion such as the leisure suit or the body shirt or the shirt that is open to the belly button. But those fads quickly pass, and, over the long haul, the leisure suits and body shirts will be outsold by the ever-popular Sears, Roebuck long underwear.

I suppose it boils down to men being more level-headed and less plagued by foolish vanity than women are.

And I would elaborate on that, but I have to go now. I have an appointment with my hair stylist. He is putting new tape on my hairpiece, because it keeps blowing off in the wind.

Love Lost in Lingo

June 3, 1981

He was staring morosely into his beer and every so often he'd sigh deeply. The bartender was too smart to ask him what the problem was. But I wasn't.

What's bothering you? I asked.

He shook his head and said: "I just ended a . . . we just ended. . . ." And his voice choked and cracked.

Ended what?

"We ended . . . a . . . relationship."

A relationship?

"Yeah. She broke off our . . . relationship."

I bought him a beer, advised him not to let life wear him down, and quickly moved on.

I'm not without sympathy, but I hate the word "relationship." If he had told me he had suffered a shattered romance or a broken love affair, I'd have stuck around and endured the boredom. But I refuse to listen to someone blubber about a "relationship."

What an awful word. It's the kind of sterile word used by lawyers and sociologists and other menaces.

Exactly when the word "relationship" began being used as a substitute for a romance or love affair, I don't know. But that's the way people talk now.

And not only does it sound like something out of this impersonal, computerized, digital, credit card era, but what does it rhyme with?

That's the real question. Try to rhyme relationship with something. Battleship? Landing strip? Broken hip? Scholarship?

With words like that, how are we ever going to have schmaltzy poems and heart-plunking love songs? And without them, some day the ultimate romantic statement will be: "Your place or mine?" Maybe it is already.

Sure, you can string together a few words like relationship. But can you imagine anyone ever saying "They're playing our song" when they hear: "We started our relationship, on a landing strip, while watching a Messerschmidt fly by"?

If the word "relationship" had been in use over the years, I hate to even think about the kind of popular love songs we would have been hearing.

How about this: "I'm in the mood for a relationship, simply because you're near me."

Or: "You've got to give a little, take a little and let your poor heart break a little: That's the story of, that's the glory of a relationship."

How about the classic "Stardust"? "Tho' I dream in vain, in my heart it always will remain: My stardust melody, the memory of relationship's refrain."

From the Beatles we would have: "Yesterday, relationship was such an easy game to play: Now I need a place to hide away. Oh, I believe in yesterday." Or: "And I relate to her. . . . A relationship like ours could never die, as long as I have you near me."

I can go on and on. So I will:

• "Fish got to swim and birds got to fly, I got to have a relationship with one man till I die; can't help relatin' to that man of mine."

• "I can't give you anything but a relationship, baby; that's the only thing I've plenty of, baby."

• "Oh, how we danced on the night we were wed; we vowed our true relationship, though a word wasn't said."

• "You made me relate to you, I didn't want to do it, I didn't want to do it."

• "What the world needs now is relationship, sweet relationship. It's the only thing there's just too little of."

• "Relationship is a many-splendored thing."

• "When the moon hits your eye like a big pizza pie, that's a relationship. When the world seems to shine like you've had too much wine, that's a relationship."

• "On a day like today, we passed the time away writing relationship letters in the sand. Now my poor heart just aches, with every wave that breaks over relationship letters in the sand."

                    *   *   *

Then there's another phrase. "Significant Other." It is now used by many people to describe the other party in a relationship. It has become a substitute for words like girlfriend, boyfriend, etc.

You could really make some heart-tugging songs out of "significant other."

How about this? "Let me call you significant other, I'm relating to you. Let me hear you whisper that you're relating to me, too."

There's the oldie: "Five feet two, eyes of blue, but could she relate, could she coo, could she, could she, could she coo—has anybody seen my significant other?"

And there's the old jukebox favorite, "You Are My Sunshine," which would sound like this: "You are my significant other, my only significant other. You make me happy when skies are gray. You'll never know, dear, how much I relate to you. Please don't take my significant other away."

One thing I forgot to ask the guy in the bar: When his significant other ended their relationship, did she at least osculate him good-by?

A Classy Way to Go

August 12, 1980

NEW YORK—I hate to admit this, but there are reasons for a Chicagoan to envy New York.

I'm not talking about the obvious reasons for envy, such as baseball, although I could. As I'm writing this, the Yankees are on TV playing a "crucial" game. That means that they are in first place and even if they lose the game, they'll still be in first place. In Chicago, a crucial game means that the Cubs have a chance to move out of the cellar. Or that the White Sox franchise won't be sold.

Nor am I talking about whether New York works. No big city works if it has a large minority population, which translates into a large unemployed population, which leads us to a large welfare population, which takes us to most of the urban nightmares of the twentieth century. The American cities that actually work are oversize suburbs like Minneapolis, Portland, Oregon, or San Diego. They are dull, pleasant, and medium in the size of their population—which is almost all-white, American-born. And the residents belch more than the smokestacks do.

No, the reason I envy New York is the style with which its gangsters kill each other.

It may seem strange for a Chicagoan to envy New York for anything that has to do with crime and violence. Since the days of Capone we have considered ourselves first in this field.

There are valid reasons for this pride. When it comes to splatter marks, you can't beat the St. Valentine's Day Massacre. It was Chicago that pioneered the use of gangster nicknames— "Scarface," "Greasy Thumb," "Cherry Nose," "The Enforcer," and "The Camel." We're probably the only city that routinely identifies certain congressmen, judges, and aldermen as representing the crime syndicate.

Yet, I must put aside my pride and accept New York's superiority in matters that have to do with the killing of little fellows in fedoras and shirts stained with tomato sauce.

In Chicago, people are killed while parking in their drive-ways (shotguns or ignition bombs), while driving on highways (shotguns), while walking to their apartments (pistols or shotguns), while cooking a midnight snack of sausage (pistols), or while sitting on chairs in front of their houses, cooling off on a hot summer evening (pistols, shotguns, bombs, knives, spears, and wives who inform for the enemy).

But in New York, they do it publicly.

Do you remember the New York restaurant scene in *The Godfather,* in which Michael Corleone has dinner with a dope dealer and a corrupt police captain? Michael takes a pre-planted pistol from the toilet tank in the men's room, blows the dealer and cop away, and walks out of the restaurant while everyone chokes on his veal ("the best veal" in New York, the gangster told the cop before Michael zapped them).

I don't know if life imitates art, or if it's the reverse.

But that's how they do it in New York. They don't hide in hedges, waiting for someone to come home. They don't pop out of sewers and shoot some guy walking his dog. And they don't plant bombs in ignitions, which is the most cowardly way to murder someone—what if a guy lets his wife keep the car for the day?

In New York, they kill people in restaurants. They kill them while they are chewing veal. Or eating linguine with red clam sauce. Or while smoking a cigar and sipping an espresso.

Their gangsters end up on a restaurant floor, with napkins tucked in their collars, eyes cold as coins, and a cigar gripped by their lifeless teeth.

That gets to me as a Chicagoan. About a year ago, Carmine Galante was having something to eat in a place called Joseph and Mary's in Brooklyn. Galante was the *capo di tutti capi* of the national syndicate. It means that he was the slob of slobs.

Some men walked in and shot him to pieces. And all over the country there was the picture of Carmine Galante dead on the restaurant floor, a cigar clenched between his teeth.

So I hopped in a cab yesterday and told the driver to take

me to Joseph and Mary's. He said: "I know why you're going there. The hit, right?"

Right.

"Then why don't you go to Umberto's first."

Ah, I had forgotten Umberto's. That was where Joseph (Crazy Joey) Gallo got his.

I told the cabbie to take me to Umberto's. And it turned out to be another reason I envy New York.

Umberto's is on Mulberry Street, which is the heart of the old "Little Italy" section. Block after block, you have one great Italian restaurant after another. Umberto's may or may not be the best of them. But it's the only joint on Mulberry Street that can boast that Crazy Joey Gallo was ventilated while eating magnificent linguine with clam sauce.

"Where did Crazy Joey get it?" I asked the cook, who stirred clam sauce on the other side of the wood counter.

He pointed at a Formica table in the corner. "There. That table. They walked in. Boom! Good-by Joey."

On the wall behind the table were autographed pictures of celebrity customers: Dean Martin, Frank Sinatra. That's very big in New York. Every cheap hot dog joint has a photo of Frank Sinatra.

But exactly, precisely, perfectly placed behind the table was a picture of a benign, heavenly Bishop Lawrence Graziano.

Who's the bishop? we asked.

"I dunno," said the chef. "He must like the clam sauce."

Did Gallo die right there, on the floor?

The chef sneered at my ignorance. "Nah. He was shot there, but he got up and walked out. Right out the front door."

Where did he go?

"Nowhere. He dropped dead on Mulberry Street."

I asked him what the effect was when someone was bumped off in a New York restaurant.

"On our business? I'll tell you the truth. Business gets

bigger and better. You want to make it in New York? Have somebody big knocked off in your place. It's great. We were never that well known. But if another guy gets knocked off in here, we might have to expand."

I went outside and got in a cab and told him to take me to Joe and Mary's in Brooklyn. He looked out the windshield and shook his head. "I can't take you there."

Why not?

"It closed up."

But that's where Carmine Galante was killed. A hit is supposed to help business in New York.

The cabbie shrugged. "That's the way it usually goes. But it didn't happen with Joe and Mary's."

Why not?

"They killed Joe, the owner, too. That's bad for business."

Bellying Up to Success

November 8, 1973

A recent magazine survey shows that the average American male worries more about the size of his belly than any other part of his body.

That probably surprises people who think that the sexual revolution would have provoked concern about other physical attributes, but the magazine, *Psychology Today*, says it isn't so.

The survey shows that the stay-young-and-lean syndrome

has changed the attitude toward a pot belly, which was once considered a fine thing for a man to have.

If the survey had been taken thirty-five years ago, they would have found pride, if anything, in a bulging middle. Of course, such a survey could not have been taken then. Any pollster who asked men to describe how they felt about parts of their own bodies would have been knocked down and beaten.

The pot belly was viewed as a mark of success. Every alderman had one. An alderman who didn't look well fed would have been suspected of honesty, and therefore of stupidity.

It was the sign of maturity. A young man wasn't grown until he could belly up to the bar. And how could you belly up to a bar without a belly?

The finest athletes had them, especially bowlers, softball players, perch fishermen, and furniture movers.

So did all the civic leaders, such as the desk sergeant, the bookie, and the tavern owner.

The greatest stomach in our neighborhood belonged to Slats Grobnik's uncle, Beer-Belly Frank Grobnik.

He claimed his stomach was the secret of his legendary strength and agility. He could lift a jukebox in his arms and dance with it, which he did every Saturday night in the tavern.

"I'd like to see some greasy tango dancer try it," he'd boast as he clumped around the saloon.

He was proud of this talent, so he was offended and started a brawl when he tried to go dancing at the Aragon Ballroom and they wouldn't let him in unless he checked his jukebox at the door.

Like most men of great bellies, Frank used it to communicate emotions. When he finished a hearty meal of beer and hard-boiled eggs, he would thump it with his broad hand.

Everybody knew Frank had just eaten by the deep sound that rolled through the neighborhood.

He scratched it when he was tired, and rubbed it when he was hungry. And when he was angry, he would thrust it forward and use it as a weapon. Those who felt the wrath of his belly said it was like being struck by a fat truck.

It was always Slats' dream to have a belly like his Uncle Frank's. But nature didn't intend it. He was so skinny you could actually see through him in a bright light. At the beach, he once drank too much strawberry pop and looked like a tall thermometer.

Nature decided that Slats' physical distinction would be his remarkably long, hooked nose.

When Slats was born, his father took one look and said to the nurse: "What do we feed it—birdseed?"

His Aunt Wanda, who had knowledge of the occult, asked Mrs. Grobnik: "Think back. Before Slats was born, did anything frighten you or give you a bad shock?"

"Yes," said Mrs. Grobnik. "My husband did."

As Slats grew up, he became sensitive about his nose. Anytime another kid so much as sneezed, Slats thought he was being made fun of and would start swinging. Goofy Archie, who had hay fever, spent his entire summers sneezing and ducking.

Because of Slats' sensitivity, people tried to persuade him that a prominent nose was a mark of distinction.

"Abraham Lincoln had a long nose," his mother told him.

Slats nodded sadly. "Yeah, that's probably why they plugged him."

The candy store man told him: "What you got, kid, is a Roman nose."

Slats thought about that, then threw a rock through the candy store window. "Nobody can call me a Dago," he said.

A teacher, trying to be progressive and kind, finally thought she had the solution.

She asked Slats to play the part of Cyrano in a school play.

"Cyrano's nose was rather long," she told Slats, "but he was very brave and honorable and smart."

"Sounds like me, all right," said Slats, giving the teacher a pinch.

The teacher's idea didn't work.

Slats read the script until he reached the part where Cyrano hides under the beautiful Roxanne's balcony and whispers sweet love words for a handsome, but inarticulate, young man to repeat to her.

That's when Slats flung the script down and walked out, saying: "I ain't playing the part of no pimp."

Bottom-line Bargain

December 18, 1980

Many people consider it very important to have someone's name on the rear end of their jeans.

They want anyone who looks at their bottoms to know instantly that they have spent what it takes to have jeans by Calvin Klein, Gloria Vanderbilt, Diane Von Furstenberg, Bill Blass, Bonjour, or some guy named Sasson.

I've never worn any pants with an absolute stranger's name printed on the rear end. I wasn't reared that way. In fact, I don't remember wearing anything with any exterior labeling on it except my shoes. They are a fashionable Dr. Scholl model, and on the rubber soles are stamped the words: "Vulcanized. Oil Resistant."

Oh, yes, I've also worn softball shirts that have the names of taverns on the back. But that's not so much a concession to fashion as it is to the tavern owner, who pays for the uniforms and buys an occasional round.

But in the case of the designer jeans, people are willing to spend extra money just to have the name Calvin Klein where they sit. In other words, Calvin Klein, Sasson, and these other strange birds not only receive advertising on your rear end, but you pay them for the privilege of giving them the advertising.

I asked a young woman why she wants the names of these people on her rear end, and she said: "Sure, I could wear a pair of, say, the Levi Chic jeans. They're a lot cheaper and fit me perfectly well. But if I went to a party and somebody looked at my behind and noticed that it said Levi Chic, I'd be embarrassed."

I can understand that. If it said Levi Chic on my rear end, I'd be embarrassed, too.

"No, what I mean is that by having something like Calvin Klein or the others, you are making a social statement. You are saying that you can afford to squander money on jeans."

I had never thought about one's behind being used to make a statement. I usually write a memo.

Another thing I've noticed about the designer jeans is that they don't look comfortable.

"They can be terribly uncomfortable," admitted the young woman. "Talk about pain. Some of them feel like they are going to kill me when I sit down. So I try not to wear them at a sit-down party and I only wear them to bars that are so crowded I know I'll be standing."

That's another reason I'm not the designer jean type: I prefer something that combines high fashion and loose-fitting comfort—such as a pair of mechanic's coveralls from Sears.

The reason I'm talking about this subject is that I noticed a story the other day about the counterfeiting of designer jeans.

Somebody named Sheldon Goldstein, who works for Puritan Fashion Corporation, which makes Calvin Klein jeans, says that fake Calvin Kleins are being sold in at least ten states.

"It is a multimillion-dollar rip-off," Goldstein said. "People are purchasing five-dollar jeans for amounts of twenty-six to thirty-eight dollars. Our intent is to make people aware that counterfeit Calvin Klein jeans are being distributed throughout the United States."

Goldstein provided advice for people who want to be sure that the genuine Calvin Klein name, not some counterfeit Calvin Klein name, is drawing admiring glances to their buttocks.

"We suggest purchasing designer jeans from reputable department stores. Anytime they are purchased from an outlet or a flea market at a discount price, chances are very high they are counterfeit."

This might upset Mr. Goldstein, but if I were the kind of person who spent money on designer jeans, I would look for the counterfeits. They sound like a good deal.

For one thing, Goldstein didn't say anything about the counterfeits being easy to spot because they look awful and don't fit properly. So I assume they fit as tightly and provide as much physical pain as do the genuine articles.

In that case, why not buy the counterfeits? As long as your bottom is making a social statement, why not save a few bucks and make the statement at the same time.

Goldstein sounded like he was sneering when he said: "People are purchasing five-dollar jeans for amounts of twenty-six to thirty-eight dollars."

But he didn't say how much more than five dollars his genuine Calvin Klein jeans cost to make. I tried to get that information from his company, but nobody would talk about it.

So I asked an acquaintance who works for a Chicago clothing store for some dollar figures on Calvin Klein jeans.

"Our store pays twenty dollars for them and we sell them for forty-two."

And what does it cost the Puritan Corporation to make them?

"It's just a rough guess, but I would say that it would be about ten dollars tops. But that's not just the manufacturing cost. That would include what they have to pay Calvin Klein for the use of his name. And it would include that incredible advertising budget and what they have to pay Brooke Shields."

Ah, I had forgotten about Brooke Shields. She is the child movie star who was hired by the jean-maker for seductive commercials, in which she flaunts the jeans' fly and her lean shanks.

Since all that advertising costs a bundle, it can probably be assumed that the genuine Klein jeans don't cost much more to produce than the five-dollar manufacturing cost that Goldstein put on the counterfeits.

So I suggest that if anyone runs across the counterfeit Calvin Kleins, snap them up. Most people, looking at your behind, will not know the difference.

And not only will you be getting a bargain, but you will have the satisfaction of doing business with high-class people. Counterfeiters they may be. But that's a lot better than making soft-core porn with a teenage kid to peddle a pair of pants.

Manic on Mechanics

January 9, 1980

A friend of mine swears this happened.

It was shortly before midnight and he heard some loud voices outside the window of his first-floor apartment in the city.

He looked out and saw two men standing at the curb quarreling.

One of them held a pistol in his hand and was saying: "I told you that I was going to shoot the sonofabitch, and I'm gonna do it."

The other man said: "You shouldn't oughta do it."

The man with the gun said: "No, I told you that if it happened one more time, I was going to do it, and I'm going to. Now get out of the way."

With that, he raised the pistol and calmly blasted several holes into the hood of an old Pontiac parked at the curb.

Shoving the smoking pistol into his pocket, he snarled at the car: "There, you sonofabitch, I'm through with you."

And the two of them walked away.

My friend called the police and they rushed to the scene about half an hour later. They wrote down the license plate number and presumably they are trying to trace the man who shot his car.

I'm not sure what they will do when they find him. It

seems to me that a person ought to have the right to shoot his own car if the thing deserves being shot.

And without knowing anything more about the case than these few sketchy facts, my guess is that the police will find a man who is now at peace with himself.

There comes a point in trying to deal with mechanical objects especially those mass-produced today—when the only answer is violence, even murder.

I've murdered several such objects myself over the years and have felt better for it.

I killed a TV set once, and my conscience doesn't bother me.

The TV had developed the vicious habit of flipping just when the Cub game was in a crucial situation, which was almost all the time.

I'd haul it to the repair shop, the man would tinker with it, and I'd haul it back. It would work fine for a while. Then Ernie Banks would come to bat in the last of the ninth with the score tied, dig in, wiggle his fingers; the pitcher would shake off a signal, nod his head, go into his windup. And the TV picture would start flipping.

I'd turn the horizontal control and for a moment it would stop flipping. But as soon as I sat down, it would begin again. It was as if it had a brain of its own and was trying to torture me.

It reached a point when I'd sit there, not thinking about the game, but just swearing at the TV, calling it every filthy name I could think of. And the more I swore, the more it flipped.

So one day I just pulled the plug and carried it out to the back porch.

I yelled to the people from the first floor, who were sitting in the yard, to get out of the way.

"Don't jump," they said, scrambling out of their chairs.

I threw it, and as it dropped I shouted, "Die, you lousy————!"

Oh, I felt good when it shattered with a loud noise. And the downstairs neighbors stared up at me for a moment, went inside, and didn't sit in the backyard again for the rest of the summer. They were probably afraid I'd get mad at the washing machine.

I killed a typewriter once, too, and that isn't easy. Typewriters have a great will to live.

This one had developed all kinds of evil habits, especially when I was nearing a deadline. The ribbon wouldn't reverse. The *c* would stick. It would single-space when it was supposed to double-space. Then the *k* started sticking, too. Finally it did everything all at once.

First I tried tearing it limb from limb, but typewriters are strong. Once I had torn off the top shield, it really resisted. I tried ripping out the keys, but they just bent a little. So I tried tearing out the letters, but the *u*, or maybe it was the *f*, gashed my hand in retaliation.

I managed to yank off the carriage return, but that was about it. So I just picked it up and threw it at the wall, spraining my back.

Finally, I raised it above my head and smashed it to the floor. That really did it. Pieces flew all over the office. And my instep, where it landed, was swollen for a month.

The last machine I killed was a cassette recorder, and no machine ever deserved execution more.

I had used it while I interviewed a presidential candidate, and he had said some of the most wonderfully stupid things I had ever heard.

But when I played the interview back, the cassette was blank. All that stupidity was lost to history.

I put it on the floor and jumped on it, and laughed as its Japanese innards came squirting out.

That was the last machine I killed, but I've beaten up several others. Mostly coffee machines and other mechanical thieves.

Some readers may recall a column a few years ago in which I recommended not letting coffee machines and other vending devices get away with taking your money and not giving you anything. I recommended the best way to kick them. (Not with your toe. With the bottom of your foot, as if kicking down a lady's door.)

In that column, I said kicking it wouldn't get you your money back, but you'd feel better.

The response was heartwarming. Hundreds of people wrote about how much better they felt after kicking a cheating machine.

However, one young man wrote and said that he followed my advice and was happily kicking the office coffee machine when his boss came by and fired him.

"Your crazy advice cost me my job," he said. "Now what should I do?"

I told him to put my column on the floor, face up, and jump up and down on it and he'd feel better.

He said he'd try. Then he called back and said: "You're right, I feel better."

Good, I said.

"Yeah, but the landlord lives downstairs and because of all the noise, he says he wants me to move out."

Some people just can't be helped.

A Trial's Trail of Gold

November 18, 1981

The defense lawyers, prosecutors, judges, cops, and others
who hang around the Criminal Courts Building are still
talking about macho man Adolpho Lopez and his amazing
gold chain.

And members of a jury whose duty it was to look at his
gold chain will surely never forget the sight.

Lopez the macho man stood trial last week. Except for the
gold chain, it wasn't really an unusual case, especially to
someone in Adolpho's social set.

Adolpho, twenty-four, is a member of a street gang. I'm
not sure which one. The Insane Idiots, the Moronic Madmen,
the Panting Paranoids—it doesn't make much difference. A
spray can is a spray can, and a macho man is a macho man.

And on most evenings, Adolpho and his fellow gang
members are roaming around, looking for something to do
and somebody to do it to.

In this case, what Adolpho allegedly did was to notice a
lady who struck his fancy on the street at Division near Clark.
He didn't know the woman, but formal introductions are not
considered necessary in Adolpho's macho circles. She said he
forced her into a car and, while his pal Repolia Robinson,
thirty-four, drove, he beat, robbed, and raped her.

The police eventually caught him and, unfortunately, Adolpho didn't give them any reason to shoot him, so the trial was held.

Most rape trials are nasty because the defense lawyers often try to convince the judge or jury that it was really the victim's idea. If you believe defense lawyers, the streets of Chicago are constantly teeming with hot-blooded women looking for a fast physical encounter with a bum like Adolpho.

But this case was not only nasty, it was unique because of Adolpho's gold chain.

How can I describe the chain? It isn't easy.

It's similar to the gold chains that vain men wear around their necks. Or it could be worn around a wrist, or even an ankle.

Actually, describing the chain isn't that difficult. It's describing *where* Adolpho wears it.

He doesn't wear it around his neck or wrist or ankle.

As Adolpho explained the chain, the last time he was in prison—I'm not sure if it was for burglary, robbery, or aggravated battery, since he's been convicted of them all—he decided to wear a gold chain where no other macho man has been known to wear a gold chain.

Let me put it this way: You've heard of those primitive people who pierce their lips and noses and put chains and rings through them?

Or those supposedly civilized people who pierce their earlobes and put baubles of jewelry through them?

Adolpho, while in prison, decided that he would put a hole through that part of his body in which he takes the most macho pride. And he would string a gold chain through it.

That's as descriptive as I can be without becoming too embarrassed to continue. And if you still don't understand, I will add that he wore the gold chain where it would not normally be on public display.

Anyway the gold chain became the key element in the trial.

The victim, a thirty-six-year-old mother of two, was asked

if she had noticed that Adolpho wore a gold chain where one would not expect a man to wear a gold chain.

She said she didn't remember any gold chain.

So Adolpho's lawyer, who couldn't have dreamed he'd earn his living this way when he was back in law school, tried to establish that it would be impossible for a rape victim to overlook a gold chain that was worn in so prominent a place—at least prominent for a rapist.

He even produced four females who testified that they had been romantically involved with Adolpho. They swore that the chain was not something a girl could overlook.

Then came an unusual legal problem: showing the gold chain to the jury.

All the lawyers went into the judge's chambers to discuss it in private, which is where such matters should be pondered.

The prosecution suggested that photographs would be adequate. But the defense said, no, the jury should see the actual chain.

So Judge Robert Sklodowski had to decide. He says: "Before I could allow it at all . . . in my chambers I inspected it and had pictures taken. I don't mean I inspected it with my hands. I inspected it visually, if you know what I mean."

(I mention that detail in case Judge Sklowdowski runs for public office again, and tries to shake the hands of you voters. It's all right.)

He finally decided that the Polaroid pictures did not show the chain clearly enough, especially the clasp that could permit it to be removed, although Adolpho said removing it would cause him terrible pain.

So the moment came. Adolpho the macho man stood before the jury, dropped his trousers, and put his gold chain on display.

And he stood there for more than a minute while his lawyer asked him pertinent questions about the gold chain—whether he always wears it, how he keeps it polished, and so on.

Witnesses to this performance say that several of the jurors looked off into space. Others looked embarrassed. One female juror reportedly needed medication afterward.

Then came the closing arguments, the highlight being when Adolpho's lawyer described him as: "A macho guy who takes pride in himself in his own way."

The prosecutor, a female, was more succinct. She said: "The guy is a pervert."

Surprisingly, the jury returned a verdict of not guilty. They didn't say why. They just announced the verdict and went home to tell their friends about the amazing thing they had seen while on jury duty.

So Adolpho is a free macho man again, and probably the hero of his gang.

All we can do is hope that the price of gold goes higher and higher and higher.

Then maybe a thief will grab Adolpho's gold chain and run like hell with it.

Laugh and Learn

January 12, 1977

It seems to me the practical joke has become a dormant form of humor.

The White House tried to revive it in 1972, and some of the pranks were clever. But a joke can't really be called practical if it gets you two years in prison.

Whenever I hear people talking about great practical jokes, they are inevitably the old classics, most of them collected years ago in a book by H. Allen Smith.

So I was pleased to recently hear about two fine, sadistic practical jokes that sounded original.

One was the work of a Chicago salesman who became bored with the ritual of sending out Christmas cards.

"My wife and I weren't going to bother last year, but we already had the cards and that's when I got this idea," he related.

"You know how some people will write a few personal lines on a card?

"Well, here's what I did. If a guy had been in the service, I'd write something like: 'Hi, Joe, old buddy. Got your address from Jim Scanlon (you remember the old barracks moocher). Me and the wife and kids are going to be passing through Chicago during the Christmas holidays, and we'll stop by and spend a night or two with you, and we can sip a few brews and rehash our days in the old outfit.'

"Then I'd sign it with a phony name, something like: 'Your old pal, Wilbur Crull.'

"I was driving South on a sales trip the next week, so I took them along and mailed them all from small Southern towns.

"You can imagine how people reacted when the cards came. Wives were yelling: 'Who the hell is this guy? They're going to move in with us during Christmas?' Husbands were saying: 'For God's sake, I knew a hundred yokels in the army. He could be any one of them!'

"For guys who hadn't been in the service, I just substituted something about college days.

"My wife and I talked to several of them after they got the cards. They were in a panic. One couple had such an argument about his lousy old-time friends, they almost got divorced. Another friend of mine wouldn't answer his doorbell if he didn't recognize the person outside. It was beautiful.

"You know what I'll do next Christmas? I'm going to say something like: 'Joe, old buddy. My pickup truck broke down and we couldn't make it to Chicago. But we'll be there for sure this year, ya' hear?'"

The other joke was the work of a restaurant owner in Madison, Wisconsin.

He and three friends were on a fishing trip way up north. They were staying in a cabin on the shore of a wilderness lake.

It was 10:00 P.M. They had fished all day, had a few beers, played some poker, and were going to turn in and get up before dawn for more fishing.

One of them, let's call him Joe, was the first to his bunk. He was exhausted. Within a few minutes, he was snoring.

The restaurant owner quickly told the others his plan.

One of them got Joe's wristwatch, which he had put on a dresser, and changed the time to 4:45.

Then they changed their own watches and the alarm clock to 4:45.

They set the alarm clock to go off at exactly five o'clock, turned off all the lights, took off their clothes, and went to bed.

Fifteen minutes later, the alarm clock went off. They all got up, shuffling around, making the grumbly, miserable sounds that men make early in the morning. One of them put toast and coffee on.

The most miserable was Joe. He sat on the edge of his bed, shaking his head, moaning: "I don't feel like I've been to bed at all."

He kept looking at his watch, the clock, asking them what time they had, mumbling and groaning.

He complained as he drank his coffee, and on the way to the boat.

"I must be getting old," he said, as they dropped anchor and began fishing.

Every few minutes, he'd glance at his watch and look at the eastern horizon and say: "What time have you got?"

"Five-forty," somebody would say.

"Boy, it's dark," Joe would say.

A little later: "What time have you got?"

"Six."

He began looking concerned. "Shouldn't it be getting light soon?" he asked.

"Daylight Savings," one of them replied.

By the time his watch said 6:40, he had stopped casting. He just sat there staring into the darkness.

Finally, in a voice filled with genuine terror, he cried: "I'm telling you, something is wrong! It's not getting light today! It's not getting light today! Something is wrong!"

"End of the world," they hooted. "Doesn't matter, because the fish aren't biting anyway."

That's when he caught on. And he took it well, although they had to wrestle an oar out of his hands.

A Tickle a Day

November 28, 1977

I thought that by now I had run across most known social injustices. But a letter that recently was printed in this paper brought a new one to my attention.

It concerns the tickling of babies. The person who wrote

the letter condemned baby-tickling as cruel and sadistic, and urged people to stop doing it.

That's a problem I had not thought about before. Like most people, I have seen babies tickled. But it never occurred to me that it might be harmful to them. I assumed that since they giggled, they were enjoying themselves. That was faulty reasoning, of course, since even adults giggle when there is no reason. TV newscasters do it often. But maybe they tickle each other during commercials.

I knew that the popular practice of throwing babies in the air and yelling "whoopsie" at them wasn't a good idea. Especially in houses that have low ceilings. It can cause a child who was tossed around that way to grow up with a fear of heights, as well as a flat head.

An uncle of mine used to do that all the time. When he was around, there was always a shrieking baby in orbit. Sometimes he'd get two or three of them going at the same time, and work in a couple of oranges or apples so it was a regular juggling act.

He once tossed my cousin so high that the kid sailed right off the back porch and landed in the crook of a tree. We had to call the fire department to get him down. The firemen couldn't understand how a tot could have climbed that tree.

And sure enough, when my cousin grew up, he had a terrible fear of heights. And also a fear of uncles, trees, porches, firemen, and the word "whoopsie."

I'm certain that most people who tickle babies don't realize they are being cruel and sadistic. Somebody points a baby at you, and your choice of responses is limited to chucking it under the chin, saying goo-goo, or giving it a tickle.

I'm a chin-chucker myself, although I occasionally say goo-goo. It depends on the circumstances. If the kid is drooling all over its chin, I prefer goo-goo.

As far as I know, there isn't anything harmful about

chin-chucking, so long as you don't wind up and chuck so hard that the child gets punchy.

On the other hand, if a baby is chucked under the chin by everyone it meets, it could develop a callused jaw. So maybe chin-chucking is another little-known abuse we ought to think about.

After reading the anti-tickling letter, I asked a child expert if tickling really was bad for babies. He said it sure was. For one thing, a child who is tickled can develop sexual inhibitions at a later age.

I don't argue with experts, but I don't see how they could be sure of something like that, since most people wouldn't remember if they had been tickled as babies. For all we know, a man who blames early tickling by his old granny for his inhibitions might be inhibited simply because he has knobby knees and wears baggy shorts.

The child expert also said that tickling is handed down from one generation to another, and becomes increasingly worse. For example, someone who was tickled as a baby is more likely to become a tickler of babies himself. And a person who was tickled on his ribs might later tickle babies on the ribs and the bottoms of their feet. And that baby, in turn, could grow up to be the kind of sadist who would tickle a baby on the ribs, feet, and under the neck—maybe even with a feather.

So in three or four generations, you could end up with someone who is sexually inhibited but giggles all the time. It would be better to be tossed off a porch.

I'm not sure what can be done to prevent the tickling of babies. It's an issue that has not been taken up by any politicians that I know of. Had someone called it to President Carter's attention last year, it would have fit right into his campaign. Maybe he would have admitted tickling Billy when they were little. There has to be an explanation for Billy.

A law forbidding baby tickling could be passed, but it would be difficult to enforce. Most parents, uncles, aunts, and grannies wouldn't turn each other in. Not unless there was a reward involved.

City inspectors could probably be assigned to just walk around and listen for the telltale sound of a baby giggling. That might seem like strange work, but it's not much different than what many of them are doing anyway.

Or maybe newborn babies could be stamped with a harmless vegetable dye that says: "Do Not Tickle." But that might be a bad precedent, because someone would also want them stamped: "Do Not Toss in Air," and someone else would want to add: "Do Not Feed Presweetened Cereals." Pretty soon every baby would look like a Ralph Nader position paper.

The problem should probably be studied further. In the meantime, don't tickle any babies. Not unless you want to bring another TV anchorman into this world.

Lapping It Up

April 7, 1978

By now, every major publication in America has taken an in-depth look at the new national craze of running.

It is claimed in most of these stories that running has passed almost all other participation sports in popularity. Those who love running rave about how it improves their health, makes them feel younger, improves their work and sex lives, sharpens their minds, and even gives them euphoric highs.

I won't argue with their claims, but many people happen to think that the most healthful, rewarding physical activity is not long-distance running, but long-term sitting.

Unlike runners, who can drive you crazy with all their smug talk about how great they feel, sitters are modest. At least the truly dedicated sitters are. They seldom talk about how great sitting is. They just sit. They don't try to talk everyone they know into taking up sitting. The most they say is: "Have a chair."

But recently I talked to Joe Spinecurve, head of the Chicago Area Long-Term Sitters Club, about the benefits of sitting, and he answered some questions.

Can anyone sit?

"Yes. That's one of the best things about sitting. You can do it regardless of how young you are or how old. You can do it alone, or with a friend or even a large group of people. You can sit in all kinds of weather, any time of the day or night. And you don't have to take special training or read a book about it or see your doctor for approval. It is a very natural activity.

"It also conserves energy.

"Do you realize how much energy all those crazy runners burn up? No wonder the Arabs have us over a barrel. If those loonies would stop burning up all that energy and sit down, this nation could be self-sufficient in energy."

Does a person need any special equipment to sit?

"Absolutely not. That is one of the best things about it. You don't have to buy special pants or any such wasteful junk. You don't even need pants, although I prefer them, especially when sitting in mixed company or on a cold surface. All you really need in the way of equipment is a chair. Actually, if you can't afford a chair, you can get by with any flat spot and a wall or a tree trunk to lean back against.''

Do you recommend any particular kind of chair?

''It depends on personal preference. I prefer a big, soft, womblike, motherly chair. I position my chair so that I am near my books, magazines, TV set, salami, Swiss cheese, potato chips, liquor supply, and other life supports. Hard-bottomed and straight-backed chairs are adequate for short-term sitting, such as when you have dinner. But if you intend to do some very serious sitting—a full day or maybe a whole weekend or an entire week's vacation—then you need something you can really wallow in.''

Is sitting good for your health?

''Let me answer that with a question. When you go to see your doctor, what is he usually doing? He's sitting, right? Well, it must be good for you, or why would doctors do it so much? Those guys are no fools. With the kind of money they make, they want to stay around long enough to enjoy it.''

But is it as good for you as running?

''Better. Scientific studies show that long-distance sitters suffer 92 percent fewer sprained arches, broken toes, twisted ankles, torn ligaments, pulled hamstring muscles, and sore knees than runners do. Sitters are hit by 82 percent fewer cars, bitten by 71 percent fewer dogs, and trip over 89 percent fewer fireplugs and short people than runners. And sitters are cleaner than runners because they step in 78 percent less doggy do-do and are hit on the head by 83 percent less pigeon do-do, so you are far safer in letting a sitter walk on your rug or borrow your comb. Also, sitters are nicer to be around because they don't smell as bad as runners, who sweat all over the place.''

Runners say that running sharpens their thinking. Some say they get a ''high'' from it. Does this happen from sitting?

''I will answer it this way: The immortal Beethoven composed his nine magnificent symphonies while sitting. Shakespeare wrote every one of his plays while sitting. Believe me, that man could sit. Einstein figured out his theory of relativity while sitting. Lincoln wrote his Gettysburg address while sitting. Winston Churchill devised his greatest military strategies while sitting. Mark Twain wrote his greatest books while sitting. Gandhi had his greatest thoughts while sitting.

"The greatest minds in the history of civilization have had their finest moments while sitting. You name me one great piece of music written while running, one great book, one great anything. While running, you don't have time to think because you are breathing so hard and worrying about some mugger tripping you and wondering if that pain in your chest is something serious or just gas."

Runners say their sport improves their sex lives. What about sitting?

"That's crazy. How can you have sex while running? But sitting in a chair, there are all kinds of possibilities. Check any manual."

Does your sport have a motto?

"Take the load off your feet."

Dropping Back In

May 1, 1979

One of the interesting social developments of our time has been the large number of people who have changed life-styles and careers when they reached their middle years.

Not long ago, I met Waldon Pond, forty-six, and his wife, Murky, forty-two, who, with their two children, have thrown aside their former life-style and taken another.

Until recently, the Pond family lived high in the mountains of Utah. Their home was the wilderness log cabin in which Waldon was born. It was more than fifty miles from their nearest neighbor and one hundred and fifty miles from the closest town.

Waldon had made a modest living digging rare roots out of the earth for shipment to natural health stores. This had been his career since graduating from Rutabaga Agricultural College, also in a remote section of Utah, where he met his wife.

In their wilderness home, his wife contributed to the family income by crafting tree-bark belts for shipment to natural clothing stores. She also grew her own vegetables, while Waldon trapped and fished, and the children gathered edible berries and leaves.

For recreation, the family gathered in the log cabin in the evening and read the classics aloud or, as a string quartet, played music by Bach, Haydn, and Mozart as well as authentic folk songs handed down by their ancestors.

The children had few friends of their own age, but they enjoyed frolicking with their pet deer, squirrel, fox, raccoon, otter, mountain goat, elk, and moose, which the family had tamed and which lived with them.

Then their lives abruptly changed.

"One day I was digging up a rare root," Waldon recalled. "In a tree above me, a beautiful bird began singing a sweet song. I lay down on the grass and looked at the puffy white clouds drifting across the blue sky, and I listened to the bird sing, as I often do.

"And I asked myself: 'Is this what I want to do with the rest of my life?'

"At that moment, a bird dropping landed in my eye. I took that to be a sign.

"That night I sat down with my wife and asked if she was content with our simple, natural life away from the hurly-burly and close to nature. She said, frankly, she could take it or leave it. She was getting a little tired of having all those animals around the cabin, especially the tame moose.

"So we packed our few simple possessions and in a week we were living in Chicago. And this is where we have been for the last year."

Waldon, who now calls himself Wally, has become the sales manager of the used-car division of a large auto agency on Cicero Avenue.

"I love it," he said. "I love the rat race. To me, seeing some unsuspecting soul walk into my lot, and pouncing on him and talking him into buying a clunker that might explode when it hits the first pothole, is infinitely more challenging than finding a silly, edible root."

Don't you miss the quiet simplicity of your cabin?

"Not a bit. I live in a large condo-apartment and since I bought it, it has increased in value by $40,000. Hell, my doorknobs are worth more than my whole log cabin was. In fact, my wife now has a real estate license and she's selling condos herself."

What about communing with nature? Don't you miss being close to creatures of the wild?

"Miss watching a lot of damn boring birds and squirrels and chipmunks from my front porch? Listen, all they ever did was dig holes or eat nuts or worms. What's so exciting about eating worms?

"I can sit on my condo balcony and see a lot more wildlife than I ever saw in the woods. Last night I saw an old lady get mugged by a street gang that sprayed "Insane Idiots" on her coat with a paint can.

"And last week I watched two guys strip a car of every-thing but the ashtray in less than five minutes. The owner showed up while they were doing it, and they stripped him of everything but his hairpiece. This is far more exciting than life in the wilderness.''

Do you still spend evenings reading and sharing music with your children?

"As a matter of fact, no. My son has moved in with a young woman. If they still like each other after three months, they're going to tell each other their names. And my daughter has joined a religious cult and is making a very good living. She poses as a paralyzed deaf-mute and sells religious tracts in the Loop or at the airport. She gets 20 percent of the take and just bought her own Mazda sports car.''

But don't you miss hunting and fishing?

"I still do it, in a different way. You see, my wife is studying gourmet cooking at night, so I hit the discos and do a little hunting. And I'm buying my own thirty-foot cabin cruiser, just as soon as the precinct captain can pay somebody off and get me a mooring. Then whatever I hunt down in the discos, I can take with me on my fishing trips. So I'm still a sportsman at heart.''

But you're no longer a mountain man.

"No. I'm a high-rise man now. The closest I get to my old life-style is when I put on my Eddie Bauer boots and bush jacket on Saturdays and ride my high-rise elevator.''

Do you think you'll ever change life-styles again—maybe return to your wilderness cabin?

"It's too late. I just sold it to a middle-aged stockbroker from LaSalle Street who quit his job to seek the simple life.''

Do you think he'll like his new life-style?

"Maybe, especially if he can get that damn moose housebroken.''

Survival of the Fairest

January 10, 1980

As you trade in your big gas-eater for a tiny car, or stuff newspaper around your leaky windows, or squirt heat-saving gunk between your walls, don't feel alone. Those rich pleasure-lovers known as "The Beautiful People" also are doing their part to conserve the nation's energy.

As my authority, I cite *W*, the New York-based fashion newspaper, put out by the *Women's Wear Daily* people, that devotes much of its coverage to the goings and comings and doings of those it calls "The BP." (That means Beautiful People, you homely dummy.)

In a recent issue, *W* interviewed a couple of dozen of the beautiful ones about how they are going to cope with the more frugal times that are expected in the eighties.

To be honest, I don't know who most of these Beautiful People are, since we don't hang around the same polo clubs, international casinos, yacht basins, or Milwaukee Avenue saloons.

And *W* does not identify them beyond their names. Presumably, those who are in the know are aware of who they are. So we can safely assume that if *W* says they are Beautiful People, they are, even if a few of them do sag.

Anyway, here is what they say they will do to conserve energy. You might pick up some helpful tips.

"Recently I visited my brother's twenty-room mansion," said a BP named Beverly Johnson. "I spent a lot of time switching off the lights and turning down the heat."

What a fine idea. I think the rest of us, when visiting our brothers' twenty-room mansions, should do the same.

Harriet Deutsch, a blond Beautiful Person whose photo shows what appear to be two diamond chandeliers dangling from her ears, says: "I prefer to entertain in our own home and, in doing so, we actively make efforts to conserve energy and use everything economically. We are fortunate to have a marvelous chef who guides us along those lines."

That's something for the rest of us to think about. When hiring chefs, we should think beyond the texture of his salmon mousse and ask whether he knows how to roast a quail with solar energy.

Françoise de la Renta (why don't Beautiful People ever have names like Myrtle or Gert?) is doing her part. She said: "When we go to the country, we have only wood fires; they're better than heating with oil. And I open my window in the summer instead of turning on the air conditioner. I live with the natural elements."

Fancy that. Opening one's window in the summertime. Françoise, with the help of people like you, we'll get the price of oil down to forty cents a barrel yet.

Then there is Nan Kempner, who said: "Less is more." (I'll bet she doesn't say that to her stockbroker.) Her idea for energy conservation: "I now wear long underwear, and not just for skiing."

What a coincidence, Nan. My grandfather used to wear long underwear, too—and when he wasn't skiing. He used to always tell us: "Always wear long underwear day and night, winter and summer, because if there is a fire and you have to run outside without your pants, you won't be embarrassed in front of the neighbors." It never occurred to me that his philosophy could have made him one of the Beautiful People.

Susan Mary Alsop seems to have a pessimistic view of the eighties. She said: "People will have less and less staff. And practically no one will be having live-in servants. Instead, we'll have to be more self-reliant and use more caterers, which is dreary."

I know how you feel, Susan. The day I let my live-in butler and chef go, I felt lost. That night I phoned a caterer and asked him to make me a salami sandwich as a bedtime snack, and it just wasn't the same. It was a dreary, dreary, dreary salami sandwich. Care to join me in a suicide pact, kid?

There is more to Susan's dreary view of the future. She said: "As for vacation houses, people will have to choose between traveling abroad or keeping up a vacation home. I'll not be taking trips abroad and keeping my house in Maine."

Me either. I'll probably flip a coin to see if I go to the Wisconsin Dells or stay in town and bicycle around Goose Island.

Pat Buckley, who is pictured with a neck full of mink, has come eyeball-to-eyeball with the energy crunch. She says: "As far as conservation goes, the real change in my life is my moped, which I ride to the fish store."

I kind of like the idea of Mrs. Buckley setting out from her estate on her moped to buy a fish.

"Where are you going, my dear?"

"I am going on my moped to buy a fish."

"But Charles will drive you."

"No, no, no. We must conserve. Charles can drive me to the furrier, or the jeweler. But when I buy a fish, it's by moped."

"God Bless America, my dear."

And finally there is Betsy Bloomingdale, who is doing her part to fight OPEC this way: "One of the ways I save energy is by asking my servants not to turn on the self-cleaning oven until after seven in the evening. We all must do little things and big things to conserve energy."

Indeed we must, Besy, and my hat is off to you and your servants and your self-cleaning oven.

But I wonder: If Susan Mary Alsop is right, and hardly anyone will have live-in servants anymore, who will Betsy Bloomingdale get to turn on her self-cleaning oven after 7:00 P.M.?

Are there caterers—dreary as they might be—who will come out and turn on Betsy Bloomingdale's self-cleaning oven?

Or will her oven just get dirtier and dirtier?

Oh, the 1980s frighten me.

A Disarming of Vitamin-E

February 6, 1973

For the first time, a TV commercial got me to run right out and buy a new product.

It happened a few nights ago when I saw a dramatization encouraging the use of a new underarm spray.

Normally, I don't use underarm products because most of them give me bumps. If the bumps get too big, my arms stick out sideways, causing me to resemble a tall bat. I don't mind looking that way, but on the street at night it can alarm strangers.

This deodorant, however, was unlike any I had heard about.

It contains vitamins.

And not just any vitamin, but Vitamin-E, which currently is the hottest vitamin on the market.

As any health fiend knows, E is said to combat ulcers, skin problems, high cholesterol, and the effects of pollution.

A woman who had a nervous, jumpy leg said that a mouthful of Vitamin-E quickly calmed the pesky limb.

Wicked old men claim that Vitamin-E gives them greater sexual vigor. Greater than what, I don't know. Probably greater than that of wicked old men who don't take their vitamins.

Despite the powers attributed to Vitamin-E, I didn't expect to see it used as an underarm spray. Usually, something that good turns up in a hair product.

I rushed to my corner drugstore as soon as I saw the commercial. There was no doubt in my mind that my armpits suffered from an E deficiency. You see, this vitamin is found in such foods as beef liver, egg yolk, cereals, and wheat germ. Because I am ticklish, I never put such things under my arm.

My druggist looked surprised when I brought a can of deodorant to the counter.

"For you?" he said.

"A healthy armpit means a healthy body," I said.

He stared, then locked the door behind me.

At home, I quickly gave myself a squirt under each arm, then waited for the results.

I didn't know what to expect. A vigorous armpit, maybe? That would be fine, but what do you do with it? Crack walnuts?

Or maybe they would develop a healthy, attractive complexion—a peaches-and-cream armpit. That, too, would be nice, but who would ever know? Even with the new morality, a person doesn't go about showing off his armpits.

As it turned out, nothing happened. They felt the way they had always felt. Kind of soggy.

And I couldn't tell if they looked any different because I don't recall ever looking at them before.

But I decided to give the spray a thorough trial. For several days, I loaded my underarms with vitamins. I used so much that when I swung my arms while walking, they made a wet, popping sound. At times, I had enough vitamins under my arms to keep an entire village in India healthy; and if that doesn't make you proud to be an American, nothing will.

After a week, I asked a bartender: "Notice anything different about me?"

He shook his head.

I whispered: "I am putting massive doses of Vitamin-E on my armpits."

He emptied my glass.

Later, while walking past the desk of a young woman in the office, I decided to test Vitamin-E's vaunted sexual claims. I raised my right arm high over my head and winked. She quickly moved to a desk across the room.

I was so disappointed that I finally called the Mennen Company to ask why their product wasn't transforming me into a new, vigorous, healthy, young armpit.

A woman in consumer relations said nobody had raised that question before, so she switched me to a Mr. Richard Jay, who is the assistant to Robert Lipsky, the top man in the "Mennen E" department.

As Mr. Jay explained it, the vitamin underarm spray was developed as part of "the whole movement to have things more natural."

That made sense. What could be more natural than spraying vitamins under one's arms? It is like returning to Mother Earth by eating a quick-frozen sunflower seed TV dinner.

But, Mr. Jay said, the "Mennen E" spray will not create a superarmpit. All it does is prevent odor, which is what any deodorant does.

"Actually," he said, "if you took a Vitamin-E capsule and

cut it in half and smeared it on your skin, you would get the same benefits as from the deodorant spray we produce."

You would also get some strange stares in the men's locker room.

Mr. Jay said Vitamin-E does away with odor by killing the tiny germs that cause it.

That clinched it. I tossed the stuff out. I don't want the little bodies of dead germs under my arm. At least, if they are alive, they might have enough sense to get out of there.

Avoid the Christmas Rush

December 28, 1976

The owner of a Michigan Avenue restaurant called me with a problem that frequently comes up at Christmas.

He had planned a party at his place for one hundred needy children. But for some reason he had only half that many coming.

Now, with the party only two days off, he was frantically trying to find an extra fifty needy children.

"Do you know where I can get them?" he said.

I asked if he had tried an orphanage. He hadn't, so I gave him the name of one.

He called back a few minutes later and said:

"No luck. They're already taken."

All I could do was suggest that he keep trying, call other orphanages and social agencies.

But I warned him to expect disappointment. He had waited much too long. When you get down to the last week before Christmas, the needy children—especially orphans—already have been pretty well picked over.

The problem is that there is such a great demand for them at this time of the year. Everybody wants one at the same time. Just before Christmas, orphanages are bombarded with phone calls from people who want a child for the holidays or for Christmas dinner, or from church or fraternal organizations that want a quantity of them for parties and such. Invariably, many people are disappointed. And there is nothing as depressing as getting the urge just before Christmas to do something good and then not being able to do it.

Last year, on Christmas Eve afternoon, a very angry young woman called. She and some friends had just rounded up old clothes and old toys to give away, but they couldn't find anyone to give them to. They had called several social agencies but they had closed for the day.

Knowing how upsetting such disappointment could be, I tried to be helpful and suggested that they wait until after Christmas when the social agencies reopened, since the clothes and toys would be needed then, too.

"But Christmas will be over then," the woman said, "and it won't be the same."

How true. It is so much more satisfying to help a needy person when the radio stations are playing Christmas carols and lights are strung up all over the city.

It's not the same later, or earlier. One would no more drink eggnog in August than take in an orphan for an ordinary summer weekend.

That's the trouble with supply and demand. Right after Christmas, there are all kinds of needy people available. But by then, most of us already are planning New Year's Eve activities, and that's not the kind of thing you'd have an orphan for, either.

So the idea is to make your plans to help the needy early. As with reservations for New Year's Eve, you can't wait until the last minute.

One should start thinking about these things as early as Thanksgiving—or before, if possible.

By planning your Christmas good deed early, it gives you a greater variety of choices. (For example, you may prefer an orphan girl to an orphan boy. You might have a preference in sizes, colors, etc. But by the time the holidays are upon us, there's no guarantee that you'll get exactly what you want.)

One of the problems in looking for someone to good-deed is that there is no convenient way to shop around. The Yellow Pages don't list places that carry needy children, and one can't just go into an orphanage, children's hospital, home for the elderly, etc., and browse around.

The newspapers do what they can, ferreting out stories of cold and hungry families, lonely old widows in rooming houses, and so on, but never enough to meet the demand.

What may be needed is some kind of special Christmas catalog, such as Sears and Ward's put out for their merchandise, but containing instead a complete assortment of the needy.

You never can tell, but maybe some people, after looking it over, might decide that they'd rather have an elderly widow rather than a child. And if they knew where to go, they might prefer to drop off the box of groceries right at the home of a poor family, rather than at a church basement distribution center, thus savoring the gratitude directly.

If people had something like that, they could plan calmly and avoid the frantic, last-minute rush to perform a good deed.

Best of all, there wouldn't be any disappointment. Christmas comes but once a year, and everybody should get a chance to do good. It's such a long wait until the next time.

A Christmas Carol, 1978

December 24, 1978

Marley was dead, to begin with. There is no doubt whatever about that. Keeled over walking off a racquetball court. His girlfriend was so upset she wasn't seen in Faces or Arnie's for nearly a week.

But the name of his computer services company didn't change—Scrooge and Marley. E. B. Scrooge, a cost-conscious businessman, figured it was a waste to replace all the company stationery.

Besides, Scrooge was Marley's sole heir and executor of his estate, and figured he owed Marley something, since he inherited everything including Marley's hairpiece, which fit him quite well.

Anyway it was the first Christmas Eve after Marley's death but at Scrooge and Marley's, there was no office party. Scrooge didn't believe in them. He had permitted one a few years ago, but everybody got loaded and a secretary had become pregnant by a stockroom clerk, and a state agency had ruled that since it happened on company time and company property, Scrooge and Marley had to pay for the pediatrician and the child's education. And OSHA safety inspectors came in and ordered the company to provide birth control devices to all female employees.

So Scrooge was sitting in his office when his nephew walked in and cheerfully cried: "Merry Christmas, Uncle."

"Forget it, I'm not hiring you," Scrooge said. "You're a nice kid, but you have no aptitude for business. Why don't you learn a trade?"

"Uncle, I didn't come here for a job. I came to invite you over for Christmas brunch. The whole family is going to be there."

"No thanks. The family depresses me. Especially all the lousy little brats greedily ripping open their gifts. I'll stay home and watch a football game."

"There's no football on Christmas, Uncle."

"I've got videotapes of the last six Superbowls."

"If you change your mind. . . ."

"If I change my mind, I'll watch videotapes of the Rose Bowl instead. G'by."

A few minutes later, Bob Cratchit, a computer programmer, came in and said: "Is it OK if I leave early today? I've got some last-minute shopping."

"I know where your last-minute shopping is. Down in Eddie's Bar."

"No, really, Mr. Scrooge. My oldest kid is going to be home for Christmas. He escaped from Synanon. My wife just called me and asked if I could find a straitjacket in his size."

"Yeah, you might as well leave. You haven't done anything all day anyway. Which is just as well, because you'd just screw it up if you did."

"Merry Christmas, Mr. Scrooge."

"Humbug. Beginning Tuesday, you're demoted. G'by."

At 5:00 P.M., Scrooge locked the office and went to a bar near his high-rise building, where he drank eight martinis and ate two dozen free hors d'oeuvres for dinner. He nodded at a good-looking blonde, but Marley's old hairpiece slipped over his eyes and when he got it back in place, the blonde was gone.

He staggered from the bar and passed a Salvation Army man ringing a bell.

"Merry Christmas," said the Salvation Army man.

"Here's something for you," said Scrooge, dropping the hairpiece into the collection bucket.

Scrooge made it to his thirtieth-floor condo, fell into bed, and passed out.

He was awakened at 3:00 A.M. by a strange sound. He sat up and gasped at what he saw.

There, at the foot of his bed, was an apparition. It appeared to be his dead partner, Jack Marley. It was dressed in shorts, a T-shirt, and was wildly swinging a racquet and bouncing a ball off the bedroom walls.

"Oh, Lord," yelled Scrooge. "I've got the DTs. I'm going to join AA in the morning."

"No, you don't," said the apparition. "It's me, Jack Marley. I'm now a ghost."

"What kind of ghost plays racquetball?" asked Scrooge.

"It's my punishment," said the apparition. "That's all I do is hit this damned ball."

"For eternity?" asked Scrooge.

"He didn't say, but it's going to be a long time. Man, do I have blisters on my feet."

"But you weren't a bad guy," Scrooge said. "What did they nail you for?"

"Greed, vanity, lust—the usual thing."

"Listen, I warned you about that. Discos every night. Chasing the young broads."

"I know, I know. That's why I came back to warn you. I mean, you are going to really get dumped on when it's your time."

"What did I do?"

"Oh, c'mon, Eb. You're a mean, rotten bastard and everybody knows it. Even today, on Christmas Eve. Throwing my hairpiece in the collection bucket. Demoting Cratchit. You know what they're going to do to you? They're going to put you inside a computer and leave you there for a few centuries."

"Don't say that," cried Scrooge.

"Then straighten out, man," said the apparition. "There's still time. Now I gotta go."

"Wait, wait, tell me more."

"I can't. Once a week I play racquetball with the devil. On burning coals, yet. Oh, my feet. See 'ya, Eb."

The apparition vanished and Scrooge, trembling, leaped from his bed, ran onto his balcony, leaned over the railing and began shouting: "It's Christmas Day, a wonderful day. I love everybody, I love my fellow man."

The building's doorman looked up and shouted: "Don't jump, don't jump!" Then he ran inside and called the police.

The police burst into Scrooge's apartment, and he began excitedly telling them about Marley's ghost. They put him in the wagon and took him to the drunk tank.

He demanded that they call his nephew, who arrived in about an hour.

"Get me out of here," pleaded Marley.

"I don't know, Unk. You sound in bad shape."

"So help me, I'm all right. I feel great. I love Christmas. I love my relatives."

"Unk, I'm not sure if you should go home. A man as confused as you are might blow his whole business. As your closest relative, maybe I should be named conservator of your estate."

"Ahah!" said Scrooge. "All right. I'll make a deal. You get me out and I'll make you vice president."

"You got a deal, Unk. You won't regret it."

After he was released, Scrooge stopped at a meat market and bought a goose. Then he drove to Bob Cratchit's house.

Cratchit opened the door and Scrooge said: "A Merry Christmas, Bob, here is a goose for your Christmas dinner."

Mrs. Cratchit said: "Big deal. First of all, it is loaded with cholesterol. Second of all, it is the cheapest Christmas bonus I ever heard of.''

"Ah, but there's more, Bob, my good fellow. Starting Tuesday, you are going to be the new chief technician at five-thou-a-year more. How does that strike you?"

"I'll tell you how it strikes me. After you shafted me yesterday, I went to IBM and got hired at eight-thou-a-year more. So you can take your job and your goose and shove them."

At that moment, Cratchit's son, Tim, lurched into the room in his straitjacket, dove at Scrooge, and bit him on the leg.

Scrooge ran into the street and yelled: "Don't expect a reference from me, Cratchit. But a Merry Christmas to you anyway."

From that day forward, Scrooge was a changed man. He was kind and generous to his employees, scrupulously fair in his business dealings, and became deeply involved in charities, civic activities, and his church, leaving the day-to-day operations of his company to his nephew.

Within a year, the company went bust, Scrooge lost his condo and moved into the Lawson YMCA, and took a job as a bartender on Rush Street.

And every Christmas Eve he drinks eight martinis, eats two dozen hors d'oeuvres, and drops a hairpiece in a Salvation Army bucket.

He mumbles: "I want that jerk Marley to come back just one more time so I can tell him what he can do with his advice."

That was his last mistake. Sandy and I finished off several others, finally escaping and were pronounced thieves.

6 | THE BIRDS AND THE BEES

Gluttony and Punishment

May 16, 1978

I recently wrote about a young man who was considering remarriage and gave him advice on how he could be sure his female friend was the right person for him. I called it the "click test."

Since then, a large number of other young men, married and single, have responded to my offer to provide mature and worldly counseling in matters of the heart.

At the same time, many female persons have written that my "click test" was unfair to them and have demanded that I refrain from giving further advice.

I will deal with the female persons in a later column. Hopefully, I will make them realize that they are being silly ninnies.

At present, I will take up the problem of another young man, who has been married about five years.

His problem is that he has been steadily gaining weight during the last three years of his marriage,

"When I first married, I was on the lean and athletic side. But about three years ago, my wife quit working and took a course in gourmet cooking. Now I'm not lean anymore. I have gained about fifty pounds and I almost waddle when I walk.

"She is a terrific cook and is always making some elaborate Italian or French dish for dinner. And when I get up in the morning, she has a farmer's breakfast on the table. She makes pastries and keeps them around the kitchen, where I can't help finding them and giving in to my weakness for sweets.

"If I would eat normal portions, I would not have this problem. But I am weak and eat too much because it is so good.

"To make matters worse, she makes teasing remarks about my weight. She calls me her Abominable Snowman, or Big Foot.

"How can I convince her, without hurting her feelings, that all that rich food isn't good for me?"

The problem here seems quite clear: Your wife is trying to murder you.

I don't know what her motive is since I do not have sufficient information. It might be your insurance or another man or that she wants to be free to develop her own personality.

But there can be little doubt that she is out to get you and is doing a clever job of it.

It's the old calories-cholesterol-criticism trick. Thousands of guileless men are done in this way each year by clever women who escape unsuspected.

Playing on your weakness for good food, she first stokes you with calories and cholesterol. This shoots up your blood pressure and makes your heart overwork.

Then, as you become fatter, she makes sly remarks about

your girth, which causes you stress. Your temples pound and you find yourself short of breath. So you worry, which makes it even worse.

Unless something is done, one of these days you are going to be sitting there eating a third soufflé and your eyes will roll up into your head and that will be the end. She will cash in your insurance policy, take dancing lessons, and go off on a world cruise.

So what can you do to defend yourself?

There is no point in going to the police. Under our laws, you cannot bring criminal charges against her for overfeeding you.

And don't accuse her outright. She'll just have you committed, which will accomplish her ends.

But don't be alarmed. There are ways you can save yourself, if you act quickly.

You could just pack up and leave, of course. But that would ruin your marriage. I assume you don't want to do that, since she sounds like a good wife in most other respects.

Nor do you want her to know that you know. This could provoke her into taking drastic measures, and there is no way you can protect yourself in your sleep.

So you must appear to be going on as usual, docilely eating those murderous meals, stuffing yourself into an early grave. But in reality, you must begin doing just the opposite.

The first thing you must do is begin eating large quantities of yogurt to dull your appetite before returning home each evening.

Then get yourself a dog. Not any dog, but a breed called the Gluttony Terrier. It is a tiny thing, not much bigger than a squirrel. But it has an astonishing appetite and a metabolism that permits it to eat twenty times its weight each day without gaining an ounce.

When you sit down to eat dinner, have the dog concealed on your lap. Then, instead of spooning the food into your mouth, let it fall. The terrier will snap every morsel out of the air. Don't worry about being tempted to eat the food yourself. When feeding, Gluttony Terriers are vicious, and if he sees you eating, he'll nip you fiercely on the belly and you'll soon learn to resist temptation.

Repeat the procedure at breakfast.

Soon you will begin losing weight while appearing to be eating the same huge meals.

As the pounds fall away, your treacherous wife will grow nervous and cook even richer foods in greater amounts. Since she eats her own cooking, it is inevitable that she will begin gaining weight.

Eventually, you will be lean again. But one day it will be her eyes that roll into her head as she collapses into her own soufflé, the victim of her own plot. Justice will have been served.

Then you can cash everything in and take the world cruise.

Or you might meet another woman who strikes your fancy. If so, write me again and I'll give you further advice.

A Real Gentlewoman

March 23, 1980

"Isn't this shocking?" the young liberated woman said to me in a voice filled with horror.

She was reading aloud from an appointment book published

by Virginia Slims, the cigarette company that aims its advertising at modern women.

Scattered through the book were selections from nineteenth-century manuals on female etiquette, household tips, and other advice for ladies of that era, as well as examples of old-time male chauvinism.

"Listen to this," she said, and read:

"'How to Be A Better Wife' (1897):

1. Start each day with a cheerful countenance and pleasant conversation.

2. Turn the harsh utterances of a scolding tongue into kind and gentle words, and you will be rewarded with a more agreeable nature.

3. Learn to bake juicy fruit pies and do so frequently.

4. Smooth out wrinkles in your brow by thinking serene thoughts.

5. Do not interrupt your Husband when he is speaking, thinking or reading."

She looked up from the book, scowled, and said: "Can you believe that?"

I told her I thought it was sound advice.

She stormed away before I could explain that most men would probably feel that way. While I agree it was terrible that women were treated like foolish, weak creatures, it was a good deal for the men of that day. And I'd have to be dumb not to recognize a good deal when I saw it.

I've since obtained a copy of the Virginia Slims appointment book so I can share with men the joys that their great-grandfathers had.

This selection is called "The Wise Woman's Guide to the Art of Breakfast":

As wife to your Husband, it is your most fervent duty to present him with your most agreeable manner at breakfast as well as to provide him with the comforts of a well-provisioned table.

A carelessly poached egg, a spotted cloth or hasty, fretful words can be ruinous to the harmony of his day.

Set before him a hearty breakfast of fresh sausages, boiled eggs, a cold ham, porridge with fresh cream and butter, kippers, a pheasant pie, fresh curds and whey, corn muffins, fresh bread, marmalade, honey, coffee and tea.

Keep your words cheerful and encouraging for they are as much an aid to the digestion as they are a balm to the spirit.

Never use red and white checkered cloth on the breakfast table. The small pattern is upsetting to morning digestion.

Always fold the morning paper from right to left and place it on the seat of his chair.

After that, I'd give her the rest of the morning off.

Another page carried this description of: "The Happiest Day of a Woman's Life":

It is indeed the fortunate young woman who becomes a bride. For once a woman becomes a bride, she is at last able to perfect the virtues of a Good and Honourable Wife: Steadfastness in the face of hard work. Obedience. Pleasantness at mealtimes. Lilting laugher. Modesty of dress and demeanor. Strength of character, arms, legs, back. Unworldliness in politics, economics and foreign novellas. Disinterest in card games, musical games, word games and all other games of chance.

And if you could teach her to bark at burglars, what more could a man ask?

Another section dealt with having a picnic in the park. It

tells her how to prepare food, and pack the hamper. But the most specific advice is on how to sit on a blanket. It says:

The manner in which a gentlewoman composes herself upon a blanket should be a demonstration of her modest demeanor. She should accept the support of her escort by lightly laying her gloved hand upon his arm and allowing herself to be lowered to the blanket as effortlessly and gracefully as a leaf wafts down from a tree on a gentle breeze.

When seated, her limbs should be discreetly turned to the side and their form well-disguised beneath the folds of her many skirts. She should sit with her back straight and her hands at rest in her lap. She should never lean, slouch, cup her chin in her hand or raise her arms above her head.

You don't see that in a disco joint.

Proper dining habits for a "gentlewoman" were discussed:

The unfolding of the napkin should be transacted in a manner that reflects breeding and taste. A woman who picks up the napkin between thumb and forefinger and then shakes it open exhibits a laxity of principle and looseness of character.

A gentlewoman cuts all pieces of food into tiny morsels, which she decorously raises to her mouth only when her husband's eyes are averted. She never bites, chews or crunches her food but nibbles noiselessly and daintily.

How many women today are careful to wait until the man's eyes are averted before they chomp their pizza? Damned few.

Men in some parts of the country advertised for wives. One such ad gave these requirements, which strike me as being reasonable:

Fine, upstanding gentleman seeks fine, upstanding woman for purposes of marriage and bearing children. Must have reliable physical qualities, including strong back, arms, legs. Duties to include caring for large five-bedroom house, grounds and stable. Must have sense of humor and play a musical instrument. Two weeks' vacation at mountains every June. No woman who talks loudly in restaurants, reads romantic novels or smokes cigarettes need apply.

Finally, there is a quotation from someone identified only as H. Wilson (1891) on the subject of ambitious women: "Aspiring to the pinnacles of success can cause a woman to experience spells of dizziness and fits of giddiness."

I hope nobody thinks that because I printed these items I approve of them.

Not at all. Two weeks' vacation in the mountains is too generous.

An Enlightened Male Looks at Mrs. Trudeau

August 31, 1978

It isn't easy being an enlightened male. I have to constantly guard against falling back to my male chauvinist attitudes.

For example, I just finished reading *People* magazine, which has another article on the life and travels of Margaret Trudeau, wife of the prime minister of Canada.

It was a difficult struggle not to fling the magazine down

and shout, "Shameless hussy," as I would have before I became enlightened. Instead, I succeeded in reminding myself that she is an adult female who is living her life as she sees fit.

It has been a while since I read anything about Mrs. Trudeau, who will turn thirty this month.

The last thing I remembered reading was when she had dashed off to New York to become a photojournalist, gad about with members of the Rolling Stones, and find her real self, while old Pierre stayed home and took care of their three little kids and Canada.

Now I find she is no longer gadding about with the Rolling Stones in New York. She says she still loves her husband, and might return to him some day. But until then, she is in southern France gadding about with a handsome actor named Jean-Luc Fritz, who is tall, lean, blond, and wears his shirt open to the belly button. Jean-Luc looks like the kind of guy I would like to invite to a bar on Milwaukee Avenue so we could all break beer bottles on his head.

Mrs. Trudeau is no longer a photojournalist either. Apparently she discovered that there is more to photojournalism than buying a $150 camera, hanging it around her neck, and hoofing about Manhattan with a look of intense artistic awareness on her face. Eventually you have to push the right button and reload the camera, and that is where most such instant photojournalism careers have foundered.

She says she is now an author, which probably means that somebody gave her a good deal on a trade-in of her cameras for a typewriter. She is also a film actress, appearing in a movie about a young wife who dumps her aging husband for younger men. I wonder where they got that idea?

And apparently she has found herself. She says it was hard at first because she had to learn to do her laundry, cook, shop, and things like that. But she has struggled through it all and will put it all in a book about herself.

Besides finding herself, she also found Jean-Luc Fritz, with whom she poses for pictures staring soulfully into his eyes. I can't tell if he is staring soulfully back. He appears to be. On the other hand, he might just need a good night's sleep.

Before I became enlightened, I would have looked at Jean-Luc and Mrs. Trudeau, and wondered why they weren't sneaking around, instead of posing for magazine pictures. In pre-enlightened times, there might have been married women with three children who took up with sleepy-eyed men who wore shirts open to their belly buttons. But they generally tried to keep these activities quiet, rather than call a press conference to discuss the subject.

In those times, I would have had the predictable male chauvinist response, probably saying something like: "I know what Pierre Trudeau should do. He ought to borrow a pistol from one of his Mounted Police, hop a jet to France, burst in on the two of them, put a bullet into that gigolo's tanned but miserable hide, and give her a thorough beating. No jury in France would convict him. They would probably award him the Croix de Guerre."

But now that I'm enlightened, I don't think that way anymore. Instead, my reaction is to shrug and say: "Well, Mrs. Trudeau is a grown woman. It is her life to lead as she thinks fit. Her husband should accept that and live his own life. And if Pierre should happen to run into his wife and Jean-Luc at a party or something, he should try to act adult and sophisticated and not do anything more than disfigure that prettyboy's face a little."

The magazine also showed a picture of Mrs. Trudeau posing seductively in a skimpy bathing suit while jutting out her pert behind, as film actresses often do.

Evidently, she is proud of her behind. In an earlier interview, she was quoted as saying that her best feature is her "ass." In the current story, she says that her best feature is her "bum."

Between interviews, she probably consults a thesaurus.

Once again, I showed restraint. My old reaction would have been to shout: "Has this woman no shame, no sense of decency? What is a married mother of three doing talking to a magazine about how nice her bottom is? Is this what she wants her children and the voters of Canada to read? Pierre ought to go to France and give her a few sound kicks in her best feature."

But once again I remained enlightened. I told myself: "Well, she is a grown woman with her own behind living her own life. And if she wants to sit down with a reporter from *People* magazine and discuss her behind, that is her right. After all, she is now a film actress as well as a modern liberated woman, and as such, the visual qualities of her behind have become important."

I hope others feel the way I do. After all, who are we to judge Mrs. Trudeau, her conduct, or even her behind?

One thing I am certain of, though. Her best feature sure ain't her brain.

Ninnies vs. Old Goats

September 12, 1978

The following news release has been sent by a women's organization to newspapers and broadcasting stations throughout the Midwest:

MADISON, WIS.: Women on Watch, a state task force of the National Organization for Women, today attacked Mike Royko, *Sun-Times* columnist, for the blatant and extreme sexism he displayed in a recent column about Margaret Trudeau.

Had Mike Royko written a column that was as racist as his Trudeau column was sexist, he would not have a job today. Racism has become journalistically unacceptable, but in the male-dominated journalism profession, sexism, even crassly obvious sexism, is still welcomed.

Royko has written an unusually nasty column about the wife of the Canadian prime minister, ridiculing and castigating her conduct, and her lack of brains and ability.

What does Royko know of her ability and mental capacity? Has he ever seen her photographs? Has he read what she has written?

Margaret Trudeau is a woman who has attempted to break away from the slavery of the stereotypical female role of good mother, good hostess, silent supporter of husband and, in her case, birthing every Christmas.

Think of the millions of men who have left their families and disappeared, not knowing whether their children would continue even to be fed.

Margaret Trudeau knows that her children are cared for, she sees them, they know how to reach her. Hers is not the typical male-disappearing act.

Where is male compassion for a woman who is always seen only as a wife? Perhaps Margaret Trudeau felt she had a future only as a brood sow. Perhaps she saw her support-duty as blocking her creativity. For all his adult life her husband has lived like a playboy with impunity, and no one has written nasty columns about him. Why the vicious attack because she is a woman?

Why should Margaret Trudeau stifle her creative desires and be a social doormat?

Her husband is old. Why should she not seek out the personal society of someone not old, hoary and used-up? Men have been doing that forever.

Insecure men, such as Royko, cannot tolerate the idea of women being free and equal. They hide behind pallid, so-called humor to express their hatred of women. The slaves are finally telling these men to clean out their own stables, pick their own cotton and wash their dirty underwear, and the prospect is too much for sexist pigs like Mike Royko.

I don't know what they're crabbing about. In my column I defended her right to go live her own life.

True, I indicated that I think she's a ninny, but I think that anybody who babbles intimate details of their lives to publications like *People* magazine is a ninny.

By the same token, I think that the women who put out this news release are ninnies. What else can you think about someone who would say: "Her husband is old. Why should she not seek out the personal society of someone not old, hoary and used-up?"

Is this organization encouraging women to abandon their husbands the moment the old codgers' hairlines begin receding and wrinkles begin showing on their brows?

Are husbands just expendable sexual playthings, to be used up and abandoned in favor of the first handsome face that wears his shirt open to the belly button?

Little wonder we have so many nervous middle-aged men these days, gluing on their hairpieces, driving their tired bodies around the jogging track, popping vitamin pills by the hundreds. They fear that, at any moment, outfits like Women on Watch will point at them and snarl: "You're all through, you old, hoary, used-up old goat. Into the nursing home with you—I'm off to southern France!"

I think Women on Watch is a blatantly sexist organization itself, and it should be watched.

Therefore, I'm going to form an organization called Old Hoary Used-Up Men on Watch to keep an eye on Women on Watch.

Membership is open to any males, except those who wear their shirts open to the belly button.

Advice to the Love-Worn

July 11, 1978

It is time for another in my series of columns giving mature and worldly advice to young men who are confused in their relationships with female persons.

Today's problem comes from Greg C., who is in his mid-twenties and is keeping company with Joyce, a modern young woman of about the same age.

They get along well in most respects and have mutual interests. Both enjoy outdoor activities, such as backpacking, sunning themselves, and walking around the North Side while holding hands. They like ethnic restaurants and are currently eating their way through the *Chicago Guide* listing and have progressed through the letter *P.*

Until now, the only serious disagreement they've had is over movie critics. He is a follower of Roger Ebert, while she prefers the views of Gene Siskel. But Greg feels that while this is a serious difference, it is something they can work out with time and patience and understanding.

However, he is now confronted with a rift in their relationship that threatens their future together. As he explained it: "She happened to run across a copy of one of the skin magazines, *Penthouse* or something like it, and read the letters they print from people supposedly telling of their sexual experiences.

"She became fascinated by these stories and began reading the letters printed in other magazines—*Gallery* and even *Hustler*.

"Then she started asking me if I had ever heard of people doing things like that, or if such things had ever happened to me.

"I told her that I had never done things like that, but if I had I sure wouldn't write to a magazine about them.

"I thought this strange interest of hers would pass, but it hasn't. She not only keeps reading them, but she takes detailed notes. She is now convinced that she and I are not normal because we don't act like the people who write to those magazines. She thinks that we should start doing some of those things.

"To be honest, I am not a prude. But I am not a maniac, either. And I have told her that I am content with that part of our relationship as it has been until the present.

"She has told me that this only proves that I am inhibited and that she wonders if we are really compatible.

"This is causing me to have doubts about myself. I had always believed that I was normal in this regard. Now I wonder if maybe she could be right. Am I some kind of square, without realizing it? It has me worried."

This is a serious problem and potentially hazardous for you.

Your female person friend is not the first to become intrigued by the exploits of those who purportedly write to these magazines about themselves.

Most of these letters begin like this: "My wife (or girlfriend) recently went to California to visit her sister. I happened to go next door to borrow a cup of sugar from the two pretty airline stewardesses who live in the next apartment. They opened the door, wearing negligees and boots. . . ."

Such letters usually end this way: ". . . I left the apartment seventy-two hours later. They said they did not have any sugar. I didn't care."

I recently have learned that there may be reason to doubt the authenticity of these letters.

Scientific studies have been quietly made, using volunteers who duplicate the activities related in the magazines.

The studies are not finished, but so far they have had interesting results.

In one experiment, a young man and three women reenacted a letter that supposedly had been written by a stagehand in a topless theater. It described how, during a long weekend, the performers helped the stagehand celebrate his twenty-first birthday.

The volunteer in this experiment was also twenty-one. He was, at the time, training to compete in the decathlon events in the next Olympics. He was six feet two inches tall, weighed 210 pounds, and formerly had been an all-state football player, wrestler, gymnast, and long-distance runner.

The experiment lasted one long weekend, as was described in the magazine letter.

At the end of that time, the volunteer was thoroughly examined by a team of physicians and other scientists. They found that he had become five feet five inches tall, weighed 142 pounds, his hair had turned white, and all of his teeth were very loose. As a direct result of this experiment, he has given up training for the Olympics and resides in a nursing home, where he walks with the aid of a cane and cries out in fright whenever a nurse approaches.

Other experiments have brought similar results. In one, the volunteer developed violent and embarrassing twitches—not only facial, but in other parts of his body.

Thus, there are now clear scientific reasons to suspect that the letters printed by those magazines are fictional, probably written by rural and small-town exhibitionists who have no other outlet for their passions.

So Greg C. should not let his female friend persuade him that this is the way to behave. They should discuss this matter calmly and frankly. And he should sleep with a can of Mace under his pillow.

Pitch or Curve?

April 24, 1981

Is Phyllis Schlafly, one of the nation's most persistent moralizers, correct about female virtue?

Do truly virtuous women send out unspoken signals that prevent men from making advances? And when a woman receives a sexual pitch, is it because she is not truly virtuous and somehow men know it?

That is what many men and women have been pondering since Mrs. Schlafly gave her views on good ladies and bad ladies before a congressional committee.

In case you missed it, she was in Washington to testify about the possibility of stronger federal laws to protect women from sexual harassment on their jobs.

She is against the law because she thinks women who are sexually harassed just bring it on themselves.

As she put it: "When a woman walks across the room, she

speaks with a universal body language that most men intuitively understand. Men hardly ever ask sexual favors of women from whom the certain answer is no."

I have to disagree with Mrs. Schlafly, as I usually do. I'm no expert, but I've seen lots of women walk across rooms. I've probably seen many more women walk across rooms than she has, because I spend more time at it, while she is busy being a national nag on TV.

I've seen thousands of women walk across newsrooms, barrooms, ballrooms, dining rooms, disco rooms, waiting rooms, and almost any kind of room you can think of. And I've seen them walk across sidewalks, bridges, lobbies, plazas, parks, and their husbands.

And I haven't the faintest idea, just from watching a woman walk, whether she is or is not a lady of easy virtue.

Some women move their hips more than others, true. But does that have to do with a woman's virtue, or the alignment of her bones, or the way she was taught to walk as a child, or the basic fact that she might have more hip to move?

There are places in Chicago where men sometimes gather for purposes of girl-watching. And some women, when they walk past these places, are always subjected to whistles, panting, and shouts of: "Hey, babe, howja like. . . ."

Is this caused by some "universal body language" that somehow tells the men that she is a woman of loose virtue?

Or could it just be that nature, or heredity, happened to give her a forty-inch bust, thirty-inch waist, thirty-eight-inch hips, and a pretty face?

I know of women (one hears things) who are plain in appearance, modest in bearing, and remote in manner. Yet they are said to have sizzling blood and wild instincts.

I also know of women (I told you—one hears things) who have flashing eyes, flouncing hair, bouncing bottoms, pouting bosoms, silken voices, snake-like movements, and a wanton look about them. Yet, they have blood that runs tepid.

For that matter, I'm not sure what a "virtuous woman" is, although scores of grim-lipped biddies will quickly write to explain it to me.

When I was a youth, I thought I knew, because society's standards——at least in my neighborhood——were simple.

Any female who remained chaste until married was virtuous. They were much admired by the neighborhood's married ladies.

All other females were "fallen women." They were maligned by the neighborhood ladies. They were also much sought after by us guys. As Slats Grobnik said: "Why should I waste the price of a movie and a hamburger on a girl who don't know the meaning of the word 'OK'? If I wanna be around someone like that, I'll go to church and talk to a nun. It's cheaper."

So any woman who defied the standards was known contemptuously as a slut, tramp, bum, or a dozen other words.

Meanwhile, any man who had the very same habits was known admiringly as a playboy, a dashing rogue, a lover, a real charmer, a lothario, or simply as "what-a-guy!"

But since the invention of the pill, everything has changed. Women marry later, or not at all. They take male roommates. They have flings—occasional or frequent. They have children. They are bold in making their desires known (again, one hears things).

Does that mean that any unmarried woman who isn't a virgin is not virtuous?

I've known women who were, as they said in old novels, chaste. Some of them were also mean, nasty, cruel, bad-tempered, and malicious. Who needs those kind of virtues?

I've known women who have been around, and intend to go around again. And some were warm-hearted, kind, good, considerate, gentle people. Those are virtues to be cherished.

So I guess my definition of what a virtuous woman is, and Mrs. Schlafly's definition, are different. At least I hope they are.

As for women attracting all those passes, one final thought:

It's possible that Mrs. Schlafly's views are based on her own experiences.

I'm sure Mrs. Schlafly considers herself a virtuous woman. And if men don't make passes at her, she probably believes that it is her virtue that sends them the stern message that they should not even bother.

Well, maybe it is her virtue that discourages them before they even try.

But there might be another explanation why men don't make passes at her.

It's found in the lyrics of a rock song called "Goodbye Stranger." They go this way:

> Now some they do
> And some they don't
> And some you just can't tell.
> And some they will
> And some they won't
> With some it's just as well. . . .

Groom Needs Counsel

June 2, 1978

It's time for another column devoted to helping young men solve their romantic and marital problems. As I explained when I began offering this occasional service, many of today's young men are in need of mature, wise counseling if they are to avoid a lifetime of overdue bills, lawnmowers, dope-ridden offspring, and other distractions.

Today's problem comes from a young man who is planning on marrying soon, but he faces an increasingly common question among young people—whether to sign a marriage contract.

As he explained: "The girl I am going to marry wants us to have a separate contract spelling out how we share domestic duties, the raising of the children, and requiring mutual agreement on such things as where we will live, how we will spend our money, where we will go on vacations, and so on.

"She has a better job than I have, and it has a better future, so she wants the contract to say that if we have children, the partner with the better income will work while the other one takes care of the home and kids.

"At first I thought it was the fair thing to do because I had read about how a lot of couples are doing it. My girl showed me an article in *Ms*. magazine that told why marriage contracts are good and I thought it made sense. But now I'm getting worried. I don't know much about legal matters. When I buy things, I usually don't bother to look at the fine print, or even the big print if the thing I'm buying looks OK.

"So how do I know what I'm getting into? I don't know if I could take care of a house and kids. I want to marry her, but don't even know enough about law to be sure if some of the things in the contract are for my benefit or hers. What do I do?"

The first thing you must do is try to avoid a contract. Give her a firm handshake and tell her: "Look, if you can't trust the man you're going to marry, who can you trust? Let's just shake on it like gentlepersons."

But that probably won't work, since she wouldn't be asking you to sign a contract in the first place if she trusted you. In fact, if she really trusted you, she wouldn't be marrying you. She'd be content to just live together as modern best friends and racquetball partners.

The question, then, is whether you want to agree to spend the rest of your life with someone who has so little faith in you that she would treat you like a customer who walked in off the street at a loan company.

If she is this suspicious already, what is she going to be like the first time you come home at 4:00 A.M. and explain to her that your car broke down and you were attacked by a gang of sadistic thugs who stole your money and spilled liquor on your clothes while making little bite marks on your neck? Or the second time it happens?

She will wave the contract under your nose and scream that you are in violation of Paragraph 6, Clause 9, Line 8, as well as Paragraph 8, Clause 12, and Line 4. What will the neighbors think? And in the morning, she will probably refuse to cook your breakfast, too.

But if you feel strongly about getting it over with and marrying her, and you are willing to sign a contract, then you should make the best deal for yourself that you possibly can. To do that, I suggest that you get an agent to negotiate for you.

That's what everyone does today—athletes, TV anchormen, authors. If they think it is prudent to have agents negotiate for them when entering a simple two-year contract to work, you definitely should have one when signing a paper that will bind you until your teeth fall in your soup.

Unfortunately, there aren't many agents specializing in negotiating marriage contracts. Agents operate on a 10 percent commission, and who can live on one-tenth of somebody else's misery?

However, in Chicago there is one agent who does this kind of work for a fee—Mr. Loopholes Zelinski of Milwaukee Avenue, who is an expert in domestic matters, having spent more than twenty years as a bailiff in a police court.

He has negotiated several marriage contracts and is a demon at getting his client extra nights out for bowling, softball, reunion parties, and in inserting penalty clauses should she gain too much weight, make a habit of oversleeping, interrupt your stories, refuse to clean the fish you catch, or fail to bring you a snack while you watch a football game.

In a case such as yours, where the possibility exists that your wife will hold a job while you take care of the house, he will demand clauses requiring her to come straight home from the office and not sit around after work in a bar getting sloshed with the women from her office, which is a growing problem in our society. Also, he will insist that you be permitted to go to school in the afternoon and take self-fulfillment courses, so you don't turn into a household frump-person.

That is my advice. The only other option you might consider is to tell her that you want to take a little more time to read over the contract for typographical errors.

Then draw your money out of the bank, pack a bag, buy a plane ticket, fly to Nice in the south of France, take a cab to an outdoor cafe that overlooks the beach, order a carafe of the local rosé wine, and invite someone named Gigi or Brigette or Denise to join you. Ask her if she believes in handshakes.

Royalty or Commoner...
Love Is Their Bond

July 30, 1981

Dear Prince Charles and Princess Diana:

The trumpets have stopped blaring. The incredible crowds have dispersed. Satellite TV has taken a rest. You two have walked up the aisle in the most publicized and widely seen wedding in history.

And now you are what you are: A young married couple.

That simple fact seems to have been overlooked by most of the world because you, Charles, are a future king of England, as meaningless as that title might be. And you, Diana, are going to be a queen or whatever a wife of a king is called. As an American, I don't keep track of such things.

But I do know that you are a man and a woman, and have just entered into—as corny as some may find this statement to be—the most serious arrangement, agreement, contract, relationship, or whatever else someone might want to call it, of your lives.

It's really not important that you, Charles, are a prince and king-to-be. And that you, Diana, are a queen-to-be. What I see is something far more important.

You are a couple of people who just got married.

That gives you something in common with all the young lovers, and older lovers, of a world that sometimes seems loveless.

You're really no different from the kid from the Southwest Side of Chicago, who is assistant manager of a pizza joint, and his bride from Oak Lawn, who is going to nursing school. They might not have had the trumpets and the audience of millions. But their vows and their commitment are no different from yours.

That's because when all the guests have gone home from your wedding; when all the gifts have been given; when all the wedding photographs have been taken; when all the wedding songs have been played; when all the relatives have expressed their optimism or pessimism, it boils down to the same thing: It's just you and her. Or her and you, to provide balance.

It's the most wonderful thing in the world. And don't let anyone tell you otherwise. And if you don't realize that, then you're missing out on life's most glorious experience.

That experience is very old. It goes back beyond recorded history. It goes back to some time before man could write or scratch pictures on walls, when a female and a male found themselves in a cave or in the crook of a tree, surrounded by the dark of the night, giving each other comfort, warmth, and security.

This, somehow, became translated into something called love.

Nobody is really sure what love is. Shrinks mess around with trying to define it and just make it sound more complicated than it is. Poets, as neurotic as they are, do a much better job.

I'm not sure what it is myself, except that it leaves you breathless, makes everything else seem unimportant, and can cause you ecstasy, misery, and drive you crazy. And also drive you happy.

I hope, despite your cool, English manners, that this is what you feel. I hope both of you feel crazy and happy.

Be warned: it's not going to be all kissy-face and patty-fingers and the nibbling of earlobes.

There will be times when she's going to be mad as hell at you. If not, she's yogurt or you're a saint. And there will be times when she will drive you up a wall. I hope so, for your sake, or she or you will be about as exciting as a bowl of goldfish.

When that happens—yell. That's right, yell. Tell her you're mad. And tell him you're mad. Then get it out of your systems, glare out the windows, breathe loudly through your nostrils, mutter under your breath, take a walk around the block, call a close friend and complain about how impossible he or she is. Sit and brood about how you got yourself into such an impossible relationship. Daydream, if you must, about the perfect man or the perfect woman you *could* have had.

Then call it a day, say you're sorry, go to bed, hold each other in your arms, do whatever else is called for, and wake up at the first chirp of the birds glad to be alive, and with each other.

You'll find that to be one of the sweetest moments of your life. Almost as sweet as awakening at three or four o'clock in the morning and seeing the other lying next to you, the moonlight playing on the other's body, and reaching out and gently putting your hand on the other's hand.

I must warn both of you: You aren't going to spend the rest of your life, Charlie, lean, youthful, and clear-eyed. And you, Diana, are not always going to have that fresh, ripened-on-the-vine look.

One of these days, Charlie, you're going to be shaving and you're going to look and look again and say: "By George, I have a receding hairline. And I have bags under my eyes. And a trace of jowls. And my waist seems to be damned near as big as my chest. Can I be getting old?"

And you, Diana, are going to step out of the shower and notice that the proportions of your hips, waist, and your etc., etc., are no longer as perfect as they are now. And you will have crow's feet in the corners of your eyes. And the sheen of your skin will be something more like the texture of cottage cheese.

But if you haven't become fools, she will say to you that you are even more handsome now than you were before; and you'll tell her that she's more beautiful and desirable than she was then. And you'll mean it. And if you mean it, then it will be true.

You are really lucky, you know. Not because you're young and rich and famous. Those are strictly fringe benefits.

You are lucky because you, I assume, are in love and are beginning a life together. And that's more important than anything else you do—your work, your place in history, the opinions, approval, or disapproval of others.

Now when you're down, someone will take your hand and help you up. When you're crying, someone will dry your tears. When you're frightened, someone will hold and reassure you. When you're alone, someone will tell you you're not.

That, young prince and young lady, matters more than all the ringing of the bells and the blowing of the trumpets. It's something almost everybody wants, and not everybody has.

So, kids, good luck and don't blow it.

And remember: Squeeze the toothpaste tube from the bottom.

7 | OLD BLUE-EYES AND OTHERS

You Can Bet on Sinatra

May 5, 1976

A short man with a thick neck just walked in and handed me an envelope and said: "Dis is fum Mr. Sinatra."

Sure enough, it was—a letter from Ol' Blue Eyes himself, telling me off good for my column about how he has a twenty-four-hour police guard outside his hotel suite while he's in Chicago.

Here's what he says:

Let me start this note by saying, I don't know you and you don't know me. I believe if you knew me:

First, you would find immediately that I do not have an army of flunkies.

Secondly, neither myself, nor my secretary, nor my security man put in the request for police protection. It is something that's far from necessary.

It's quite obvious that your source of information stinks, but that never surprises me about people who write in newspapers for a living. They rarely get their facts straight. If the police decided that they wanted to be generous with me, I appreciate it. If you have any beefs with the Chicago Police Force, why not take it out on them instead of me, or is that too big a job for you?

And thirdly, who in the hell gives you the right to decide how disliked I am if you know nothing about me?

The only honest thing I read in your piece is the fact that you admitted you are disliked, and by the way you write I can understand it. Quite frankly, I don't understand why people don't spit in your eye three or four times a day.

Regarding my 'tough reputation,' you and no one else can prove that allegation. You and millions of other gullible Americans read that kind of crap written by the same female gossip columnists that you are so gallantly trying to protect: the garbage dealers I call hookers, and there's no doubt that is exactly what they are, which makes you a pimp, because you are using people to make money, just as they are.

Lastly, certainly not the least, if you are a gambling man:

(a) You prove, without a doubt, that I have ever punched an elderly drunk or elderly anybody, you can pick up $100,000.

(b) I will allow you to pull my 'hairpiece.' If it moves, I will give you another $100,000; if it does not, I punch you in the mouth.

How about it?

(signed) Sinatra.

cc: The Honorable Richard J. Daley

Police Supt. James Rochford

Mr. Marshall Field, Publisher.

Mr. Charles Fegert, Vice President.

Before I respond, I have to admit that receiving a signed, hand-delivered, copyrighted letter from Frank Sinatra was a thrill. Even if he did call me a pimp.

Way back, when we were both young, Sinatra was one of my heroes because (a) he was real skinny (b) he had a big Adam's apple (c) he had greasy hair, and (d) all the girls loved him. Me, too, except for (d).

For thirty years, I've considered him the master of pop singers. Why, in 1953, I played his great record of "Birth of the Blues" so often that a Korean houseboy learned every word. And he probably taught the song to his children. So if Sinatra has a fan club in the Korean village of Yong Dong Po, it's because of me.

I mention this only to show how deeply it pained me to be critical of him. The pain may have been brought on by the french fries at lunch, but I prefer to think it was sentiment.

Anyway here is my point-by-point response to his point-by-point response to my column:

• If you say you have no flunkies, I take your word and apologize. I even apologize to the flunky who delivered the letter.
• You say you didn't ask for the police guard. I'll buy that. But I didn't say you asked. I quoted the police public relations man, who said you did. I now suspect that what actually happened is that some politician sent the cop over to impress you. This point could have been easily cleared up before I wrote the column, but every time we called your suite, your secretary got snippy and hung up. I thought you didn't like smart-aleck broads.
• I didn't say you were disliked; the police PR man said it to justify the guard. I like you, Frank, honest. When you wore big bow ties, I wore big bow ties. When you wore big lapels and baggy pants, I wore big lapels and baggy pants. When you dated Ava Gardner, I dated Agnes Grobnik.

We're a lot alike.

• The reason people don't spit in my eye three or four times a day is that I duck fast.

• After rereading your massive file of news clippings, I agree that you have never punched any "elderly drunks." Most of the drunks you punched were younger.

• If you can prove, without a doubt, that I have ever been a pimp, I will give you $11.69. In cash. You're not the only high roller in town.

• I don't want to pull your hair. People would think we're a couple of weirdos.

However, for the sake of a sporting proposition, I'll do it. But only if I can make new terms for the bet.

If your hair doesn't move, you can give me a punch in the mouth. (I figure that fans who can't get tickets for your show will pay fifty cents to touch my swollen lip.)

But if it does move, never mind the 100 Gs—you give me one of your old bow ties and an original recording of "Birth of the Blues." I still say it was your best song.

John Wayne's True Grit

June 13, 1979

During the late 1960s, I had a serious falling out with a liberal friend. He was against the Vietnam War, and so was I.

He didn't like Richard Nixon or George Wallace or J. Edgar Hoover, and I didn't either.

But I was a John Wayne fan and he couldn't understand that. John Wayne, he argued, stood for everything that was wrong. He glorified war, violence, justice by the gun, male chauvinism, simple-minded solutions, and even racism in the casual way he shot down Indians. So how could I like a man who represented all of that?

My answer drove him up the wall and almost ended our friendship. "You're right," I told him. "But I still like John Wayne. His movies really make me feel good."

That was about it. I can't remember *not* being a John Wayne fan. Other movie cowboys were more popular than Wayne when I was a kid. But there was something unreal about them. Roy Rogers, for example, never shot anyone, except in the wrist, and seemed to be in love with his horse, Trigger. Gene Autry never shot anyone, except in the wrist, and he played a guitar and sang in an adenoidal voice.

Then John Wayne came along, and he shot people in the heart, and drank whisky, and treated his horse like a horse. In fact, he treated women like he treated his horse. He seemed real because he reminded me of the men in my neighborhood.

I never went to a John Wayne movie to find a philosophy to live by or to absorb a profound message. I went for the simple pleasure of spending a couple of hours seeing the bad guys lose.

And I still refuse to go to movies that have unhappy endings, or movies in which the villain wins, or movies in which the hero whines, or movies in which the hero isn't a hero but a helpless wimp. If I want to become depressed, why should I spend three dollars at the movies? I can go to work, instead.

That's why the Duke's fans went to his movies. We knew he would not become bogged down in red tape, or fret about losing his pension rights, or cringe when his boss looked at him, or break into a cold sweat and hide in his room, or moan about his impotence, or figure the odds and take the safe way out.

He would do exactly what he did in *True Grit,* my choice as his greatest movie, when he rode out to bring in Lucky Ned Pepper, whom he had once shot in the lip.

As all John Wayne freaks recall, he was alone, as a hero should be, and he was sitting on his horse confronting Ned Pepper across a long, lovely valley. Ned Pepper was accompanied by several villainous friends.

Wayne informed Lucky Ned he was bringing him in—dead if need be.

And Lucky Ned sneered and said something like: "That's mighty bold talk for a one-eyed old fat man."

Who can ever forget the look of thunderous rage that enveloped John Wayne's face. True, he was fat. True, he was old. True, he had only one eye. But did Lucky Ned have to be so rude as to mention it?

Ah, it was a wonderful moment. And it got better when Wayne, in a voice choking with anger, snarled: "Fill yer hand, you sonofabitch!"

And it got even better when he stuck the reins between his teeth, drew a pistol with one hand, a repeating rifle with the other, and galloped full speed into the valley, steering his horse with his teeth and blazing away with both weapons.

At the time, a movie critic—a man in his thirties—wrote that he was so overwhelmed by that scene that he abandoned his critical poise and stood on his seat in the theater, waving his arms and screaming: "Go, John, go!"

I didn't get quite that carried away, being of a more mature age. I simply stomped my feet and put my fingers between my teeth and whistled as loud as I could.

Foolishness? Maybe. But I hope we never become so cool,

so laid back, so programmed, that nobody has that kind of foolish, odds-defying, damn-the-risk spirit.

After all, what makes some firemen drop the hose and run into a burning building to carry somebody down an icy ladder? It's not the pension, or the thirty days of vacation, or the civil service guarantees. What makes one man drop his briefcase, kick off his shoes, and dive off the Michigan Avenue bridge into the Chicago River to try to rescue a prospective suicide while everyone else just watches? What makes an occasional politician enrage his constituents and risk defeat by damning the consequences and taking a position that is right, but unpopular? What makes some lawyers take on lost causes for no fee, and pound away for frustrating years until they get an ounce of justice?

I don't know the answer, but I'll bet that down deep, they're all John Wayne fans, and would have put the reins between their teeth, too.

Now that he's gone, I don't know what we'll do. I just can't see somebody like Johnny Travolta confronting Ned Pepper.

He'd probably ask him to dance.

Dylan the Great

January 30, 1974

The first time I ever heard Bob Dylan sing, I knew he would be a success.

He sounded exactly like Woody Guthrie, an earlier folksinger, and I figured that if he added a few more imitations—maybe Bette Davis and James Cagney—he would have an even funnier routine.

Then I found out he wasn't kidding around. He wanted people to take his Woody Guthrie style seriously.

So I changed my mind and decided he would not be a success after all. People would hoot and jeer, I assumed, when they heard Dylan, the former Bobby Zimmerman, a middle-class youth, trying to sound like Guthrie, an authentic, callous-palmed, Depression-era Dustbowl Okie.

But I was wrong. Most of Dylan's fans had not heard of Woody Guthrie. They assumed that Dylan, and other suburban-style guitar jockeys, had created folk music.

Dylan became a great success and made millions, which proves that it is better to sing about hard work than to do it. He became so rich that in 1966, while still a lad, he retired.

When I saw what Dylan accomplished by imitating Woody Guthrie, I really kicked myself. I used to do a helluva imitation of Al Jolson.

Now I am filled with even more regret because I was on vacation when Dylan came to Chicago to launch his out-of-retirement concert tour.

For one thing, I wanted to see if he still did Woody Guthrie, or if he had switched to someone else, like maybe Mario Lanza.

But more than that, I have learned that I missed one of the greatest cultural events in the history of the world.

At least that's what I gather by reading the papers and magazines.

Newsweek magazine, for instance, put Dylan on the cover and quoted a record company executive as saying: "This event is the biggest thing of its kind in the history of show business."

That is a lot of history, going back to the first Stone Age man who juggled a few rocks to amuse his cavemates.

Newsweek also quoted a young woman as saying: "I think he [Dylan] is the most important musician who ever lived— more important than Beethoven."

(In fairness, it should be pointed out that Beethoven lost his hearing. Had he not done so, he might have been as important as Dylan.)

And Ralph Gleason, the noted West Coast columnist and musical authority, wrote: "The impact that Bob Dylan has had upon the culture of the past ten years in the English-speaking world . . . is extraordinary and comparable, at least in terms of concepts and additions to the language, only with Shakespeare and the Bible."

It is hard to argue with that, especially when you consider such Dylan lyrics as:

> It's never been my duty
> To remake the world at large,
> Nor is it my intention
> To sound the battle charge.
> I love you more than all of that
> With a love that doesn't bend
> And if there is eternity
> I'll love you there again.

Now admit it. You have never read anything like THAT in Shakespeare or the Bible.

Most of the Dylan admirers also offer the ticket sales as further evidence of the importance of his historic return from Malibu.

They expect more than 650,000 people to attend his concert tour. They say another 5 million pleas for tickets have been turned down.

As one critic raved: "There may not be another performer in the world who can draw like that."

At this point, I must offer a mild disagreement. While Dylan may be in the same class as Shakespeare and the Bible, there are other popular performers around.

Take Ringling Brothers, Barnum & Bailey Circus. About 9 million people saw it last year.

The Illinois State Fair drew 662,895 people, and most of the farm creatures don't sound as good as Dylan.

Billy Graham, without Levis and boots, preached to 1,046,750 people.

But figures aren't important. What is important is that Dylan has returned, which means that those who missed seeing Beethoven can now see the very best.

I was interested in reading one of Dylan's reasons for coming out of retirement. (I knew it couldn't be money because great artists don't give a damn about such things.) Dylan said: "Saturn has been an obstacle in my planetary system. It's been there for the last few ages and just removed itself from my system. I feel free and unburdened."

I'll bet. And it must have hurt.

As for the future, Dylan said: "I am not looking to be that new messiah. That's not in the cards for me."

I don't know if that is modesty or just a lack of ambition.

Algren's Golden Pen

May 13, 1981

I remember almost to the moment the first time I saw the name Nelson Algren.

It was in a tent in Korea about three decades ago. The guy in the next bunk flipped a paperback book at me and said: "Hey, here's a book about Chicago. You want it?"

I glanced over the blurbs on the jacket to see what it was about. The blurb said something to the effect that the book was set in a "slum" in Chicago. And it described the slum as being the Division Street area.

Slum? I was offended. That was no slum. That was my neighborhood.

Curious, I went ahead and read the book, and I was stunned. It was the first time I had read a novel that was set in a place I knew. And Algren, with *The Man with the Golden Arm,* had captured it. He had the people, the sounds, the alleys, the streets, the feel of the place.

It's a strange sensation to read a novel about a place you know well. It had never occurred to me, growing up in that neighborhood, that it contained the stuff a great book can be made of. The great books, as they were force-fed to us in the schools, were about other countries, other cultures, other centuries. And the duller they were, the greater they were.

But here was somebody named Nelson Algren writing

about Division Street and Milwaukee Avenue, and the dope heads and boozers and the card hustlers. The kind of broken people Algren liked to describe as responding to the city's brawny slogan of "I Will" with a painful: "But What If I Can't?"

I didn't know it then, but many Chicagoans weren't pleased by Algren's book, even though it won the first National Book Award for fiction, sort of an Oscar for writers.

Among those who were displeased were the so-called leaders of the city's Polish community—people who were big on joining the Polish National Alliance and other such organizations.

They believed that because many of his characters were Polish, Algren was presenting them in a poor light. I guess they would have preferred that he write a novel about a Polish dentist who changed his name and moved from the old neighborhood to a suburb as soon as he made enough money.

So for years they sniped at Algren, tried to keep him out of the libraries, and made themselves look foolish. As one of them—an insurance broker—once said to me: "I didn't know anybody like the characters in his books." Well, I did. And I saw some of them off when they went to prison or the morgue.

After reading my first Algren novel, I made a point of finding his other works. He had done other novels, and a wonderful prose poem about Chicago called *Chicago: City on the Make.*

But my favorite of all his writings was his collection of short stories called *The Neon Wilderness.* Bittersweet stories. Funny-sad stories. I think they're among the finest short stories written by an American.

I told him that the first time I met him, about seventeen years ago. He had invited me to a gathering in his walk-up flat overlooking Wicker Park, near Damen, North, and Milwaukee.

That's where he lived for most of his years in Chicago. It's a funny thing about the rewards of the writing trade in this country: You can pick up *People* magazine and see this or that commercial, best-selling hack lounging by his pool in Beverly Hills, or swaggering about his estate on Martha's Vineyard. Or you can read about some wordsmith who stole the plot of *Moby Dick,* turned the whale into a white shark, and made a fast million or two.

Meanwhile, someone like Algren never got out of Wicker Park and couldn't always make the rent until a small check for a book review came in the mail.

But, he would have to admit, that's the kind of thing that always happened to the losers in his stories, so why not to the author of those stories?

Not that he ever beefed about life around Wicker Park. It had many advantages.

For one, there were the Luxor Baths on North Avenue, once considered the finest steam bath joint in town. When it opened in the 1920s, Mayor Big Bill Thompson himself showed up to honor it by accepting a squirt of steam on his big gut.

Although I always argued that the Russian Baths on Division Street had more class, Algren preferred the Luxor and would spend many hours soaking up steam and listening to the bookies, loan sharks, precinct captains, and his other favorite creatures discussing events of the day.

He could always find a poker game in the back of a barber shop or saloon, or an ex-prize fighter to describe how he almost became a contender.

And when there was nothing else going on, he could sit on his third-floor porch and watch the passing scene—which often included somebody with a brick chasing somebody with a wallet.

In many other countries, a writer of Algren's stature would have been given a chair at a university, assured of a reasonable income, and asked only to write to his heart's content. They do that in this country, too, but usually for dull writers who know how to play university politics and act properly at the dean's wife's teas. Algren tried it briefly, but he talked too tough for them, and I think he pinched a few coeds, so they asked him to go away.

He moved from Chicago a few years ago, and had a great time announcing that he no longer liked this city, and that it had never appreciated him. Neither statement was true, and he knew it. But he liked saying such things to create a controversy. We had dinner the night before he left and the fact was, he was moving because he felt like moving.

He tried New Jersey for a while, and finally wound up in a pretty old whaling town on Long Island, New York. That's where he died a few days ago and was buried on Monday.

If the mayor and some of those stiffs in the City Council can see their way clear, it would be a nice gesture for them to rename one of the little streets around Wicker Park after him. Algren Court or Algren Place. Nothing big. He wouldn't expect it.

And if you get a chance, you might want to read some of his writings. Any good bookstore can probably order them for you.

You might even come across a 1967 printing of those short stories I mentioned, *The Neon Wilderness.*

If you do, check the printed dedication. As I said earlier, the first time I met him, I told him I thought the short stories were the best things he ever wrote. I was afraid he might be offended, since he considered himself foremost a novelist. But he listened, nodding politely, and said: "That's interesting."

A few years later, a new, hardcover edition of the short stories came out. He had a little party to celebrate, and when we went home, he handed us each a book.

It wasn't until a few days later that I opened it and saw the printed dedication. It said: "For Mike Royko."

It's still one of the nicest things anyone ever did for me.

Jane Fonda's $100-a-week Morality

March 28, 1978

Jane Fonda, who has alternated between providing moral leadership for the nation and starring in hit movies, has found a way to do both jobs at the same time.

She now gives interviews in which she solemnly prattles about her concern for grave social problems, while also talking about how good her latest movie is. That way, she manages to maintain her queenly position within California's social relevancy crowd, while encouraging people to drop $3.50 to see her latest filmed entertainment.

Her skill at juggling both roles has become such that she can now provide social-relevance answers to moviemaking questions.

An example was a recent magazine interview during which she was complaining about the scarcity of good movie scripts about subjects that have "vision and scope." The interviewer asked why there aren't more such movie scripts.

The obvious and true answer would have been that movies of vision and scope don't draw audiences as big as movies about overgrown sharks.

But Ms. Fonda's explanation was: "Because too many of you [writers] care about money," explained Ms. Fonda.

The interviewer pointed out the obvious: "Well, you have to live."

Ms. Fonda disagreed and said: "We have to go beyond the Hollywood writers and find young people who aren't interested in $100-a-week versus $500-a-week, so long as they can survive and are in touch with what's happening."

The interviewer said: "It's not easy to survive on $100-a-week these days."

Ms. Fonda explained: "It's not easy, but it depends on what your interests are."

See? Jane the moral leader made it clear that what we have here is a social conflict between a dedication to vision and scope and relevance, and grubbing for a few extra dollars.

In a moment, she was really going—expanding the significance of the inadequacy of movie scripts to inadequacies in our society as a whole, and happily jabbering about "mobilizing large numbers of people whose lives are directly affected," and bringing about "democratic control of large corporate boards" and about how bad Nixon was and how saintly Cesar Chavez is, and so on.

The interviewer didn't ask her whether she prefers lightly or heavily buttered popcorn during a movie, and that was wise because she would have probably gone on forever about the insensitivity of eating heavily buttered popcorn while people in undeveloped nations have to eat it unpopped.

Having once earned $100-a-week and less, which Ms. Fonda has never done, I can't see why she believes that starving can help a person write better movie scripts about anything besides starving. Maybe she just wants them starving at their typewriters so she can sit on the beach at Malibu and fret about their deprivation.

Her own earnings give no indication that she stays "in touch with what's happening" by surviving on $100-a-week.

For her next movie, Ms. Fonda is going to be paid close to $1 million. To earn that much, one of Ms. Fonda's $100-a-week writers would have to flail his typewriter for about 190 years. Assuming, of course, he didn't demand a raise to $101 week.

Her next movie, incidentally, is a creation of writer Neil Simon, who has become a millionaire by carefully avoiding subjects of scope and vision and, instead, making people laugh. Simon usually gets about $100-a-word, not a week. Ms. Fonda hasn't explained why she is going to appear in a movie written by a capitalistic running dog like Simon, rather than by someone of scope and vision who is also suffering from terminal scurvy. Maybe she can't find a writer who can come up with good lines while foraging through garbage cans.

Whenever Ms. Fonda is asked about her own considerable earnings, she quickly asserts that she doesn't keep all that money for herself. No, she puts it into an organization that she and her husband, Tom Hayden, have formed to make this a better world for the rest of us. Presumably better even for $100-a-week writers. Maybe the Haydens plans to pay them $109.

Well, I hate to doubt the word of a moral leader like Ms. Fonda, but I have trouble believing that she gives most of her money away that way. And since she insists on being a moral leader and telling other people that they ought to work for $109-a-week, it is about time she produced income tax statements and other records clearly establishing that she, too, is scraping by on just enough to keep food on the table and a roof over her flighty head.

If she provides such proof, I will apologize for doubting her. And I'll even work for her for $100-a-week. I'll write a touching movie script about a movie star who becomes a great moral leader, but suffers tragedy in the end when she vigorously nods her head in agreement with one of her own thoughts, and her brain falls out of her ear.

Pickford's Old 'Error'

March 31, 1976

I didn't think it was possible, but Mary Pickford, the onetime screen darling of America, has managed to offend lots of people. She did it by growing old.

Actually, that's not entirely accurate. Growing old in itself was not Miss Pickford's social error. It was in letting the Oscar night TV audience see that she had grown old.

The gossip columnists seem to agree that her taped appearance for a special award was, as one of them put it, "in bad taste."

And if the calls to the Wally Phillips popular morning radio show are any barometer of public opinion, and I think they are, then many people share the view that the TV audience should not have been subjected to Miss Pickford's appearance.

They were on the phone to Phillips as early as 5:30 A.M., the morning after the Academy Awards presentations, to express their displeasure.

The producer of the Phillips show said: "They thought in general that it was in poor taste to have that segment on the program. They felt that perhaps it destroyed an image of her that they had held.

"They would have preferred to never have known how she didn't measure up to the questions that were asked her, and seemed like a lady of eighty-two.

"They knew her as a star of an era, and instead saw a doddering, sickly old lady."

Imagine that! A doddering, sickly old lady in the midst of all those sleek, nubile young actresses, and those handsome, broad-shouldered, virile actors. Eeek!

Well, maybe I'm not normal, or have weird taste, but I watched the show and saw the presentation to Mary Pickford, and it didn't bother me.

One reason might be that I'm not surprised to discover that somebody might be wrinkled, frail, weak-voiced, and maybe a bit senile when they get to be eighty-two. That happens to people who get to be eighty-two. They sometimes get old, old, old.

The word doesn't bother me, either. Old. Oollllllldddd. I prefer it to "senior citizen." Or "twilight years." Old. Say it. Go on, your teeth won't fall out.

Or how about "wrinkled" or "sagging" or "liver spots"? Or "varicose veins"? These words don't offend me, either.

But if they offend you, if you turn your head away from Mary Pickford and find it all so distasteful, then there's something wrong with you, kid, because it's perfectly normal. It happens to all of us, unless we croak first. We get old.

Take Margaux Hemingway, the tall stunner who was on the show. One of these days she's going to wrinkle up, and maybe her teeth will fall out, maybe even her hair, and her knee joints will go crackety-crack.

Is that too terrible to face—Margaux Hemingway's knee joints going crackety-crack?

For some reason, it doesn't bother people nearly as much when an elderly actress has her breasts propped up like the bow of a ship, her facial skin stretched out like a drumhead, her siliconed body girdled and buttressed into preposterous curves and lumps, and an inch of pink mortar stuck on her face.

Then the gossip columnists marvel at how young she looks,

and the audience cheers. They cheer the illusion of Zsa Zsa, but they flinch at the reality of Mary Pickford.

What's wrong with looking old age in the face? Afraid? You bet.

Better to slap a hairpiece on that wrinkled pate, slip into a leisure suit, and scuttle across the dance floor like a spastic and fur-topped prune.

And better to slip granny and gramps, and all the grannies and grampses, into hideaways where we don't have to see their gums, hear their wheezes, and be reminded of what the future holds.

Many of those who saw Mary Pickford said they would rather remember her as she once was.

Why? She's not dead. She may be old, but she is a living, breathing human being. She has thoughts, emotions, and, I'm sure, experiences happiness.

That's what I think I saw on my TV. When her brief segment ended, the camera came in close. And there was a tiny teardrop in her eye.

And when the audience was shown applauding, I saw her husband, Buddy Rogers, no kid himself, looking at her with love and pride, looking like he was almost crying himself from these feelings.

I thought that was very, very nice. Maybe I'm not easily offended.

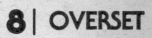

8 | OVERSET

Never Let Go of a Guitar

August 24, 1973

It can lift the spirits to occasionally read an inspirational story. There are all too few of them in our hectic society. But here is such a story, about how one stranger reached out toward another.

It began with something very commonplace—a two-line ad in this paper for the sale of an electric guitar.

The ad was placed by Bob Macey, nineteen, of Oak Brook, a pre-med student. He wanted to sell his guitar, a fine Gibson, before returning to school. He wanted $350.

On the second day of the ad, he received a phone call. The man said he was interested, but for an unusual reason.

He explained he was a physician and that his nephew had recently been seriously injured in an auto crash. The boy had been burned from the neck down.

The man said he felt personally responsible for the accident. He had been like a father to the boy, whose parents were divorced, and he had talked him into driving to Chicago to visit one of his parents. During the drive, the crash occurred.

In the accident, the boy's guitar had been destroyed.

Now, he was in Ravenswood Hospital, slowly recovering.

But his morale was low. So the uncle hoped that if he bought him a guitar, it would improve his state of mind.

"Would it be possible," he asked Macey, "for you to bring the guitar to the hospital this evening so he can look at it?"

Of course he would, Macey said.

"Fine," the man said. "When you get to the hospital, just ask the receptionist for Dr. Carr."

When Macey arrived, the receptionist pointed out Dr. Carr, who was waiting in the lobby.

But Dr. Carr was upset and embarrassed. His nephew had had a bad day and he was just not feeling well enough to be surprised.

"I realize I'm inconveniencing you," Dr. Carr said, "but could I ask you to come back again tomorrow morning? I'm sure I can show it to him, and if he likes it I'll buy it from you for the price you're asking."

Before he left, they chatted about the accident and the difficult family life the injured boy had. By the time they parted, Macey felt that he had found a friend in the white-haired, ruddy-faced tweed-coated physician.

The next morning, he was back at the hospital. Dr. Carr met him in the lobby.

Macey opened the case and showed him the guitar, explaining how the various switches worked.

It was a beautiful instrument, made of solid ebony with mother-of-pearl inlays and gold plating on the metal parts. Macey had shined it before coming to the hospital.

"I'm sure he'll like it," Dr. Carr said. "Let me take it up to his room right now. Then if he wants it, I'll come back down and pay you."

As Dr. Carr hurried off with the guitar, Macey ran after him.

"I forgot to give you the pick. He might want to try it."

Dr. Carr took the pick, but he shook his head, saying: "No, he's burned too badly to be able to pick it up yet. But just looking at it will probably make him happy."

Macey sat down and waited in the lobby. A half-hour passed and Macey became concerned. Had the boy suffered a relapse . . . or worse?

After an hour passed, Macey asked the receptionist if something had happened to the boy.

She said she would check. She made three phone calls. Then she told Macey there were no burn cases in the hospital.

Macey told her she had to be mistaken. Dr. Carr's nephew had been burned.

She told Macey there was no Dr. Carr on the staff.

"But the receptionist had pointed Dr. Carr out—by name."

Yes, but only because the white-haired man had walked into the hospital, said his name was Dr. Carr, that he was waiting to meet somebody, and would the receptionist please direct that person to him.

The police were called. They filled out a report and an officer told Macey: "Never trust anyone, kid."

I told you it was an inspirational story. It should inspire all gray-haired codgers who worry that the younger generations really are a lot smarter. Maybe the kids invented the phrase "rip-off," but smooth old guys in tweed coats have made it an art.

A Day on the Sidetrack

January 29, 1981

One of the most difficult challenges facing any married man is coming up with a believable excuse for staying out late at night.

They can range from the banal ("There was a sixteen-car accident on the expressway") to the imaginative ("And after the janitor locked me in the office, and I got out, I got on the elevator and it broke down between floors and . . .").

But no one has ever called his wife late at night and told a story that compares with that of William Goodloe, twenty-six, of Maywood, a computer operator.

To appreciate Goodloe's story, we have to start at the beginning, as he tells it.

He left home for his job at Pandick Press Midwest Inc., 111 North Canal. He walked the few blocks to the Melrose Park commuter station where he catches the North Western.

But as he approached the station, he saw a very long freight train slowly going by.

"It must have been three miles long," Goodloe said, "and as it was going by I heard the bell ringing that meant my train was going to be coming in."

The westbound freight blocked his way to the passenger station, so Goodloe was afraid he would miss his eastbound train.

"This has happened to me before, and what I've done is

cross the freight train. It's a little dangerous, I know, but I've been careful."

What Goodloe did was scramble aboard one of the flatbed cars on the freight train. Then he intended to jump off on the other side.

"The trouble was, just when I was getting on the freight, it started going faster. And by the time I got past the truck trailers it was carrying, it was going faster.

"So when I looked down at the ground, and was going to jump off, it was going so fast I got scared."

So he stayed on the freight.

"I figured, OK, I made a mistake, and I'll just ride to the next station, and when the freight stopped, I'd get off."

Not a bad plan. Except that the freight train didn't stop at the next station. It was going about forty miles an hour when it went through.

"It didn't even slow down," Goodloe said. "And, man, I was getting cold. Going that fast on an open car, my behind was freezing off.

"But I wasn't worried. I knew it had to stop or slow down pretty soon. So I just sat there shivering and waiting.

"But when we went through Geneva, I thought, 'Oh oh, I'm in trouble.' That's the last commuter stop.

"And then it went faster and faster. Man, it must have been doing sixty miles an hour, and that train was rocking and vibrating, and I thought I was going to bounce off. I wasn't only freezing, but I thought I was going to go flying off the car. So I just found something to hold on to and I hung on."

Every so often, the train would whiz through a town and Goodloe would wave and shout at people, hoping they would realize he had a problem.

"They'd wave back at me. They thought I was being friendly. Or they'd point at me and laugh. They thought it was funny that somebody was riding on a flatbed freight car, I guess."

The train rumbled on. Goodloe hung on and his teeth chattered.

"I decided I'd better try to crawl to either the engine or the caboose and see if I could find somebody and let them know I was on board. I started for the caboose, going from car to car."

But before he made it, the speed dropped. The train had slowed because it was approaching the bridge that spans the Mississippi River.

Goodloe was about to enter Iowa.

"I didn't wait. I jumped off. One of my shoes fell off when I hit the ground. Then you know what happened? Somebody in the caboose yelled, 'Did you enjoy the ride?' They knew I was on there all along. Maybe they thought I was a hobo."

Goodloe put his shoe back on and headed for a road. He was about 180 miles from home and he had $1.45 and his brown-bag lunch in his pocket.

"I was hoping to find a cop to find out what I could do."

And as he hoofed down the highway, he found a cop. Or the cop found him.

Goodloe started to explain what had happened. But it isn't easy to tell in a few words a story about trying to crawl across a freight train in order to catch a passenger train, etc. Especially when your teeth are chattering.

Then Goodloe noticed that the cop kept looking at him suspiciously.

"Just wait a moment," the policeman said, going to his car radio.

And in a few minutes, other policemen arrived and Goodloe was taken into custody.

He had become a suspect in the wounding of a policeman in a nearby Iowa town the day before.

"They said I looked like the guy who shot a cop."

Goodloe was taken to police headquarters in Clinton, Iowa, where he was questioned and photographed so his picture could be shown to the wounded policeman.

"I mean, I was really feeling like the world had turned upside down on me. I start out the day by walking to my train to go to my job. Then I wind up in Iowa suspected of being a gunman. Wow, what a trip."

The wounded policeman looked at the photo and said Goodloe wasn't the guy, so the police told him he was free to go.

"I got on the phone and called my wife. I told her that I was in Iowa. She said: 'Where?' I told her: 'In Iowa. I got here on a freight train.' And she said: 'All right, where are you?' I said: 'I'm in Iowa. I got on a freight train. The police thought I was a gunman.' And she said: 'Now, I'm going to ask you again. Where are you?'

"Boy, it took me a long time to convince her. Then she and my father drove there and got me."

Goodloe's story is true. The police confirmed it. "Yeah, he kind of wandered in on a freight train," a policeman said.

And did the experience teach Goodloe a lesson about not climbing across freight trains?

"I suppose," he said. "But it wouldn't have been bad in the summer. The Mississippi was kind of pretty."

Disorders in the Courts

May 3, 1978

It was a routine case in traffic court, except the policeman testified that the motorist used filthy language.

Then, according to a spectator, the judge peered at the motorist and sternly asked: "Do you know what happens to people who foul-mouth policemen?"

The motorist shrugged.

"The police sometimes shoot them," the judge said. "And maybe more of them ought to be shot!"

The spectator was so shocked by the judge's words that after his own case was finished, he called us and indignantly protested the way the judge had talked.

We called Judge Arthur Ellis to find out if he was really encouraging policemen to ventilate citizens who swear at them.

"Yeah, I remember that case," the judge said. "I guess I shouldn't have said that. It slipped out. . . . It was an uh, ober dicta."

A what?

"An ober dicta."

Is that Latin?

"Yeah."

What does "ober dicta" mean?

"I don't know."

I later checked a dictionary and found "obiter dictum," which indicates that the judge's Latin isn't much better than my own. It means "something said; saying."

Based on that, I guess the judge doesn't really want cops to shoot persons who swear at them. He probably just likes to enliven his courtroom.

And I can't say I disagree with that. Most courtrooms, and especially traffic court, can be a dull place.

I knew one judge who liked to wake everyone up in night traffic court by occasionally issuing a surprising ruling.

One night a man showed up who obviously had been drinking. He was charged with running a red light.

"How do you plead?" the judge asked.

The man mumbled something. The judge told him to speak up.

The man insolently said: "You don't hear too good, judge. I plead guilty."

The judge asked: "Don't you know it isn't smart to plead guilty?"

The man, still insolent, said: "So what? You wouldn't give me a break anyway."

The man's wife started to say something to him, but the man told her to shut up.

The judge said: "All right. I shall enter a plea of guilty. And here is my sentence.

"You shall be given into custody of the sheriff of this county, and on the fifteenth of the month, he shall cause a bolt of electricity to be passed through your body until you are dead dead dead."

The man staggered backward, his red eyes popped wide open and his jaw dropped. His wife gasped. Everyone in the courtroom sat up straight.

"Just for running a light?" the man cried.

"No. For being dumb enough to plead guilty. Ah, but on second thought, I'll just fine you fifteen dollars and costs. You are not worth frying. Go, and sin no more."

Nobody else became insolent in the courtroom that night.

Which reminds me of the most sadistic, cruel, mean, and funny thing I have ever heard done in a courtroom. An elderly policeman told me the story. He swears it is true.

It happened many years ago, before policemen began living in squad cars, talking into microphones, using computers, and taking themselves too seriously. One night a paddy wagon brought a big, drunken steelworker into the South Chicago police station. He had been arrested for throwing several of his drinking companions through the window of a neighborhood tavern.

He was of Eastern European origin and apparently had anarchistic tendencies because he bellowed at the room full of cops: "When we haf revolution, we going to take all you red-nose Irish bastards and shoot you by wall."

The desk sergeant, who wasn't too sober himself, said: "Book this man on disorderly conduct and high treason."

While papers were quickly filled out, the rest of the cops went upstairs, where there was an empty police court.

They took the steelworker upstairs to the courtroom. A detective was pretending to be the judge. Another became the prosecutor. Others became clerks, bailiffs, and the public defender. Several more sat in the jury box. A few winos were brought from the lockup to sit in the spectators' seats.

The trial was held, evidence presented, and when it ended, the "judge" said: "I find you not guilty of disorderly conduct. But I find you guilty of high treason. I sentence you to be executed by means of electrocution as quickly as the sentence can be carried out."

They rushed the dumbfounded man out of the courtroom and to the lockup, where he was asked what he wanted for his last meal. Somebody ran out to an all-night diner and got a hamburger with fries for him.

As he ate, the lights in the cells blinked on and off several times.

"What's that?" he yelled.

"We are testing the electric chair," he was told.

When he finished his meal, they led him into the squad room, where they had rigged a large chair with wires. A detective had turned his collar around, so he looked like a clergyman. He loudly prayed over the steelworker, who began weeping.

They strapped him into the chair, and atop his head they placed a bowl-like gadget they had taken off a lamp.

"Be brave, my son," the clergyman-detective intoned. "You will meet your maker any minute now." The steelworker began wailing.

At that moment, the door burst open and a cop rushed in,

shouting: "Stop the execution! The governor has given him a reprieve!"

The next morning, he was taken before a real judge on the brawling charge. He immediately began babbling: "Last night I was in the electric chair . . . the governor saved me . . . high treason . . . a thing on my head."

The judge sent him to the state hospital to be examined. When he got out of there, he resumed drinking in the neighborhood tavern. But from then on, he always went home after two beers.

Warm Advice for a Cold Day

January 9, 1976

Before I left for work this morning, I read the paper and there was a story with tips on surviving the cold spell.

It said dress warmly. So I put on long underwear, boots, and earmuffs. Actually, I already had them on when I got up. It said to avoid frostbite, wiggle toes and fingers. All the way to work, I wiggled my toes and fingers, even on a crowded bus. A young lady standing next to me on the bus was offended.

I followed all the instructions, and when I got to work I was cold and numb and miserable.

That always happens, because it is the same lousy advice we get every cold winter. I've been reading the same stuff all my life, and wiggling my toes and fingers, and wearing long underwear, and taking shortcuts through office buildings, and not rubbing snow on frostbite but using warm water instead, and putting a scarf over my face, and every winter I'm still cold and miserable.

We need some new cold weather advice. And since nobody else is offering any, here are a few of my suggestions for surviving subzero temperatures in Chicago.

(1) Don't go to work. To hell with it. The world isn't going to end if you don't show up. And even if it does, you might as well be home to make sure looters don't break in. Call in with some kind of excuse. Tell them a pack of wild dogs is outside your door and will eat you if you go out.

Then stay in bed all morning. When you get up, don't wash. It's bad for you. Eskimos don't. Spend the afternoon watching the soap operas. There are some good ones on. Really dirty. They do more shocking things in one segment than Helen Trent or Our Gal Sunday did in a lifetime. If your wife knows the soap opera plots, and what they've been doing in detail, you might make a mental note to check on what else she has been up to while you are at work. TV can put ideas in a person's head, you know.

Or, in the morning, you might call a few pals and suggest that they take the day off, too, and invite them over and get a poker game going. There's nothing like sitting around on a cold day, playing poker and drinking beer, when everybody else is at work. You'll like it.

And order out for some pizza. It's the best thing for warding off frostbite. You never hear of frostbite cases in Rome.

If your wife says that having you and your friends around the house all day makes her nervous, tell her to go out and get a job and she won't be so nervous anymore. On the way she can start up the car and run it for a while. That's another good cold weather tip.

The next morning, call in with another excuse. Say there is a grizzly bear blocking the driveway. And—another cold weather tip—open a fresh deck of cards. Pizza gets them marked up easily.

(2) Maybe you aren't the kind of person who can sit home all day. OK. Then get up and leave for work. But don't go there. Go out to O'Hare and buy a ticket for the next plane to Jamaica.

If you don't have enough cash, use credit cards or write a check. You can pay later. And even if you can't pay later, don't worry. Let them sue. This is an emergency.

When you get to Jamaica, tell a cabdriver to take you to a little bar called Toto's. On the way, stop at a men's shop and pick up some cutoff pants, a T-shirt with bold stripes, a bandanna, some wraparound sunglasses, and a long, thin cigar. But remember to take off your black, ribbed business socks.

When you get to Toto's Bar, ask for Toto (he wears a black eye patch) and tell him I sent you. He'll fix you a great rum and scotch and gin mixed with coconut milk. Don't have more than three. The coconut milk is fattening.

Tell Toto that you want to meet Gina. You can't miss her. She has long black hair, green eyes flecked with gold, long tanned legs, an orange bikini, and has an erotic tattoo on her left ankle. She's a nice kid. Tell her I sent you.

Gina has her own air-conditioned cottage on a lush hill overlooking a secluded beach, with a quiet old lady servant who keeps fresh gardenias floating in the pink swimming pool, and who knows voodoo. Tell the old lady I sent you. She'll fix you up with a potion.

When you settle down by the pool, ask Gina to bring you the phone. Call home collect. Tell your wife you've been kidnapped by some crazy radicals, and you don't know how long you'll be gone, but you'll keep in touch. If she asks you why you are chuckling, tell her the radicals are tickling your feet.

(3) Or go to Sears and buy an extra set of long underwear.

Taking a Flier in the Interest of Science

January 24, 1977

I took part in a significant scientific experiment the other evening.

It began in a Washington bar, where a few reporters were celebrating the end of the inauguration, so we could begin being nasty to Jimmy Carter.

Time flew, as it does in bars, and I looked at my watch and cursed. I had missed my train to Chicago.

"Train?" someone said. "You ride trains?"

I'm used to that. Yes, I ride trains. I love the bumpy ride, the dirty windows, the erratic schedules, the faulty air-conditioning.

Actually, I hate trains. But I'm terrified of airplanes.

"You don't fly?" someone asked.

Sure I fly. I flew as recently as 1953. That was only twenty-four years ago.

Everybody started making suggestions. I've heard them all. Hypnotism. Tranquilizers. Therapy. Religion.

My terror, I explained proudly, is so powerful that it resists every cure known to man.

"Get drunk," said Dick Ciccone, a Chicago reporter.

There is not enough booze in Washington to overcome my fears.

"I'm flying back to Chicago tonight," Ciccone said. "I'll bet you can do it if you try."

I cannot resist a bet. "Waiter," I said, "a double martini."

The scientific experiment had begun.

From this point on, I'm fuzzy on details.

But about three hours later, we were lurching in and out of this cab. Then somebody took my credit card and handed me a piece of paper.

Then we were walking through this tunnel and I was sitting down in this long, large room with lots of other people.

"Is this the waiting lounge?" I recall asking.

Ciccone laughed. "This is the inside of the airplane."

"I can't do it," I yelled, and turned to run. But it was too late. They had closed the door.

I began babbling about my civil rights being abused when this pretty lady leaned over me and said something. I don't remember what she said, but she had freckles and nice teeth.

At first I thought she was trying to take off my jacket. I didn't know what she had in mind, but I was all for it and offered to remove my shirt.

But she was just buckling my seat belt.

"How do you get a drink in this joint?" I bellowed.

"Oh boy," moaned a guy on the other side of the aisle. "We've got one of THOSE."

I considered punching him out. But by then the engines were roaring and the damn thing was moving.

I've always thought of airplanes as large, metal coffins that are propelled at the speed of sound, several miles above the Earth. The thought always makes me sick.

This time I tried closing my eyes and thinking of it as a huge hip flask. I felt better.

Word spread quickly that a first-time passenger was aboard.

Word spread quickly because I was howling about how terrified I was. People decided to be kind.

"Look who is aboard," someone said, leading me down the aisle.

I looked. It was Muhammad Ali, of all people. He was bouncing a baby—his, I was told—on his knee and saying, "Goo-goo."

"See?" a stewardess said. "Even the little baby isn't scared."

"You're right," I said. "Ask Ali to bounce me on his knee."

Me and the champ talked.

"Hi, champ."

"Hiya."

"Joe Louis would have torn your head off."

We didn't talk any more.

The plane hit a bump in the air and it vibrated.

I shouted: "I need a drink!"

People kept coming up to me and giving me little bottles filled with fear-killer. I guess they wanted the experiment to work. Or me to shut up.

Then this guy came down the aisle, apparently curious as to the source of the bedlam.

When his face came into focus, I bellowed: "Hiya, Charlie, you ol' son of a gun. What the hell are you doin' here, Charlie? Have a drink, ol' pal."

Charlie is president of the company that owns this newspaper. Boy, do I know how to make an impression on the boss.

Suddenly the plane began losing altitude.

"We've had it!" I cried. "One more drink!"

"We're landing," an elderly lady said. "Hush."

In a moment we were on the ground.

"Is this Pittsburgh?" I asked.

"It's Chicago," the stewardess said.

Amazing. It was faster than a ride on the Milwaukee Avenue bus.

"I'll never forget this ride," I yelled.

"Nobody else will either," said some smart aleck.

As we left the plane the pilot stood near the door. I tweaked his cheek and said: "Good job, ol' buddy." He didn't look thrilled by my praise.

The stewardess was there, too. "Want to run away to Acapulco?" I said. She didn't look thrilled either.

So, the experiment worked. And for all my fellow nonfliers—and there are millions of us—it isn't all that hard. The only problem I can see is that after five or six flights, you'll have cirrhosis of the liver.

Will I do it again, now that I've done it once?

Sure. In another twenty-four years. That will be the year 2001. I'll get smashed and go to the moon.

Self-Analysis Put to Test

October 10, 1975

I've always been hooked by the self-analysis tests that frequently appear in the features pages of newspapers and magazines.

The questions have multiple-choice answers, and each answer has a different value in points. You add up the points and determine the kind of shape you are in.

For instance, the question in a test on drinking might go:

Q—Do you usually drink:
(a) Only at parties? (1 point)
(b) Only a nip after work? (2 points)
(c) A pint before breakfast? (3 points)

Or, if it is about your mental state, a question might go:

Q—Do you spend a lot of time:
(a) Worrying about bills? (one point)
(b) Thinking you are getting old too fast? (2 points)
(c) Sitting in a dark closet by yourself, whimpering and
    wringing your hands? (3 points)

The various tests tell you if you are likely to have a heart
attack, if you have a drab personality, if you are on the verge of
a marital breakup, and just anything else that might be of
interest.

The idea is that a bad score should warn you to change some
of your habits.

I've taken them all. And, on the basis of the results, I have
discovered I died sometime in 1968, that I'm confined to a
padded cell, that everybody I know hates me, or should, and
that I'm very happy.

But I haven't changed any of my habits. Why push my luck?

Not long ago, a new test appeared in a column by Ann
Landers. It consisted of questions about boozing and drugs and
sex, and getting drunk and arrested, and getting young girls in
trouble, and all sorts of fascinating stuff.

The trouble was it was designed for teenagers, to determine
whether they were goody-goodies (0 to 21 points), normal (22 to
35 points), or depraved and dissipated (36 points and up).

Although I am no longer a teenager, at least most of the time,
I decided to take the test anyway.

My answers were based on the things I had done through my

nineteenth year. Since drugs weren't widely used then, I substituted liquor in questions that dealt with them.

Answering the questions was a real nostalgia trip. Several times, I had to sit back and chuckle at memories of what it was like when I was fondly known in my neighborhood as "the wolfman," "that creep," and "stay away from my sister, you!"

Then I added up the total points. And I couldn't believe the results. I had scored nineteen. Nineteen? Even Jack Armstrong or Andy Hardy would have had higher scores than that.

I figured something was wrong with the test, so I asked a friend of mine, who is about my age, to take it. He is a rather straight sort, who came from a decent neighborhood and spent much of his youth reading books, playing ping-pong, and working on a Junior Achievement project.

He got thirty-five points, putting him on the edge of dissipation. He smiled and said: "Someday, I'll tell you about the girl next door."

So I asked a woman in her thirties to take the test. She is a proper sort who attended parochial schools, and I've never known her to swear, spit, or kick children. And she got thirty-two points.

"You want to tell me about the boy next door?" I asked. She just winked.

It made no sense and left me feeling depressed. Me, a goody-goody? It was impossible. In every neighborhood, there is a youth who is so dangerous an influence that all the parents tell their kids that they can't associate with him.

Well, I was so dangerous an influence that my own brother wasn't permitted to associate with me. Respectable girls blushed in my presence. In a survey taken by adult reprobates in the neighborhood, I was voted Rookie of the Year.

I've had that test in my wallet for days now. Every so often, I take it out, take the test again, and the results are always the same.

So I have to face it and be honest with myself. I just wasn't the young man I thought I was. Just as that youthful home run wasn't as long as we remember, that touchdown run as spectacular, that winning basket from as far out—my evil acts weren't as loathsome as I prided myself upon.

In brushing away the webs of time, I now realize that I sincerely wanted to do all of those things. Me and Slats Grobnik used to spend hours planning, anticipating, slobbering.

But nobody would cooperate. Bartenders said: "Take off the false mustache, punk, you ain't no midget." And girls said: "Try it again, goof, and my brother will maim you."

I've since taken the test one more time. And my answers were based on what I would have done if I had been given any cooperation, Boy, oh boy, oh boy!

My score was ninety-two. Even Mr. Hyde couldn't have done any better in a London fog.

I feel good again. Maybe I didn't do anything terrible. But at least my intentions were bad.

Best Witches from Slats

October 31, 1973

Slats Grobnik never cared much for Halloween.

It made him angry that all the kids in the neighborhood went around soaping windows, tipping over garbage cans, and leaping out of gangways to scare old ladies.

That's the way he acted all year, and it was no fun when everybody else did it.

He didn't like going to parties, either. "All they do is tell stories about witches on brooms," he sneered. He said he would rather go to the tavern with his uncle, Beer Belly Frank Grobnik. "At least they tell stories about women on streets," he said.

He did attend one party, though, because his mother insisted he accept an invitation from a kid in the nice neighborhood two blocks away, where some people owned their own houses.

"I want to wear a costume so nobody will recognize me," Slats said.

"All you gotta do is wash your face for that," his father said.

His mother suggested he dress up like a bum, and Slats asked how bums dress. After she told him, he looked at his father and said: "You got anything that'll fit me?"

He went to the party but didn't have a good time. When it was time to duck for apples, Slats plunged his head into the tub. The water turned a muddy color and he was thrown out.

Slats didn't go trick-or-treating, either, which was surprising because his uncle Chester Grobnik had been the greatest trick-or-treater in the neighborhood. He was still at it when he was twenty-nine. That's when he walked into a place on Milwaukee Avenue wearing a mask, carrying a Molotov cocktail, and whispered to a cashier: "Trick or treat—fast!" It was a bank and he got three to five years.

Slats worked out a system that made walking the streets unnecessary. He stayed home while his parents went to the costume party at the VFW hall.

Slats would pull a nylon stocking over his head and face, turn out all the lights in the flat, and wait.

When there was a knock on the door, his little brother Fats would yank it open.

For a moment, the little kids outside would see nothing.

Then Slats would click on a flashlight held to his chin. In broad daylight, Slats had a face that made some old ladies cross themselves. And with the stocking and the flashlight in the dark, the effect was ghastly.

Most of the kids would scream, drop their bags of candy, and run.

Then Slats and Fats would gather up the bags, take them inside, close the door, and wait for the next bunch.

Slats justified this practice by saying: "You don't see the alderman going door-to-door to get his; so why should I?"

He stopped doing it, though, when his trick almost led to tragedy one year.

When the door was yanked open, and Slats turned on his flashlight, there were no trick-or-treat kids outside.

Instead, it was Mrs. Ruby Peak, the stout, balding little widow from Arkansas, who lived above the war surplus store.

She had come by to borrow a cup of bourbon from Mrs. Grobnik.

At the sight of the shapeless, glowing head, Mrs. Peak shrieked: "Billy Tom," and fell over in a faint, cracking her head on the bald spot.

Billy Tom was her late husband. He had died of a sudden stroke some years earlier while moving furniture. A night watchman in the furniture store had surprised him, and during the tussle he gave Billy Tom a terrific stroke on the brow with his club.

When Mrs. Peak came to, Slats kept his mouth shut about what he had done, and Mrs. Peak swore she had seen the ghost of her husband in the Grobnik flat. "I'd know that face anywhere," she said.

And in the long run, everything turned out for the best.

Mr. Kapusta, the landlord, agreed to pay for the stitches in Mrs. Peak's head, and threw in a cash settlement besides, if she would promise not to tell anyone what she had seen.

Mr. Kapusta, who wasn't a very democratic person, said:

"If people hear I got a hillbilly—even a ghost of one—in my building, the property value will go down."

Mr. Grobnik was so upset about being haunted by the ghost of Ruby Peak's husband that he threatened to report Mr. Kapusta to the building department. So his rent was reduced by five dollars a month.

And Mr. Kapusta hired Aunt Wanda Grobnik, who had strange powers, such as reading the future in coffee grounds and pinochle cards, to drive Billy Tom's ghost away. "See if you can drive him the other side of the viaduct," Mr. Kapusta said. "Then maybe I can pick up a building there cheap."

She spread some garlic and dried cabbage leaves around the flat and was paid ten dollars when the ghost didn't reappear.

Everybody got something out of it except Slats. And for a long time he was bitter about it, saying: "People never appreciate what you do for them. Next Halloween, I'll set fire to a garage."

Dear God: Why?

May 5, 1981

To: God
   Address: Somewhere in the Universe Dear God:
   I know how busy you must be with a whole universe to worry about. That's why it occurred to me that you don't

have time to read our papers and your TV reception might not be good. So I thought I'd drop you a note about how things are going here.

Well, things couldn't be going any better, at least as far as your image is concerned. You wouldn't believe how well loved you are on this planet today, and how much is being done in your name.

I hardly know where to start, there's so much going on. So I might as well start in Northern Ireland where you've always been very big. Ah, what religious fervor can be found there.

The Irish Protestants are so devoted to you that they do everything possible to make life miserable for the Irish Catholics, because they don't think the Irish Catholics have the right approach toward worshipping you.

And the Irish Catholics do what they can to make life miserable for the Irish Protestants for essentially the same reasons.

In their great love for you, they shoot at one another, bomb one another, set one another afire, kill little children, bystanders, cops, soldiers, old ladies, and some are now committing suicide by starvation.

Then each side buries its dead, goes to church, and gives fervent thanks to you for being on its side. It is very touching.

And one thing about these people: Their devotion to you is unshakable. They've been doing this for about four hundred years. So it's a good thing that you have an entire universe at your disposal, because I don't know where else you could find room to accommodate the souls of all the people who have died there in your name.

You're also highly regarded in a country called Lebanon, where just about everyone believes in you, although they don't agree on what you should be called.

In that country, there are Moslems and Christians, and they've created different sets of rules for worshipping you.

Naturally, they say you have sent the rules down to them. I don't know if that's true or not, but if I may make a suggestion: if it's true that you gave them the word, it would really simplify things if there were only one set of rules. It would cause less hard feelings.

But such details aside, they are expressing their devotion to you by killing each other by the hundreds. I guess they figure that if one side can wipe the other side out, it will prove that their way of worshipping you is correct, and you'll be pleased with them.

So every day, they lob shells at one another and blow up the usual men, women, children, bystanders, old ladies, and stray dogs. And every day, they take a few moments out to thank you for your support and to promise that they'll continue their efforts in your behalf.

Now, not far from there are countries called Iraq and Iran. The Moslems in those countries basically agree on what to call you, but they disagree on some details concerning how best to worship you. So they're killing one another, too.

It's more than a little confusing, though, because in Iran there are people who call themselves Baha'i, and they, too, have their own way of showing their respect for you. Unfortunately for the Baha'i, their way doesn't include killing others who don't share their point of view. So that makes them patsies, and the Moslems in Iran, in their love for you, have been kicking the Baha'i around pretty good.

Just a short missile ride away, there's a lot of religious action going on between a country called Israel and just about everyone else in that neighborhood.

The people in Israel also have their own set of rules for worshipping you, which they say you passed on to them. And they claim that you look more favorably upon them than anyone else. This has always caused a lot of hard feelings because a lot of other groups figure that *they're* your favorites. (It must be hard being a father figure.) Israel's claim that they're Number One has also made some people wonder this: If the Jews, after all they've been through over the centuries, are really your chosen people, what do you do to somebody you *don't* like?

Anyway the Jews and their Moslem neighbors—both of whom claim your complete support—have been going at it for about thirty years. But I don't think they'll ever equal Ireland's record because they'll all eventually have nuclear bombs. Boy, when they start throwing those around, will you have a crowd showing up.

Oh, and I can't forget to mention this final item. Somebody just shot the pope. As you know, he's the leader of one of your largest group of followers here. A very peaceful, non-violent man, by the way, although his followers have been known to shed a few million gallons of blood when their tempers are up.

Anyway, the man who shot him apparently did it because of *his* devotion to you. It's not completely clear, but this fellow seems to think the pope was in some way responsible for somebody invading the sacred mosque of his religion in a place called Mecca. That, of course, was an insult to you, so he got even in your behalf by shooting the pope.

Well, I know you're busy, so that's all for now.

P.S. I never believed any of those stories going around a few years ago that "God is dead." How could you be? We don't have one weapon that can shoot that far.